AT THE GATES OF
DARKNESS

RAYMOND E. FEIST

AT THE GATES
OF DARKNESS

The Demonwar Saga
Book Two

HARPER
Voyager

This novel is entirely a work of fiction.
The names, characters and incidents portrayed in it are
the work of the author's imagination. Any resemblance to
actual persons, living or dead, events or localities is
entirely coincidental.

HarperCollins*Publishers*
77–85 Fulham Palace Road,
Hammersmith, London W6 8JB
www.voyager-books.com

Published by *HarperVoyager*
An Imprint of HarperCollins*Publishers* 2010
1

Maps by R.M. Askren

A catalogue record for this book
is available from the British Library

ISBN 978 0 00 726471 1

Set in Janson Text by Palimpsest Book Production Limited,
Grangemouth, Stirlingshire

Printed and bound in Great Britain by
Clays Ltd, St Ives plc

Mixed Sources

Product group from well-managed
forests and other controlled sources
www.fsc.org   Cert no. SW-COC-1806
© 1996 Forest Stewardship Council

FSC is a non-profit international organisation established
to promote the responsible management of the world's forests.
Products carrying the FSC label are independently certified
to assure consumers that they come from forests that are managed
to meet the social, economic and ecological needs
of present and future generations.

Find out more about HarperCollins and the environment at
www.harpercollins.co.uk/green

Acknowledgements

As always, I am indebted to those who created Midkemia and allowed me to use it. Without their creativity the world of Midkemia would be far less vivid. So, Steve A, Jon, Anita, Conan, Steve B, Bob, Rich, April, Ethan, and everyone else who contributed, my continued thanks.

Thanks to two people who always give support and friendship, Richard Spahl and Ray McKnown. And thanks to Kim McKnown for battling through and keeping me smiling every time I see her.

I also, once again, thank Jonathan Matson for far more than wise counsel and his business acumen, but for an abiding friendship which I cherish.

Thanks to my mother, still, for being there.

Special thanks to a remarkable lady, Theresa Duchinsky, for being so wonderful.

Lastly, and most deeply, to my children for their love and beauty; they still drive me crazy while keeping me sane and I am loving the adults they're turning into before my eyes.

For the ladies who make me look so good: (in alphabetical order) Jennifer Brehl, Emma Coode, Jane Johnson, and Katherine Nitzel; rarely does an author get one good editor, let alone four.

CHAPTER ONE

Sacrifice

*H*OWLS FILLED THE NIGHT.

The blasted hills smoked and the stench of char filled the air. Hundreds of robed figures slowly wended their way between rocky debris to reach the huge clearing below the remains of a fortress gate tower. A powerful man stood silently on top of the pile of stones, looking down upon his followers.

Another figure waited in the shadows, using his considerable skill to remain unseen, and wishing fervently that he was anywhere else in the world but here. James Dasher Jamison took a slow, even breath, as much to calm himself as to catch his breath, and struggled to keep his wits about him. Within the courts of the three largest nations of the region, he was known as a minor noble of the Kingdom of the Isles; a man who had inherited, not earned, his rank, being the grandson of the Duke of Rillanon.

To others he was Jim Dasher, a businessman involved in some petty criminal dealings in the city of Krondor; and to a few, he was known as the Upright Man, leader of the Thieves Guild: the Mockers. But even fewer knew James Dasher Jamison as the head of the Kingdom of the Isles intelligent apparatus, reporting directly to his grandfather.

In his forty or so years, Jim had seen many strange and terrifying things – experiences that came with his various positions. At times he feared he had become as heartless a bastard as those he had put down in the name of the Crown, or for the Conclave of Shadows, with whom he often worked; but even his lifetime of violence and intrigue could not have adequately prepared him for what he now saw before him.

A massive fire encompassed a circle of stakes, to which were tied four human sacrifices. They were not the first, already the dead numbered in the dozens, if not hundreds; but what churned Jim's stomach more than this terrible scene, was that the slain had seemed willing, even eager to embrace a painful, flaming death.

Around the edges of the clearing more victims dangled at the ends of ropes; moments before, Jim had witnessed them place the nooses around their own necks, and jump off small ladders, to hang themselves. Many necks had broken with an audible crack, but a few had died slowly, kicking for what had seemed far too long a time. Jim had seen more than his fair share of public hangings in Krondor, but this was far more horrific than a criminal reaping his just deserts. This was a chilling display of self-sacrifice to evil. The howls lessened as the masochists finally began to lose consciousness and die.

As Jim watched, sickened, another score were impaled on

wooden stakes, their blood and faeces filling the air with the unforgettable stench of death. Some of them quivered and twitched as their own weight drove the stakes deeper into their bodies. Others gave out only one death spasm before they hung on the stakes, motionless.

Jim saw nothing sane here. He turned his attention to the man standing on top of the tumbled down masonry, who held his hands up in a welcoming gesture. The man's expression and bearing made Jim wish to turn tail and run away as fast and as far as he could. He had never seen this man before, but his description fit what he had learned from Pug of Sorcerer's Isle and a Demon Master named Amirantha: The man on the stones above was Belasco; one of the most dangerous men alive, and certainly one of the maddest.

With a sweep of his hand, the domineering magic user conjured a mirage, a shimmering likeness that hung in the air above his head, one that made the mob at his feet cry out in supplication and awe.

The image was Dahun, and from what Jim had learnt over the last six months, the appearance of his likeness, almost as if he stood here in the flesh, meant that his servants were closer to opening a portal for him.

Dahun was twenty feet tall and roughly man shaped, but he also possessed a long black, scaled lizard's tail, which descended from the base of his spine. His chest was massive and his stomach rippled with muscles under reddish skin that stretched from black at his feet and blended to crimson over his chest. His face was human, save for a massive, jutting lower jaw and large bat-like ears. His eyes were solid black orbs. Long tendrils of hair, braided with human skulls, hung to his shoulders. His brow was adorned with a massive golden circlet, set with a dark stone that pulsed with purple light. The fingers of his left hand ended in black talons and flexed restlessly, as if in anticipation of tearing his enemies apart. In his right hand he held a flaming sword. His hips were girded with a studded kilt, and two large leather bands crossed his chest with a massive golden emblem at their centre.

Jim spent a moment fixing the image in his memory. Then he glanced around and noted the slack jawed, empty eyed expression on the worshippers around him. It was clear they had been drugged in preparation for this ritual, so he attempted to mimic their shambling walk.

Feeling almost sick to his stomach, Jim steeled himself and slowly joined the people who were approaching the monster. Like them he wore a heavy black robe, but he had pulled the cowl forward to conceal his features. The original owner of the robe now lay at the bottom of a deep ravine less than a quarter mile away.

He shuffled his feet, moving slower than those around him to keep to the rear of the crowd; he wanted the opportunity to slip away easily should the need arise. He kept his hands inside the sleeves of his robe – one hand held a dagger treated with a fast-acting poison that would cause paralysis within a minute and the other a device which had been constructed for him by a master artificer in Krondor: a ball that when shattered would emit a blinding light for ten seconds, providing him more than enough time to get away. It would disable those around him for a few minutes, or at least the human onlookers, he couldn't be certain that everyone in attendance tonight was like him.

Jim swallowed hard again and paused, forcing himself to confront the vision of the monster above him.

Belasco raised his hands again. Jim could easily see that the magic user was madder than a bug trapped in a bass drum. His demon projection was the most horrifying sight that Jim had ever witnessed, yet the magician was laughing like a delighted child. He was calling out to the faithful, but Jim wasn't quite close enough to hear his words, only the tone of his voice.

Jim inched to the right as the followers in front of him continued their slow progression forward; the group was coming together at the centre of what had once been a fortress. Perhaps five hundred of the faithful had gathered. Jim glanced around; a sudden tightness in his neck had caused him to worry about who might now be behind him. It was a sense he had inherited from his great-grandfather, something the family called his 'bump of trouble'. Right now it was starting to itch badly.

As he suspected, figures moved along the rocks that surrounded the flat central area of the ancient marshalling yard. The roaring fires at its edge made everything beyond their light difficult to see, but Jim had mastered the trick of not looking directly at the flames, and kept alert for flickering movement betraying those outside the light.

The name of this ancient Keshian fortress had been lost in time. Its walls and towers were mostly gone, crumbled like the masonry upon which Belasco stood, and only one underground entrance a few hundred feet away still led into its tunnels and caverns. Jim had no intention of entering that labyrinth. In his great-grandfather's day it had been known locally as The Tomb of the Hopeless. Legend told that an entire garrison had been left to die in there. It once commanded the entrance to what was called the Valley of Lost Men.

Jim reoriented himself. To his right was a gap in the rocks that would grant him relatively fast access to a trail north: it was an abandoned caravan route that ended in the Keshian port city of Durbin. At the foot of these hills waited half a dozen of the deadliest thugs Jim could find. Five were cutthroats who occasionally worked for him in Durbin; the sixth was Amed Dabu Asam, his most trusted agent in the Jal-Pur desert region and the one he relied on to carry word back to Krondor should Jim not return by dawn.

To his left was an open expanse and then the sudden drop down of sheer cliffs. Only the gods knew what waited in the desolate valley below them, so should he have to bolt, Jim knew that he was certainly going to veer right.

He glanced around again, trying hard to look like just another devoted follower of the demon, mimicking the ritual movements of the others. He hoped his wary looks towards the archers hadn't attracted attention. He sensed that other things would start happening soon, all of them bad.

For over half a year Jim had been trying to find the lair of The Servants of Dahun, a group of outlaws known to others as The Black Caps. He had decided to investigate this ancient fortress whilst poring over the many reports from his great-grandfather's days.

Once home to a cult of fanatical assassins called the Nighthawks, the site had been considered abandoned for over a century. Obviously someone had decided that since no one was paying attention, it was time to reoccupy the fortress.

It was close enough to Krondor and the Empire city of Durbin to allow the murderous dogs quick and easy access, and remote enough that the chance of discovery was small. Jim had almost been killed twice, getting here, and now was counting the seconds of borrowed time that he had remaining.

He considered the tale of his ancestor facing down a cult of assassins here, with almost no help. Jim would take a fortress full of assassins over this mob of religious fanatics any day. The assassins might kill you, but at least it would be swift, but these lunatics would probably slow roast him over a fire and eat him.

Finally, Jim was close enough to hear Belasco's words. 'We are here to give blood and life to our master!'

As one the assembled mob chanted, 'Hail Dahun!'

Jim instinctively took a step back, checking first to his right, then the left. The crouching figures on the rocks surrounding the area were archers. He began sidestepping towards the closest boulder, which stood a very distant twenty feet to his right.

With two more rapid steps, Jim reached a deep shadow beneath an overhanging rock. He had to crouch, which made removing his robe more difficult, but in seconds he was almost invisible within the tiny pool of concealing darkness. He reached back and from behind his neck pulled a thin hood over his head that left only his eyes exposed. The material he wore was dull black, with dark metal fastenings. He gripped his dagger and waited.

Belasco shouted, 'Rejoice! Know that your sacrifice brings our master closer to us!'

As he spoke, the archers crouching in the rocks rose up and began firing at the worshippers. Most stood stunned as those next to them fell. The eeriest aspect to Jim was their silence. A muffled exhalation of breath, or just a faint grunt of pain; no one screamed or cried out. The wind whipped up the dust, and Jim could only catch glimpses of their faces, but none of them showed any fear.

They stood like sheep, waiting quietly until a bow shaft found their mark.

Jim didn't need to see any more. He crept along under the rock and slipped behind it, circling until he was behind the archer perched above his hiding place. There was ten feet of open ground he needed to cross to reach his next cover and he didn't hesitate. All eyes were on the worshippers falling around Belasco's feet, but Jim knew that very soon they would all be dead and that the archers would then start checking for survivors. He was determined to be as far away as possible before that moment.

Jim reached the second shadow and looked around. Seeing no one nearby, he sprinted across another open space and cut between two large rocks marking the entrance to a game trail that would lead him down a short incline to the old caravan route to Durbin. The eerie sound of the desert wind deepened Jim's apprehension as he half ran, half stumbled down the trail.

His nearly out-of-control flight caused him to bowl over a black-clothed figure waiting at the bottom of the trail. The two men went down in a tangle of arms and legs and Jim almost plunged his knife into the figure before he recognized him. 'Amed!'

'Peace, my friend,' said the Keshian agent as he regained his feet.

'What are you doing here?'

'When you failed to return, I thought to follow, in case you needed aid.'

Jim glanced upward and said, 'What I need now is to get as far from here as quickly as possible. Horses?'

'Down the road a little,' said the spy. 'I thought it reckless of you to come on foot, so I brought along a spare.'

Jim nodded, and followed his companion. He had insisted on approaching the ancient fortress on foot, as all the supplicants were walking and a rider would have stood out. Suddenly, Jim thought he saw a movement above and behind them and with a quick tug on Amed's shoulder, had him kneeling at his side. Pointing upward, he nodded once.

The nod was returned and Amed signalled his route up. Practiced in ambush, both men knew almost instinctively what the other would do. Jim would head back the way he came while his companion would loop around, to approach the possible stalker from behind. Jim waited to see if anyone was coming down the trail, and after ensuring that Amed was in place, he started back up the path.

Reaching the top of the trail, he found Amed kneeling, inspecting the ground in the moonlight. 'I can't be sure,' said the Keshian spy, 'but I think whoever followed you turned back when you headed down to the caravan road.' He said, 'Do we follow?'

'No,' said Jim. 'I need to report back as soon as possible.'

'Magic?'

Jim smiled. 'I wish. Those devices are only loaned out when necessary and lately, some of the older ones have stopped working. Pug is trying to find a way to restore them, but it looks as if a lot of Tsurani art is being lost.'

Amed shrugged. 'I know little of the Tsurani, few ever venture this far south. And I have no desire to visit LaMut.'

'It is a less than captivating city,' said Jim. 'Let's be on our way.'

As they made their way to where the horses waited, a man hidden deep in shadows watched their departure. He waited until they were far enough down the old caravan route then turned to trot silently back into the night. Reaching the clearing now strewn with bodies, he found Belasco waiting for him.

The mercenary said, 'Master, it is as you predicted.'

The magician smiled but there was nothing akin to humour in his expression. 'Good. Let Jim Dasher return to Krondor with his tale of bloodshed and dark magic.'

'Master,' said the killer. 'I do not understand.'

'I wouldn't expect you to,' said Belasco as he sat on top of the rock on which he had been standing. He looked at the carnage around him. 'Sometimes you have to put on a demonstration to show your opponents what you're capable of accomplishing.'

'Again, I do not understand. You instruct?'

'Ambition?' said Belasco, regarding the mercenary with a narrow gaze. 'I'm not sure I like that.'

'I do as you bid,' said the man, lowering his head.

'Where are you from? You speak oddly.'

The mercenary smiled broadly, revealing teeth filed to points. 'I am of the Shaskahan, master.'

Brightening up at that, Belasco said, 'Ah! The island cannibals! Lovely.

'Yes, I will instruct. Sometimes you wish your opponent to think they are ahead. Other times not. This time, I want them to concentrate on bloody murder and dark magic, as if I were just another mad necromancer like my brother.'

'This is to serve Dahun, master?'

'Of course,' answered Belasco annoyed by the question. 'Just not in the way you think.' He stood up. 'Get the horses,' he shouted. 'We ride south!'

The mercenaries moved with precision. Of all the hired

murderers he had at his disposal, this group was the most unswerving in their obedience and loyalty. The fanatics had their uses, but were too willing to die for their 'god,' and at the moment Belasco needed men who were willing to kill and reluctant to die.

'Eventually,' said Belasco quietly, 'Jim Dasher and his masters will decide that the time has come to investigate the Valley of Lost Men. We shall have to prepare another distraction for them when they do.'

With that he leaped down from the rock and hurried to where a mercenary held his horse. Mounting, he looked around to see that all was as he wished it. The fires would burn for hours, and the embers would remain hot for a day or more. The smoke and stench of death would drape this plateau for a week, but eventually the hot desert winds and the scavengers would reduce everything to dust and dry bones, and even the charred wood and dry bones would eventually be carried away.

He signalled and led his men down the steep trail into the Valley of Lost Men.

Sandreena, Knight-Adamant of the Order of the Shield of the Weak, waited at the docks. Her orders had been simple: meet with a Kingdom noble. She had no idea of who it would be, but she had been told that he would recognize her. She didn't know if he had met her before or simply been provided with a description; there weren't many members of the Order who were tall blonde women.

A pair of men covered in road dust approached. Their faces were obscured by the trailing edges of their keffiyehs that formed a covering for their noses and mouths – not unusual for men riding in from the Jal-Pur. Despite the oppressive heat, Sandreena stood motionless in her armour, her shield slung across her back and her sword within easy reach.

The taller of the two men came to stand before her and handed her a bundle of parchment. 'For Creegan,' was all he said before he turned and walked toward the end of the dock where a Kingdom trading vessel waited.

She wondered who this mysterious nobleman might be, but as he was probably disguised as a local trader, she knew that the situation did not warrant scrutiny. Father-Bishop Creegan was only forthcoming with the information she needed to ensure the success of her missions. Apparently, in this case all she needed to know was that those papers needed to reach Krondor.

She moved towards the stable yard where her horse waited. If the unknown nobleman needed her to ride to Krondor with his missive, then his ship was bound for another destination. She put aside her musing and stopped at a local stall. She would need a week's provisions and several skins of water, for Durbin was three day's ride from the first oasis, and Kingdom town of Land's End another four days from there.

Not looking forward to the task before her, but resolute in her devotion to her duty, she paid for the dried meat, dried fruit and roasted grain that would be her only sustenance for the coming week. She also needed a week's worth of grain, as there would be no fodder for her mount along the way.

Considering her assignment, she let her curiosity about the unknown Kingdom noble fade away.

Jim stood on the deck of the *Royal Sparrow*, a message cutter that had been turned out to look like a small coastal trader, renamed

Bettina for the duration. The crew were among the finest sailors and marines Jim could steal from Admiral Tolbert's fleet, each trained personally by Jim at one time or another. They were forty-five of the hardest, most dedicated and dangerous fighting men afloat on the Bitter Sea, and Jim had been grateful for their skills and loyalty on more than one occasion.

He considered his chance meeting with Sandreena. Dressed as a court noble, he was unrecognizable to her, but covered in dirt, with three day's growth of beard, he had risked that she might remember him as the Mocker who had sold her into slavery years before. He was grateful for the keffiyeh he wore, and relieved that he hadn't been forced to avoid being killed as he tried to explain his role in the period of her life that she'd most like to forget. Instead he considered himself lucky to now be surrounded by those loyal to him and the Crown, who would ensure he reached his destination safely.

Like Amed, the crew were among the few men Jim would trust his life to; they would follow him to the lower hells. And given what he had seen over the last month, that was very likely to be their destination.

Overhead, a nasty squall was finally leaving the small ship behind, as it moved eastward towards the distant city of Krondor. The storm had seemed to come over them in waves, and they had endured four days of bad weather in a row. Jim ignored the drenching he had received on deck, and waited to get close enough to the island to disembark.

In the distance, through the gloom, he could make out the dark, looming castle on the bluffs overlooking the one approachable cove on Sorcerer's Isle. The sight filled Jim with a vague foreboding, as it had the first time he had seen it. He knew from experience that the feeling was a very subtle magic employed by Pug, the Black Sorcerer, and that it would pass once he entered the premises. He noticed that the magical, evil-looking blue light in the northernmost tower was absent, and had been replaced by a relatively benign looking yellow glow, as if only a stout fire burned within.

Jim waited until Captain Jenson, master of the ship, gave the orders to reef sails and drop anchor before he indicated he was ready to go ashore. He was now dressed in a simple, utilitarian fashion – woollen tunic and trousers, a broad belt with sword and knife, high boots, and a large flop hat – all well-made despite their simplicity. He entered the longboat as it was lowered over the side and waited until the first breakers drove it into the shallows to jump out. He was already soaked to his small clothes, so waiting for the men to pull the boat ashore seemed unnecessary.

He was impatient to talk to Pug and his advisors, especially the Demon Master, Amirantha, and he hoped to unburden himself; he wanted the intelligence he carried to be someone else's problem. He had Keshian spies to catch, competing criminal gangs to crush, and a court life that had been neglected for far too long.

He waded ashore, ignoring the water sloshing into his boots. The route from the beach was short and divided quickly. To the left the trail meandered up and over a ridge, then down into a vale where the sprawling estate, Villa Beata, had rested. Gutted by fire in an attack a year before, it now lay abandoned, a testament to the wickedness of Belasco and his minions. To the right lay the stony path which led up to the black castle.

He trudged up the path, now regretting his impulsive jump

into the surf, as the water had knotted his stockings in his boots. Even with the rain, they had managed to stay dry until he jumped into the water. Not only would he have some serious polishing to do to save the fine leather boots from the predations of seawater, he would have a heroic set of blisters to show for his impatience, as well.

Sighing in resignation, he wondered if one of the inhabitants of the black castle might have a balm for his feet when he reached the gate. He crossed over a rickety looking drawbridge, which despite its dilapidated appearance, was well-maintained and sturdy.

The castle itself was a study in theatricality. Originally constructed by Macros, the first Black Sorcerer, it had been built using magic out of a blackish stone, shot through with steel grey. The looming gatehouse had the look of an open maw, as if any who entered would be devoured. The empty courtyard was weed choked and dusty, and the twin doors to the castle stood ajar.

Jim knew as well as those who lived here that the decision to relocate from the villa to this miserable haven was part of a ruse, to let Belasco think that the Black Sorcerer and the Conclave of Shadows had been humbled and driven into the old fortress where they huddled in fear, waiting for the next assault.

The truth was much more complex than that.

As he entered the forlorn looking castle, Jim reflected on his changing relationship with these people over the last year. The relationship between the Conclave of Shadows and the Jamison family had been difficult for twenty years. Jim's great-grandfather, the legendary Jimmy the Hand, later Lord James of Krondor, had married Pug's foster daughter Gamina. In a sense, they were distant family, but along the way a division had slowly developed.

Jim crossed the empty great room, crossing before the massive fireplace. In ages past, this type of castle would have housed as many as a hundred members of a noble family, their retainers and families, and on especially cold nights they would have gathered in this one room. He paused for a moment and considered the attention to detail undertaken by Macros the Black in constructing this place. Anyone exploring this near ruin would assume it had been built ages before its actual erection.

He mounted the stairs leading to the one tower he knew to be occupied and wondered how his great-grandfather would have viewed the current situation. By all reports of his nature, Jim concluded that he would have been both annoyed and amused by it.

Pug had shamed the Prince of Krondor at that time, later King Patrick, disavowing his loyalty to the Kingdom of the Isles and virtually daring the Kingdom to assert its claim on the island duchy of Stardock, in the Vale of Dreams.

Jim knew there had also been some dispute with those running Stardock on Pug's behalf at that time, as well. Whatever the true cause, Pug had then withdrawn to this island with his family and retainers. He had also begun the Conclave of Shadows, the secret organization that had become a major part of Jim's life, despite his original wish to have nothing to do with it.

Reaching the top landing, Jim paused and thought about his report. He carried the most dire intelligence, but he was about to make an important choice.

The relationship between the Jamison family and the Conclave became strained when Jim's grandfather had been summoned to the King's court and elevated to the rank of Duke of Rillanon.

At times during his grandfather's administration of the capital city – and by extension of the Kingdom itself – conflicts of interest had arisen between the Conclave and the Kingdom. James of Rillanon, like his grandfather before him, had been steadfast in his loyalty to the Kingdom of the Isles.

Jim reflected that it might have been simpler for his great-grandfather; in those days the aims of the Stardock magicians and the Kingdom were more or less in harmony. He wondered if Jimmy the Hand would have looked at this situation the same way Jim did.

Jim's father, William Jamison, and his uncle Dasher had both died in the border wars with Kesh when Jim was a boy, and his great uncle Dashel had no surviving sons. By the time he was twenty years of age, Jim Dasher Jamison was the sole surviving heir to the family, and both his grandfather and great uncle had marked him.

Jim pushed aside the memory of the ruse his forbearers used to persuade him to take control of all the criminal activity along the Bitter Sea coast, as well as taking charge of the Kingdom's intelligence services. He had found he had a knack for both and had made the criminal activities serve the Kingdom's interest, but that hadn't made wearing two caps at the same time any easier.

And now he was on the verge of more responsibility, as a fully committed agent of the Conclave. Pushing open the door to the tower's common room, he wondered if he was making the right choice.

He pushed open the door and was confronted by two young women knitting, while a third placed wood on a fireplace set in the opposite wall. Three men huddled close to the fire speaking quietly. One young magician recognized him and said, 'Jim Dasher, welcome!'

Jim nodded a return greeting and said, 'Jason.' He glanced around. 'Where is everyone else?'

'Scattered,' said Jason, pushing his long blond hair back from his forehead. 'Pug's sent many of the younger students home or to Stardock, the rest have been moved to safe locations. A few of us have stayed to keep a lookout for any more trouble and convey messages. What do you require?'

'I need to speak to Pug,' said Jim, not bothering to mask his impatience. He held up a sphere of dull golden metal. 'This doesn't work. I had to take a fast ship from Durbin to get here.'

The magician took the sphere and said, 'The Tsurani transport spheres . . . We've not had any new ones in years.' He looked at it and his tone was regretful. 'I fear most of the artificers who made them perished on Kelewan. The few who survived . . .' He shrugged. 'Most of those we have are decades old, my friend,' Jason said softly.

Jim knew that the few Tsurani magicians who survived now struggled with the rest of their people on their new home world, or were perhaps living quietly in LaMut. And, without saying as much, Jason had implied that if the Conclave had access to newer devices, Jim would have had them.

Feeling a fool, Jim said, 'Yes. You're right. Now, may I speak with Pug?'

'Pug's not here,' said Jason.

'Where is he?'

Glancing over at his companions the young magician's tone was apologetic. 'We don't know. We haven't seen him for nearly a month now.'

Jim said, 'Then I need to speak with Magnus.'

'He's gone as well,' said Jason. 'Come, sit by the fire and rest. We have means of sending word, but it may take some time.'

'By some time, do you mean hours or days?' asked Jim, pulling off his leather gauntlets and moving to a stool near the fire.

Jason only shrugged, and Jim felt his frustration return in full. He knew his crew would wait until he sent word or returned, so he felt little need to move away from the warming fire. Thinking of nothing better to do, he sat back against the cold stones, removed his boots, and wondered just where the two magicians might be.

CHAPTER TWO

Foreboding

*L*IGHTNING FLASHED ACROSS THE SKY.
Amirantha silently counted before the distant boom of thunder came. Looking at his old companion, Brandos, the Warlock of the Satumbria said, 'The storm is moving away from us.'

The fighter nodded, remaining silent as he concentrated on cleaning his armour. He sat on a low stool near the massive fire burning in the ancient keep's fireplace in the tiny room near the top of the only occupied tower.

Amirantha had been amused the first time he had visited the legendary castle of the Black Sorcerer. Now he simply found it old and drafty, stifling in its familiarity and a place locked in the grip of sorrow. After a year of living with these people, the Demon Master now understood their pain and anger. Whatever had passed for normalcy before the vicious attack on Villa Beata, the death of Miranda, her son Caleb and his wife Marie, along with the murder of a score of students, that normalcy had never returned.

One of the few brighter moments over that year had been Brandos' return a month previous. He had travelled back from their home near the city of Maharta in Novindus, with his wife Samantha. But even that unrelentingly cheerful woman had only been able to lift the constant pall of gloom of this place momentarily.

Pug and his surviving son, Magnus, would come and go from the castle, and at times they shared interesting discussions. Amirantha was forced to concede he had broadened his understanding of demons and the demon realm more in the last year than he had in fifty years of solitary study. Often they possessed similar information, but the magicians had misinterpreted its significance, and he had frequently helped Pug identify misapprehensions in his knowledge.

But those times were growing more infrequent as Pug and Magnus were away for longer stretches dealing with matters pressing upon the Conclave. Amirantha and Brandos had not been formally invited to join their organization, but there was a tacit understanding that they were nevertheless a part of it, willing or not. Amirantha had no doubt that the magicians had the means to ensure he didn't leave the island with the vital knowledge he possessed, so he considered his choice in the matter a moot point.

He stood and stretched, then made a small motion with his head to indicate that Brandos should look out of the small window. The old fighter put aside the leather jerkin he had been cleaning and walked over to his friend. He now looked ten years the magic user's senior despite being the younger of the two. 'What?' he asked softly.

'The rain is going to play out soon,' answered the Warlock as he looked out at the late afternoon murk.

'You look bored.'

'Constantly,' said the Warlock. 'When I first came here, I did so with great anticipation, I thought that for the first time in my life I might have colleagues with whom I could share my knowledge as well as learn from; that I might find kindred souls, and I did at first, but lately . . . Now, who do I have instead?'

'Children.'

Amirantha smiled. The magicians who remained here with Pug and his son, Magnus, were hardly children, yet with one word Brandos reminded Amirantha of his tendency to be dismissive of almost everyone he met, because of his long life and the perspective it offered. Yet, Pug was even older than him, as were others who came and went from this island. Miranda, Pug's late wife, had been one of those, and her sudden death had served as a grim reminder to Amirantha that his long life and vast experience was not a defence against mortality.

'Hardly,' said Amirantha. 'But most of them are still in the formative stages of their education, training, and power. None of them have been practicing their arts for more than twenty years.'

Brandos returned to his stool and took up the leather he had been cleaning. Applying a generous dollop of soap to his weapons belt, he said, 'It makes you wonder where all the grown-ups went, doesn't it?'

Amirantha continued to stare out of the window. 'Indeed.' He craned his neck slightly. 'I'm ready to go outside.'

Brandos sighed, looking at his unfinished cleaning. 'Well, a short walk. I could use a leg stretcher.' Looking at his friend, he added, 'Samantha says that lately I've been as irritated as a bear woken from an early hibernation, so maybe it'll do us both good.'

'We've had four days of rain.'

'It's an island in the middle of an ocean, Amirantha. It's late autumn. There's going to be a lot of rain.'

Muttering as he opened the door, Amirantha said, 'It's not an ocean. It's a sea.'

Brandos shook his head but said nothing.

While Amirantha descended the stairs that led to the common room, he let out a long silent sigh. He knew his foster son understood that his argumentative impulse was only borne of frustration. After the destruction of the villa there had been a flurry of activity. The dead had been cremated, the wounded tended to, and then the long conferences between Pug and his most trusted advisors had drawn to a close. Those discussions had animated the Warlock in a way he rarely experienced; they had made him happy.

Continuing down the stairs, Amirantha realized that some of his current irritation was brought forth by the contrast between that initial period of reorganization on the island, and what he was now forced to endure here. It had changed one night, two months ago; Pug and Magnus had simply vanished, along with more than thirty of their most powerful colleagues. What had been a somewhat crowded keep was all of a sudden occupied by fewer than a dozen souls.

The month Brandos had travelled south to fetch Samantha had been the loneliest time in Amirantha's life, and he was vexed to discover how lonely he could feel. He had strong feelings on matters concerning his own conduct and appearance, and the extent to which he had missed his foster son did not sit well with them. He had cursed himself for such a feeling more than once. It was not wise to grow close to anyone, especially as he was destined to outlive most people, assuming he survived the approaching struggle.

Reaching the floor of the tower, they entered the common room and were met with an unexpected presence.

'Jim Dasher!' said Amirantha in greeting.

Jim turned and rose from his seat before the warming fire and said, 'You're still here, Amirantha.' He extended his hand and they shook.

He exchanged greetings with Brandos, as Amirantha said, 'My lingering was at Pug's request. He can be most persuasive.'

'Ah,' said Jim, nodding. 'He wouldn't let you leave.'

Brandos snorted, and Amirantha said, 'He was insistent, but truth to tell, I have found many things here interesting.'

Glancing around the stark hall, Jim said, 'Really?'

Amirantha smiled, 'Well, not so much lately, but the first nine months were fascinating.'

He motioned for Jim to move with him towards the large doors. 'My quarters are adequate, but hardly commodious, so I thought to step outside for a breath of air now that the rain has nearly stopped.'

Jim nodded, pulled his boots on, and fell into step behind him. 'I just came in from the . . .' Jim began, and then stopped himself. 'Actually, I'm supposed to report directly to Pug on this matter.' He looked hard at Amirantha, then said, 'Still, much of what I've seen concerns you, too.'

'Really?' said the Warlock. He said no more, content to let the mysterious noble-turned-spy speak when he was ready.

As they reached the entrance to the yard, they paused, feeling the occasional rain-drop blown in by the freshening wind, then continued on, leaving the relative warmth of the keep entrance for the soggy ground of the marshalling yard. The rain had almost stopped and the wind was freshening a little; it already felt dryer.

'So, you were about to say?'

Jim appeared annoyed. 'I can never tell who knows what around here.'

Amirantha laughed. 'I can tell you this much, my friend: all of us here have some power and ability, despite appearances to the contrary. Pug ensured all the vulnerable students were safely away within a day of—'

'The attack,' Jim finished.

'I was going to say the death of his wife and son.' Amirantha sighed. 'Never having had children, I can only imagine what he's going through. I had little experience of him to judge what he was like before that, scant hours really, but . . .' He shrugged.

'You sense he's changed,' said Jim. He looked to the west where somewhere behind the clouds the sun was lowering toward the horizon. 'He knew I was engaged on important business, and yet he has left no apparent means of contacting him; that is most unlike Pug. It's as if he's . . .' Jim shrugged.

'Distracted?' offered Amirantha.

'More,' said Jim. 'He's distant in a way that troubles me.'

'I don't understand.'

Jim smiled slightly. 'I don't expect you to. I hardly know the man well, despite our tenuous kinship.'

'Kinship?'

Jim said, 'My great-grandmother was his foster daughter.'

Amirantha raised his eyebrows in slight surprise. 'Tenuous by blood perhaps, but otherwise?'

'We are not close. It is a long story, a family matter, and really not pertinent to the discussion at hand.'

Amirantha shrugged. 'Perhaps, but we have ample time to fill. Enlighten me.'

Jim stared off into the darkening afternoon gloom and said, 'While Pug and I may not be close, I do know a great deal about him; his role in Kingdom politics has been significant, since long before I was born.'

'Obviously,' agreed Amirantha. 'Given the rank and status of those who have visited here since I was first made aware of the Conclave's existence.'

'So in my other duties to the Crown, I've been required to study a great deal of history, much of it penned by my own forbearers. I know Pug to be a man of strong convictions and one who pays attention to detail. He is not the sort to let important things slip by. Yet lately . . .' Jim took a deep breath.

'I assume you mean this,' Amirantha said, indicating the cold, nearly empty castle around them with a wave of his hand.

'I would have expected the man I knew, the one I studied, to have begun reconstruction on the villa at once, defiantly, to let his enemies know that they would not prevail.'

Amirantha nodded, pursing his lips in thought. He remained quiet for a moment, then asked, 'How much time do you think his enemies spend studying him?'

Jim inclined his head slightly as if conceding the point.

'Would it not seem, given what has happened here, that Pug knows he's under a great deal of scrutiny? By such accounts, his enemies have been coming at him for years, in one form or another.'

'Only if you assume that there is a single intelligence behind the series of assaults on this world going, yes. But that can only be an assumption.'

'A better one,' observed the Warlock, 'than thinking that this land has been beset by a string of coincidental afflictions.

'I may not be a master of magic on Pug's scale, but I know enough about the other realms to suspect this is not a series of random occurrences.' He paused, and Brandos recognized his expression. Amirantha was frustrated. 'Over the last year I've heard frequent reference to things such as the Pantathian Serpent Priests, the Riftwar, the Great Uprising, and all the rest of it; enough of them to believe there is one agent behind all of this, one intelligence that has targeted this world, perhaps this very nation, even perhaps this island, for reasons known only to them; but irrespective of those reasons, the consequences for this entire world are bound to be dire.'

'I agree,' said Jim, 'but explain your reasons.'

'The Pantathians exist in the distant mountains to the west of my home, yet stories of them travel; they are a strange race, and their obliteration has been assumed numerous times, yet they linger.

'They serve an ancient hate, a female idol they call "the mother of us all". They kill without remorse any who refuse to serve her.

'The Emerald Queen, whose army savaged my homeland

before travelling half-way around the world to come to the Kingdom, was a demon in disguise.' Suddenly Amirantha became animated. 'Do you have any notion of how remarkable that is?'

Jim shook his head.

'I will bore you with a long lecture some other time—'

'And he will,' interjected Brandos.

'—But demon possession on that level, of a powerful magic user . . . It's unknown to those of my calling.'

Jim said, 'I still don't see the connection.'

Amirantha seemed to fight for words. 'I can't explain. It's as if I'm on the edge of understanding something important, but I'm not quite there yet. But it's more than a feeling, Jim.' He looked at Brandos and said, 'Am I usually prone to leap to conclusions, Brandos?'

Brandos shrugged, then realized it wasn't the time for more japes; it had been a serious question. 'No, you're occasionally too convinced of your own brilliance, but you are hardly rash.' He paused, and then added to Jim. 'He's miscalculated and almost killed us several times, but at those times he was wrong, not impetuous. If he says he's on the edge of understanding something huge, I'd believe him.'

'Well, then,' said Jim Dasher. 'Is there any way I can help?'

'Only if you can supply me with more information than I've been privy too lately.'

Jim was silent for a long moment as he stared out into the fading light.

Brandos cleared his throat and said, 'I'm going to go inside; I will ask Samantha to rustle up something for you to eat. I imagine you're hungry.'

Jim smiled. 'Thank you, Brandos. That would be wonderful.' After the old fighter had left, Jim said, 'He should be a diplomat.'

Amirantha laughed. 'Hardly, but he can be discreet at times.'

Jim paused, then said, 'Very well. I expect that Pug will ask you to listen to my report anyway, as you are the demon expert.'

Amirantha nodded. 'That elf, Gulamendis, is the only being I've met who knows as much, possibly more.'

Jim looked uncomfortable. 'Those Star Elves make my skin itch. But they're a matter for another time.' Jim told the Warlock what he had witnessed in the distant Jal-Pur desert and when he was finished, he asked, 'What do you think?'

Amirantha said, 'I think we need to find a way to fetch Pug back here as soon as possible.'

'Why?'

Heading back towards the keep, Amirantha said, 'Come with me.'

He didn't wait to see if Jim followed, but hurried inside. He glanced around the common room and asked the four younger magicians there, 'Where is Jason?'

One of them pointed towards a door that led to a small room Pug occasionally used as a private office. Amirantha went to the door, knocked once and then opened it. Jason sat behind the tiny desk in the former storage room, squinting at a paper under the dim glow of a single candle. The tiny window above hardly admitted any light on the brightest of days.

'Yes?' he asked, apparently untroubled by the sudden entrance.

'Pug,' said Amirantha. 'You need to summon him at once.'

Jason sat back. 'And how am I supposed to do that, given that I have no idea where he is?'

Amirantha gave Jim a sidelong glance, then said, 'I count Pug many things, but a fool is not one of them. Even if you don't know where he is, I'm certain that he's left you with the means to contact or summon him, should the need arise; and such a need has arisen.'

'Really?' asked the younger magician. He looked at Jim for corroboration.

'I think so, as well,' said Jim.

'Very well,' said Jason, rising from behind the small desk. 'Come with me.' He picked up the candleholder.

He led them out of the room and across the floor of the keep's great hall. Brandos stood near his wife beside the large hearth where a pot of stew was simmering. The old fighter shot a questioning look at Amirantha, but with a nod of his head the Warlock indicated that he should stay where he was.

Jason led them up a flight of stairs to the upper floor of the main building and down a long hall that traversed the building to the tower opposite Amirantha's residence. The single candle Jason held provided the only light on that floor. To the best of the Warlock's knowledge, the tower stood empty, save for the enchantment on the top floor that caused the ominous blue light to glow whenever a ship came within sight of the castle.

They climbed a circular staircase to the second to last floor and Jason opened a door. Inside the room was bare, save for a construct of wood: two curving poles sat on top of a base that looked metallic. Amirantha glanced at Jason and said, 'Tsurani?'

The young magician said, 'In design, yes. Pug built it.'

'What is it?' asked Jim.

'A rift gate,' said Amirantha. 'What our friends the Star Elves call a portal.'

Jason went to a small shelf near a shuttered window and pulled down a small cloth bag. He handed the candle to Jim, then knelt and carefully opened the bag. Reaching inside he pulled out an odd looking device: a square box covered with odd designs, strange levers and wheels.

'This was created by an artificer of Tsurani descent, in LaMut. It's a little ungainly compared to the old Tsurani devices.' He shrugged as if what he was saying was simple trivia.

He then placed the device on the metallic base between the two poles, tripped one of the levers and stood back. 'I have no knowledge or ability when it comes to rift magic,' said the young magician. 'It is difficult and outside of my interests. Only Magnus and a few others know much about it, although no one knows as much as Pug. He had this constructed should the need arise to summon him.'

Suddenly a whooshing sound filled the room, then a crackle of energy, followed by a shimmering between the poles. A grey void appeared, scintillating colours ran faintly over its surface, like oil refracting light on water.

'Pug will receive the alert in a moment. He should appear as soon as he is able.'

'Do you know where he went?' asked Jim.

Jason said, 'We only know what little he tells us.'

Long moments dragged by, then, suddenly a figure stepped through the rift. A short man with a closely trimmed beard, Pug still wore the ancient fashion of the Tsurani Great Ones: a simple black robe and cross-gartered sandals. 'What is it?' he asked as soon as he was through.

Jason inclined his head towards Jim and Amirantha, and it was the Warlock who spoke. 'We're being played for fools, Pug.'

Pug's brow furrowed as he asked, 'What do you mean?'

'I'll explain,' said Amirantha, 'when Jim has told you what he saw a few days ago in the Jal-Pur, but it would help if we had another with us.'

'Who?'

'We need an expert on death.'

Pug looked slightly bemused. 'I know just the fellow.' He turned and held up his hand. The Warlock could feel shifting magic in the room, though Jim only felt his 'bump of trouble' start to act up. After a moment, Pug said, 'You two, follow me.' To Jason he said, 'Put the toy away when we're through.' He stepped into the rift.

Jim turned and said, 'Please send word to Captain Jenson to weigh anchor and make for Krondor. I'll find him there.' He turned and followed Pug.

Just before he entered, Amirantha turned to Jason and said, 'You might also tell Samantha that Jim and I will be missing supper tonight.' He then followed the other two men into the rift.

CHAPTER THREE

Sergeant-Adamant

CREEGAN GESTURED WITH HIS HAND.
Sandreena entered his quarters still covered in dust from the road and feeling hunger pangs. Once she had given care of her horse over to the stable boy, she had paused only long enough to drink deeply from the well behind the temple, but she hadn't eaten anything but a handful of dried fruit and some nuts since leaving Land's End. Her order was mendicant and there was no dedicated shrine or temple in Land's End, so she had survived on what she had purchased in Durbin with the last of her coin.

The moment she handed her documents to the Father-Bishop she knew something was wrong, something that had nothing to do with the message she had delivered to him. He waved her to sit in a chair opposite his desk and said, 'The Grand Master has passed.'

She took a deep breath, closed her eyes and made a short prayer to the Goddess to care for the old man on his way to Lims-Kragma's domain. He had been a good man, almost saintly, and Sandreena had no doubt that he would be rewarded with a higher place on the Wheel of Life.

The Father-Bishop remained silent while she prayed; when she opened her eyes, she discovered him staring intently at her. 'Father-Bishop?'

Creegan smiled; it was not a friendly or warm expression, but rather the smile of a man finding humour in a very dark place. 'The end of life is not necessarily a cause for sorrow, daughter,' he said using the address usually reserved for minor members of the order, clearly communicating the difference in their ranks. She was uncertain why he felt the need to emphasise it, but knew he did nothing without a reason. 'The Grand Master served the Goddess well, for many years and has earned his final rest.

'But the timing is . . . inconvenient.' He stood and said, 'I must leave at once for Rillanon, for the convocation is to be held only a week after the funeral, and the selection of the new High Priest is more critical than is usual.'

She knew he was referring to the matter of the demon host: the 'Legion' as it was called, was out there somewhere, threatening to bring its ravages upon this world. Few people within the temple, and even fewer outside, knew that the threat existed. Sandreena was aware of it only because of the confidence in which Father-Bishop Creegan held her. And fewer still knew of the relationship between the Father-Bishop and the Conclave of Shadows led by the magician Pug.

She merely nodded her head and said, 'I understand.'

'I know you do, Sandreena.' He rose from the desk, and sat

on the corner, looking down at her. 'I have never told you, but there is a beauty to you that few notice.'

She was a little startled by the statement. There had always been an underlying tension between them, she found him a very attractive and powerful man, but his reputation as something of a womanizer, and their respective ranks, had always kept any inappropriate behaviour in check.

He held up his hand before she could speak. 'I don't mean your physical beauty – as impressive as it is when you choose to let others glimpse it – but rather a beauty of strength and purpose, what you've overcome and managed to achieve despite a desperately difficult beginning. It is most admirable.' He stood up and moved to the window. Looking out, he said, 'We may get more rain.' The rain along the coast had made her trip even more difficult, so she hoped he was wrong.

'I am leaving you in charge of the Order while I'm away.'

Her eyes widened. 'Me?'

'I'll send Father-Bishop Bellamy back, to assume my duties, but in the interim, you will take my place here.'

'Take your place?'

Creegan shrugged as if it were of no importance, but said, 'I will be the new Grand Master.' The way he said it, she realized it was a *fait accompli*. He glanced over and smiled. 'It was decided long ago. So, I will dispatch Bellamy as soon as the convocation is over, and you will then return to your duties, to do whatever he asks, for he will be speaking for me. Until then, you must take charge here.'

'Why me?' she asked softly.

'You are the only one I trust, Sandreena.' He came back and sat behind the desk. 'Only a few know of what is really going on out there. I'll leave you a list of names; do not trust anyone who is not on it. You've also earned the honour. Almost getting yourself killed isn't ideal, but you kept your wits about you when you realized the enormity of the political reality that has swept you up without warning.

'Few members of the Order would have coped so well with demons and secret alliances.'

'The High Priestess?' she asked.

Creegan smiled. 'She'll object, of course, but as she has no standing within the Order, I'll smile, nod, and suggest that she should pack if she's to leave with me on the ride to Salador.'

Sandreena nodded. The High Priestess Seldon had ambitions of her own and would be actively seeking a nomination to the office of High Priestess of the Grand Temple once the convocation began.

Creegan said, 'I suspect she'll dismiss you quickly and begin the endless flattery I will be subjected to on the journey.'

Sandreena couldn't help but smile. The High Priestess might be pleased to see Creegan leaving Krondor – their relationship had always held a contentious element – but his elevation to the highest calling in the Order, would make him an even more important voice in the temple, and he would have a great deal of influence over the succession when the current High Priestess stepped down.

'You'll only need to make one quick courtesy call, which I suggest you do now, before I let her know of your promotion.'

'Promotion?'

'Of course. I can't leave a Knight-Adamant in charge of the Order in the Western Realm. Effective immediately, you are now a Sergeant-Adamant of the Order, but will bear the office rank of

Adiuvare. It's an old title we rarely use, but it's still recognized. So your official title will be Adiuvare-Sergeant-Adamant. Once Bellamy arrives, you will become just another Sergeant.'

She tried not to smile. 'Just another Sergeant,' he said. As a rule, Knight-Adamants had to serve for twenty years to obtain the rank of Sergeant and few lived long enough. She was certain she not only was the youngest Sergeant in the Order, but perhaps in the history of the Order.

'I will do my best not to disappoint you, Father-Bishop.'

'If I thought there was even a remote possibility of that, I would have given the job to someone else,' said Creegan. 'Now, go make your call on the High Priestess, get something to eat, and rest. I think you'll discover the post is not as easy as you think.' He motioned to the pile of papers and said, 'More men have been defeated by reports than all the steel throughout history.' Then he made a dismissive gesture and she rose, bowed slightly, and left his quarters.

Under normal circumstances, she would have been elated by the promotion, for it would have been a signal that the Goddess had found her service worthy. In this particular circumstance it felt not like a gift, or reward, but a heavy burden. Then she chided herself: if an even bigger burden had been placed on her, it simply meant that the Goddess deemed her able to meet the demands of office.

Still, she thought as her stomach growled, she wished she could get something to eat before visiting the High Priestess.

Sandreena made her call on the High Priestess, who was, as Creegan predicted, distracted by her preparations to leave the next day for the arduous ride to the port of Salador where she and Creegan would take ship to Rillanon to attend the convocation to elect the new Grand Master of the Order of the Shield of the Weak. The High Priestess had no official duties regarding the Order, but as every prelate of rank would be in attendance while they conducted their ceremonies and elected Creegan, everyone one else would be playing temple politics. Sandreena was glad that she was to remain behind, even if she had been handed responsibility for the Order in Krondor, which involved supervising the Order in the entire Western Realm of the Kingdom of the Isles.

After she had finally eaten, Sandreena returned to the common barracks of the order and gave her dirty tabard and clothing to a servant to be cleaned. She preferred to care for her own arms and armour. She went to the communal baths and, pleased to find it empty, gave herself over to a completely thorough cleaning.

While she scrubbed her filthy hair, she considered her feelings about Creegan's departure; his promotion was as good as ordained since she had first met him, yet there was always this feeling. She sighed.

Encountering Amirantha after that near fatal attack on Sorcerer's Isle, had reignited feelings she would rather ignore. Creegan had the same effect on her. But, although her intimacy with Amirantha was something she wished had never happened, she suspected it was something she would regret with Creegan.

Her order was not celibate, though like most people given over to an important calling, personal issues were always of lesser importance; but, as a woman in her prime, she felt certain needs assert themselves from time to time.

She had never considered family a blessing, given how she grew up, yet now she often wondered about being a mother.

She knew nothing about raising a child; her mother had been lost to drugs, drink and men, and no permanent father had been at hand. Being ill-used by men since she had begun to blossom had given her a very unforgiving perspective on them.

There were only two men she had come to care for, Brother Mathias who had rescued her from her Keshian slave master, and Father-Bishop Creegan, who had been her mentor, but now she was beginning to think he was more important to her than that.

There were two men she wished dead: A black hearted rogue called Jimmy Hand by some, Quick Jim by others, who had controlled the brothel where she had served as a high priced whore when she was little more than a girl, and who had sold her to the Keshian; And Amirantha. He had charmed her, lied to her, and used her, and had lived up to her general judgment on the worth of men.

A tiny pang told her she didn't truly wish Amirantha dead, but rather she wished that he had told her the truth. Even when she had lashed out and knocked him to the floor she had felt instant regret. She wished she could have told him that he had hurt her, but that would make her look weak.

Picking up a bucket she poured water over herself, cleaning away the dirt and soap, then bent over and ran a comb through her hair. The water was hot, but the air was cold after the passing storms and she felt gooseflesh on her skin.

She decided to forego the meditative steam room and retired to the barracks. She donned a simple white shift and turned in early. She was a sound sleeper and should others of her order enter, she was sure they would not wake her. All she wanted for this night was a sound sleep with no dreams.

*　　*　　*

Morning brought the departure of the group travelling to Salador, led by the High Priestess and the Father-Bishop. As Creegan had predicted, Seldon was being as deferential as humanly possible to the prospective Grand Master of the Order of the Shield of the Weak, to the point of being cloying.

When she had awakened, Sandreena had discovered a new uniform laid out for her across the chest at the foot of her bed, and on top of it a new tabard, this one emblazoned with a chevron and crown above her heart, signifying her new rank of sergeant. She couldn't resist smiling as she beheld it. She was not a prideful woman by nature, but she did like how this badge of honour made her feel.

She had dressed and postponed a morning meal to be in the marshalling yard for the Father-Bishop's departure.

Creegan smiled when he saw her, and put his hand on her shoulder. 'The fate of the Order in the west is in your hands now, Sandreena.' He leaned in so no one else could over hear his words and he said, 'There's something on my desk that you need to read; it's the report you brought to me. Act on it at once. I'm not telling you what I would do; this must be your decision.'

Impulsively, he kissed her goodbye; but rather than a mere brush of lips, he lingered slightly, pulling back just before it became something both of them needed to worry about. 'May the Goddess go with you,' he whispered.

Words failed her, she could only nod in response. As he mounted his horse, she only just managed to return the ben-ediction. 'May the Goddess go with you, Father-Bishop.'

The High Priestess was fussing over her mount, a mild palfrey but still spirited enough to make the older woman show concern as she sat uncomfortably on the small horse. It was obvious that Seldon would have preferred a litter, but the need to be in Rillanon by the date of the convocation prevented the more sedate mode of transport. She would be very sore and unhappy by the time they reached Salador.

The party moved out and as soon as they cleared the gate, Sandreena hurried to Creegan's office. On top of his desk lay two letters and the bundle she had carried from Durbin.

She looked at the first paper, which had her name on it. She opened it and read: *Sandreena, if the Goddess wills it, we will meet again. Know the trusts rests with you and I have faith you will discharge the duties I've given you as well as if I understood them myself. I've left you a list of those who you may rely upon* – she knew he meant those who could be trusted in dealing with the Conclave – *and a report you must attend to at once. May the Goddess go with you.* It was signed only *Creegan.*

She examined the list and saw only five names on it. Four were priests and one was the orderly assigned to this office, the only members of the Order of the Shield who apparently knew about the Conclave of Shadows.

She looked up to see the man named on the list, a Pryor of the Order, Brother Willoby. He was a round-faced, stocky man with a constantly worried expression. He said, 'Sister? May I be of service?'

She sat down in Creegan's chair and said, 'I will let you know, brother.'

'I will be outside if you need me,' he answered. Unlike the Knights, the clerical branch of the Order worked within the temples, as lay priests, but they were not administrators by choice. They were men and women who had wished to serve the Goddess, but found they lacked the strength of arm to serve in the field. Like most of the Knights, Sandreena hardly gave the pryors a moment's thought, but she suspected that she would come to appreciate them much more as she looked at the rest of the documents beside the desk that required her attention.

She took the list of names and folded it up. She had already memorized the names and would burn it later.

Then she opened the report given her by the nameless Kingdom noble and read it. She put it down, picked it up again and read it for a second time.

Standing up she shouted, 'Willoby!'

Within a moment, the cleric appeared, 'Yes, sister?'

'Three things: First, do I have a second-in-command?'

The question seemed to startle him for a moment, as she was known to be the Father-Bishop's second. 'Why, no,' he said, 'I mean, you are the second-in-command, but with the Father-Bishop gone . . . I mean, no, there's no designated person now.'

'Very well,' she replied. 'You are my second, as of now.'

He blinked, then said, 'I suppose that's all right.'

'Well, since I am currently the highest ranking member of the Order west of Malac's Cross, you can be sure it's all right.'

He seemed to take her forcefulness in stride as she stood up and put the report under her tunic. 'Next, have my horse made ready with a week's provisions.'

'Your horse?' asked the clerk.

'Yes,' said Sandreena. 'I need to depart on a mission today.'

'But who . . .?' he began, then saw her looking at him.

'You're in charge until I get back,' she said.

'Me?' He was almost speechless, but nodded and said, 'I'll have your horse made ready, Sister.'

She waited until he was gone then allowed herself a low growl of frustration. 'You bastard,' she said softly with Creegan in mind. She had mistaken his kiss as a signal of the passion they had withheld over the years, but reading the report had rid her of that notion. It was merely a kiss of apology. *Of course he wouldn't tell me what he would do about this*, she thought. Sandreena had no choice other than to do exactly what he would have done anyway: send herself on a mission that would most likely get her killed.

Swearing at the curse men had proved to be in her life, she moved out of his office and headed to the armoury to see if her newfound rank would provide her with better armour and weapons.

• CHAPTER FOUR •

Death Magic

*P*UG HELD UP HIS HAND.

The two black armoured guardsmen at the door to the ancient temple were startled to see the three men appear out of a grey void that had not been there moments before.

Pug said, 'We're here to see the High Priest.'

Amirantha looked up at the sky and saw a clear, starry night. 'We're somewhere in the east, aren't we?'

Jim said, 'Rillanon. This is the temple of Lims-Kragma.'

Amirantha said, 'That makes sense.'

On the world of Midkemia, no one had more knowledge of dying and the dead than the High Priest of the Goddess of Death. The two guards still looked unsettled by the sudden arrival of the three men, but their duty was to defend the portal only when there was an obvious attack underway. Their time was usually spent making sure that those arriving to offer prayers for their dearly departed remained orderly. Finally, one of them indicated that Pug and his companions were free to enter with a wave of his hand.

They passed through a large antechamber, replete with frescos of the Death Goddess. The exquisite brush strokes portrayed the final judge of every mortal being as a warm, benevolent figure, welcoming them into the vast hall of the main cathedral. Benches for contemplation and prayer by the faithful had been erected along both sides, while against the back wall two large shelves held hundreds of votive candles, most of which were alight; each flame had been placed to light the way of a loved one into Lims-Kragma's halls.

Pug took a moment to regard the heroic statue, some twelve feet tall, of the goddess, that dominated the cathedral. She held out one hand in a welcoming gesture, and in the other held a silver net. The symbolism was obvious: no one escaped the drawer of nets, but she welcomed all equally. Personally, Pug found the sentiment slightly ironic, since he had proved very adept at avoiding her embrace so far, although his bargain with the goddess was taking its toll on his mind and heart.

Three priests prayed before the statue, while on one side several petitioners seeking the goddess's mercy for a recently departed loved-one lit candles and offered prayers. As the three men approached, one of the priests turned and rose to greet them.

'Pug,' he said, in a neutral tone. 'What brings you here?'

'I need to speak with High Priest Marluke,' said Pug. 'The matter is most urgent.'

'It always is, isn't it?' said the Priest, dryly. 'Yet I am certain the Holy Father will consider it urgent as well. Please, follow me.'

He led them past the statue to a small door between the base of the edifice and the first row of burning candles. He opened it and motioned for them to go through, then followed, closing the door behind.

The priest led them down a long hall and into a large room devoid of decoration. The only items in the room were four chairs and a simple wooden table. 'I'll inform the High Priest that you are here,' he said.

At that moment, a door opposite the one through which they had entered opened, and an elderly man in a simple black cowled robe, entered the room. 'He already knows,' he said. 'You may leave us,' he instructed the priest.

He was tall, but starting to stoop a little with age, and he was slender to the point of gauntness; his hair was light grey, almost white, but his dark eyes were alert and keen and he had an engaging smile.

As the younger priest departed, the old prelate held out his hand to Pug and they shook. 'As if you could pop into my temple without me knowing it,' he said. Then he added, 'Ah, Jim Dasher, or is it Baron James today?'

Jim shook his hand as well and said, 'Today it's Jim.'

'And who is this?' asked the old man, waving at the three of them to sit.

'Amirantha, Warlock of the Satumbria,' said Pug.

The High Priest's eyebrows rose. 'A warlock!' He sat as soon as the others had taken their seats. 'I've sent for wine and food, if you're hungry.'

Jim nodded his approval.

Looking at Amirantha, the High Priest said, 'Leave the serious discussion until my servant has left us. Until then, let us become more acquainted. I thought the Satumbria were obliterated.'

'All but me,' said Amirantha without emotion. 'We were always a small nation. Just a loose confederation of villages, really, scattered around the northern grasslands of Novindus. The Emerald Queen's army ended our existence.'

'Ah,' said the High Priest as his servant entered. All four men sat silently as food and wine was served; then the servant withdrew.

The High Priest looked at Pug and said, 'No matter how many years pass, you look no different.' He turned to Amirantha and said, 'When I first met our friend here, I was a young priest, just ordained, and working in the temple at Krondor. While I was there, this fellow had several encounters with the High Priestess.' He looked regretful. 'A wonderful woman, really, when you got to know her; she was my mentor. It's because of her that I had this impossible office thrust upon me.'

He looked again at Amirantha. 'I suspect he will look the same years after I've gone to meet our Lady.'

Amirantha only nodded politely in response to the High Priest's musing.

Then the old man's manner changed. 'Enough reminiscing. What brings you here at this late hour?'

Pug said, 'I am not sure, myself. Amirantha, Jim?'

The Warlock turned to Jim, 'You begin.'

Jim had just bitten off a large hunk of bread and cheese, and was forced to wash it down with red wine; after almost choking a little, he said, 'Very well.' Again he shared his experiences in the Jal-Pur desert, describing the scene of slaughter and self-sacrifice as best he could. Given his years of training in observing detail, the narrative lasted almost half an hour.

None of the others spoke until he was finished. Pug said, 'That is horrible, indeed.' He looked at Amirantha, 'You demanded that we have an expert in death present. Now, what other than the obvious sickening detail, troubles you? What are we missing?'

Amirantha had been preparing for this question since he had first heard Jim's account. 'Nothing that Jim observed really makes sense. I will explain, but first let me ask the Holy Father, how much demon lore he understands?'

'Little, truth to tell,' answered the old man. 'Here our concerns lie in preparing the faithful for their eventual journey to our Lady. We are put upon this world to help a fragile humanity understand that this life is but a part of a more profound journey; to let them know that if they live a just and honourable existence our mistress will place them upon a proper path towards ultimate enlightenment. Beyond that, our knowledge is gathered piece-meal; we share what we know with others,' he acknowledged Pug with an inclination of his head, 'and have in turn been given the benefit of their wisdom.' He laughed. 'Besides, I was told to work with Pug.'

Amirantha looked surprised. 'Told to? By whom?'

'By Our Lady herself,' said the old priest. 'It is rare to have a visitation, but it does occur. Usually it's a revelation for the faithful and is proclaimed throughout the land, but in this case I was simply told to help Pug in whatever way I could and to keep my mouth shut about it.' He laughed. 'I may be the only leader in the history of the temple to have had a personal revelation and be unable to boast of it.'

Amirantha said, 'Then to understand what I must tell you, I shall have to tell you a story I have already shared with Pug and Jim.'

Amirantha detailed his childhood, describing his existence on the fringes of Satumbria society, his mother's role as witch and her being tolerated by the villagers because of her skill with potions and unguents. 'She was also very beautiful, and as a result, she bore three children by three fathers, none of whom would claim us.'

He went on to compare his brothers, explaining how the eldest, Sidi, had murdered their mother for pleasure. He painted the next eldest, Belasco, as a man obsessed with surpassing his brothers in any endeavour, spurred into rage by the mere thought of being bested, and as someone who had, for reasons Amirantha only vaguely understood, been trying to kill his younger brother for the last fifty years.

'I can't even begin to guess which slight, real or imagined, set Belasco on his quest for my death, but it hardly matters.' He paused to sip some wine to ease his dry throat.

'You possess a most interesting family, certainly,' the High Priest observed. 'But I'm failing to see how any of it is connected to Jim's report.'

'I'm getting there, Holy Father,' said Amirantha. 'I recount my history so that you'll understand fully what it is that I believe to be behind that murderous exercise in Jal-Pur.' He paused, gathering his thoughts. 'My eldest brother Sidi, whom you may also know by the name Leso Varen, was mad even as a child, and only got more insane as he grew. By the time he killed our mother he had become a remorseless monster with no sense of humanity. His obsession was death magic.'

49

The old priest nodded. 'I recognize the name Leso Varen; he was a necromancer of prodigious art and from all reports, a font of evil.'

'Whatever you have read would not have done the man justice,' said Amirantha as Pug nodded his agreement. 'If there ever existed a shred of humanity in his being, it was extinguished long before he became a player in this monstrous game we find ourselves in.

'But Belasco was different; he was consumed by envy and rage, jealous of any feat completed or skill attained by my brother or I. But unlike either of us, he had real talents, although he often neglected them in order to best our achievements. I can well imagine him dabbling in necromancy or demon lore, but the murderous scene that Jim described is . . . It's not something he would normally be party to. Nor is playing servant to a demon, no matter how powerful it is.'

'Why?' asked Pug.

Sipping his wine again, Amirantha said, 'Because Belasco would choose death before he would willingly serve anyone or anything.'

'There's more,' said the High Priest, and it wasn't a question.

'Belasco would also refrain from using this sort of death magic. Here's the conundrum: death magic is not used by those who consort with demons.'

Pug suddenly became very interested, and looked as if he wished to say something or ask a question, but instead he said, 'Go on.'

'Holy Father,' asked Amirantha, 'what use has death magic?'

Pug realized Amirantha had asked the question in order to clarify a point he was about to make.

'It's an abomination,' said the prelate. 'Death magic and

necromancy are misnomers, for the foulest form of life magic. At the moment of death, when life leaves the empty shell of our bodies, an energy is released. That energy, called the *anima* by some, and soul by others, is the fundamental core of being. Our bodies are transitory and will fail eventually, but the life force is eternal.' He held up a finger for emphasis, 'Unless . . . something prevents that energy from translating to Our Mistress's hall.'

Amirantha appeared impatient. 'I'm sorry to interrupt, Holy Father, but the heart of my question is what can be done with that energy if it's trapped, bound, or intercepted somehow?'

The High Priest was silent for a moment, then he said, 'An excellent question, but one beyond my knowledge.

'What little information we have on necromancy had been gathered during our extensive efforts to stamp it out; preventing a soul from returning for judgment is an abomination against our Mistress.' He turned in his chair and shouted, 'Gregori!'

A moment later his servant appeared, and he said, 'Ask Sister Makela to join us, please.'

Gregori bowed and left, and the High Priest said, 'Makela is our Archive Keeper. If she doesn't know something, she always knows where to find out about it.'

'I have already searched the archives of the Ishapian abbey at That Which Was Sarth.' Amirantha insisted.

The old prelate smiled and shook his head. 'The Ishapians are a noble order, and we venerate them, but despite their authority and knowledge, they tend to vanity from time to time. Their library is prodigious, but hardly exhaustive. Not every tome finds its way into their library.'

'But they have into yours?' observed Jim.

Smiling even more broadly, the High Priest said, 'We all exercise our prerogatives. Our discoveries remain ours unless we choose to share them.' Then his mood turned sombre. 'And much of the knowledge we choose not to share surrounds the area of which we now discuss; some matters are best kept secret or at least closely guarded by those who understand it best.' He turned to Amirantha. 'While we wait, why don't you continue with the other points you wished to make?'

'You're perceptive, Holy Father. Discounting my ignorance of the nature and purpose of death magic, or as you called it, the stealing of life force, I have never found any connection with it and the demon realm in my studies.'

Pug said, 'There is something about my past that should be mentioned now.' He looked at the three other men and said, 'When the Emerald Queen's host sailed across the ocean from Novindus to invade the Kingdom of the Isles and sack Krondor many years ago, their regent had been replaced. A demon named Jakan was wearing their queen's guise.'

Amirantha tilted his head slightly, pondering Pug's words.

'What remains unknown to all but the few of us who were there, is—' He hesitated for a moment as he realized that his late wife, Miranda, had been among those present during the events he was about to describe, and he felt a pang. 'I was about to say, it was not simply about conquest, but rather a massive assault designed to reach the city of Sethanon.'

Jim's brow furrowed. 'Why? Sethanon had been abandoned since the end of the Great Uprising. There was nothing there.'

Pug said, 'Even your Kingdom annals were not privy to what took place at that time, below the old city, after the Battle of Nightmare Ridge.

'During the Chaos Wars, the Dragon Lords fashioned a mighty artifact, called the Lifestone. I never had the opportunity to study it properly, it was deemed too dangerous, so we left it—' He considered the wisdom of revealing the exact whereabouts of the Oracle of Aal, and decided to not burden his companions with the information, '—hidden, in a deep cavern below the city.' He looked at the High Father and said, 'But, I believe the Lifestone was constructed from captured life force, as you have described.'

The High Priest snorted. 'Ishapians! I knew they were keeping something from us. Long have we been curious about what happened at Sethanon, at the end of the Great Uprising, and why King Lyam never attempted to rebuild that city. The official reason only stated that it was no longer an important trade route stop, and rumour said it was cursed.' He shook his head and sighed.

'The Ishapians knew only what we told them,' confessed Pug. 'And we only knew the Lifestone to be a vessel of great power, one that the demon Jakan was determined to reach.'

'But why?' asked Amirantha. 'What use would a demon have for such an artifact, no matter how powerful it is?'

'If we could deduce that,' said High Priest Marluke, 'then we might understand why your mad brother is so interested in slaughter and death magic, and what that has to do with this demon he seems to serve.'

Amirantha sat back and sighed. 'Perhaps, but I don't think so.'

'Why?' asked Pug.

'Let me ponder it a while longer before I offer any more speculation,' answered the Warlock.

'Can't we – I mean, you – study the Lifestone now?' asked Jim.

Pug shook his head in the negative. 'It was destroyed before the demon could reach it.'

The High Priest's face took on an expression of distress. 'Destroyed?'

Pug raised his hand in a placating gesture. 'Perhaps that's the wrong word. The elf queen's son, Calis, managed to unbind the confining magic and the trapped life energy within was set free.'

The High Priest appeared delighted at that news. 'A blessing! The souls were freed to resume their journey to Our Mistress!' He looked eagerly at Pug. 'What was it like?'

'It was difficult to describe, Holy Father. The Lifestone looked like a crystal, one that pulsed with green energies, but when it was . . . unravelled . . . a flurry of tiny green flames floated away, in all directions.'

The High Priest sat back and said, 'Throughout our temple's history, no such manifestation of the actual act of translation has been documented. The best we have are occasional reports that one of our priests, priestesses, or lay brothers and sisters might have glimpsed a tiny green flash.' He sighed in resignation. 'There are so few overt signs of what we do. Those of us who have been blessed by a visitation from our goddess . . .' He looked into his wine cup and took a sip. 'At times, it is difficult to convince the faithful. So few actually have experienced the divine.'

Pug resisted the urge to remark that he had experienced more than his fill of the divine. Several encounters with both the death goddess, Lims-Kragma, and Banath, the God of Thieves, Liars, and a host of other malfeasances had made it clear to him that the gods were as real as the chair upon which he sat; his faith was never an issue, but he certainly felt like their creature at times, and that thought left a sour taste in his mouth if he dwelled upon it too long.

The door opened and an elderly woman dressed in the garb of a priestess entered, followed by a younger woman in similar attire. 'You called for me, Holy Father?'

'Sister Makela, we have need of your knowledge.'

'I am at your disposal,' she said as Jim rose to offer the old woman his chair. She smiled, nodded her thanks and took the seat. She was as old as the High Priest, and frail in appearance, but she also shared the same lively gaze.

The High Priest outlined what had already been discussed. When he had finished, he asked, 'Have there been any exhaustive studies on the exact nature of necromancy, specifically what use the stolen life force might have to a necromancer?'

Without a moment's hesitation, the old woman said, 'Exhaustive, no. Several volumes of opinion exist, and I can have them brought up from the archives if you wish, Holy Father. The evidence suggests that necromancers usually have one of two goals. The first is to control the dead, harbouring enough life energy to animate corpses and direct them.'

'Why?' asked Jim.

'A dead servant holds several advantages,' suggested the librarian. 'It is impervious to death, obviously, and so can only be stopped by the utter destruction of the body. These "undead" can make prodigious bodyguards or assassins, and can be sent to places where the living can not long survive; for example, they can stay under water for a few hours, or in a cursed room, protected by poisonous vapour, or some other trap harmful to the living. Moreover, they can kill with plague or infection as well as weapons.

'The difficulty they present is that they decay, as do all the dead, though life magic can be employed to slow their deterioration for quite some time.'

'What's the other reason to use life magic?' asked Pug.

She sighed, as if she found the subject distasteful. 'They may also use it to extend their own life, even after death; they could preserve their consciousness in their mortal shell, rather than journey on to our mistress to be judged.'

'A lich,' said Amirantha.

'Yes,' agreed Makela. 'It is the ultimate act of defiance against our mistress and the natural order. But the toll is great, for the mind of the magic user who extends his life this way is always the first casualty of such evil; liches are mad from all our reports.'

'Madness does not exclude cunning and purpose,' observed Pug.

'True,' said the High Priest.

Amirantha looked at the librarian and said, 'Is there any mention in the annals about ties between such magic and the summoning or controlling of demons?'

The woman regarded the Warlock in silence for a moment, then said, 'Demons are creatures of the other realms; they are not answerable to the natural laws of our own world. We have had little experience of such practices, they are the province of other orders who serve Sung the Pure, or Dala Shield of the Weak.

'They may possess such knowledge, but I do not.' She looked at the High Priest. 'Is there anything else, Holy Father?'

'I think not, Makela. Thank you for your help.'

She rose, bowed slightly before the High Priest, then moved towards the doorway where her aide waited. As she reached it, she turned and said, 'I have thought of one other thing.'

'What?' asked the High Priest.

'A passing reference, nothing more: In ancient times a war was fought against a cabal of necromancers – which was a strange enough occurrence in itself since they tend to be solitary types – but it was their name that was most odd. They called themselves the Demon Brothers.'

Amirantha said, 'Is there more explanation?'

'No, only their name.' She tilted her head slightly as she thought. 'It was something I have always found strange.' She looked from face to face as she said, 'We always assumed it was simple propaganda, a name used to describe the cabal as evil. But the more I think on it, the more I believe it may have been more than this, for the accurate translation of their ancient name would be Brothers *to* Demons.'

'I hope this helps.' She nodded, as her assistant opened the door for her, and they departed.

The High Priest said, 'Perhaps this is of some use to you?'

Pug said, 'A great deal, perhaps, thank you.' He rose and Amirantha followed.

Gregori appeared and ushered them from the room, and then left them to their own devices in the large main hall of the temple. Jim asked, 'What next?'

'We go to Sarth,' said Pug. 'The Ishapians are usually accommodating, but not particularly helpful regarding this area, but now we have something specific to investigate.'

'The Brothers to Demons,' said Amirantha. 'A very odd name for a group of necromancers.' To Pug he said, 'Do we need to advise those waiting for us at the island that we're not returning immediately?'

Pug said, 'I'll see to it after we reach Sarth.'

'Good,' said the Warlock. 'Samantha becomes very cross with me when I fail to show up for meals on time.'

For the first time in recent memory, Pug laughed loudly. Everyone in the temple turned to stare at the sound, and several of those before the votive candles glared, for laughter was not frequently heard in the temple hall.

Jim said, 'Now would be a good time to depart, I think.'

'Stand close,' said Pug and he held out his hands. Each man gripped Pug's forearm, one to each side, and suddenly they were in another place.

CHAPTER FIVE

Legacy

*A*MIRANTHA GAWKED AT THEIR SURROUNDINGS. Jim also was astonished by the room but managed to retain a shred of decorum. Pug motioned for them to follow and led them deep into the vault.

'Vault' was the only word Jim could think of to describe the room in which they stood, for the ceiling receded into a gloom that prevented the naked eye from perceiving its exact height. Around them, massive columns rose to support the invisible ceiling, and row upon row of shelves joined them in an orderly fashion. The aisles they formed, and the intersecting rows between them, produced a layout like a chess board. At each junction a slender stand had been erected, graceful ironwork that bent, swan-necked, and ended in a hook from which a small crystal hung from a metal chain. The crystal provided just enough illumination to allow those in the room to see to the next lamp.

'Amazing,' said Amirantha, as he regarded the row upon row of books.

Jim echoed his tone when he said, 'I've been to the Royal Archives in Rillanon, but this library dwarfs them in scope. How many volumes are here, Pug?'

'I'm sure I have no idea,' said the magician as they moved between the shelves; some vanished into the gloom above, and most held ladders set on rails along the wall. 'Perhaps the librarian can tell you.'

'This is Sarth?' asked Amirantha.

'That Which Was Sarth,' corrected Pug.

'I don't follow,' said the Warlock.

Turning with a wry smile, Pug said, 'Before the invasion of the Emerald Queen's army, the Ishapians abandoned their abbey near the town of Sarth.'

'I still am not clear,' said Amirantha following Pug down a long narrow passage between vaults.

Pug stopped and said, 'The Ishapians have a prophecy, or perhaps *had* is a better choice of words. It said that a great upheaval would come upon the land, and after the destruction of the west, only That Which Was Sarth would remain.'

Amirantha looked at Jim, then Pug, and said, 'Was Sarth destroyed during the Emerald Queen's invasion?'

'Essentially,' said Pug, 'though the old abbey itself survived relatively intact; how it would have fared had the brothers still occupied it . . .?' He shrugged.

'So, they made the prophecy come true,' said Amirantha, as Pug resumed walking.

As the Warlock and Jim caught up, Pug said, 'Perhaps. Or perhaps there is more destruction headed our way, and only this place, That Which Was Sarth, is destined to survive it.'

'Exactly where are we?' asked Amirantha. 'I assume somewhere underground, as I did not notice anything resembling a window in the last two vaults we passed through.'

'We are very deep underground,' said Pug. 'As to where, I promised the monks I would never reveal their location unless I have their leave. You were transported here by magic outside your understanding, so I can safely assume that you have no way of returning here after our visit.'

Amirantha chuckled. 'Indeed.'

They reached a large door and Pug pulled it open. The room behind it was small, a table occupied half its area, over which stood a white-haired magician in black robes. 'Father,' said Magnus to Pug as they entered. Then he greeted Amirantha and Jim.

Next to Magnus stood a monk dressed in the simple light brown robes of the Ishapians. He was a nondescript man of middle years, with a round head topped with a thatch of brown hair cut in a tonsure. He inclined his head in greeting and said, 'Pug. You bring us guests?'

'Brother Victor, these are our friends; may I introduce James, Baron of the King's Court in Rillanon, and great grandson of Lord James of Krondor, also known as "Jimmy the Hand".'

The monk smiled. 'We possess a wonderful story about your ancestor that you may not have heard before,' said the monk.

'And this is Amirantha, Warlock of the Satumbria, a people from across the great ocean. He is something of an expert on demons and I have need of his wisdom.'

'Your vouching for them grants an indulgence,' said the monk. 'But the Father Superior may not be so kindly disposed.'

'Which is why I came straight here,' said Pug with a nod.

The monk smiled. 'So I should mention your visit when? An hour or so after you depart?'

'That should be ample time,' said Pug. 'We don't plan to stay long, unless the need arises.'

'Well then,' said the monk wearing a wry expression, 'what do you seek this time?'

Magnus turned to Amirantha and Jim, 'We've been testing Brother Victor's vast knowledge on every subject imaginable.'

The monk held up his hands, palms outward, and said, 'Hardly that.'

'He is the living index of where everything in this vast library is to be found,' said Pug.

Amirantha said, 'Simply, prodigious; but don't you keep some sort of written record here, too?'

'Of course,' said the monk, 'and a dozen of our brothers labour ceaselessly to update our records as new material is gathered, but until they complete their task, we make do with cobbled together notes, and this.' He tapped the side of his head with his forefinger.

'What do you know of the Demon Brothers?' asked Pug.

The monk's expression stilled. After almost a minute, he closed his eyes. 'I believe there has been mention of them . . .' His eyes widened. 'Wait! I'll be right back.' And Brother Victor hurried from the room.

The four remaining men exchanged curious glances, which became expressions of deeper puzzlement as they continued to wait. Half an hour passed before the monk finally returned, a dusty, old, leather-bound volume in his hand.

'It should be in here,' he said as if he had only just stepped out of the room then reappeared.

'What is it?' asked Pug as the monk laid the book down on the table and opened it gently.

'It's the chronicle of one *Varis Logondis*, a Quegan trader who lived about four hundred years ago. He was a compulsive journal keeper who believed every detail of his life deserved to be recorded.

'In fact, most of his life was unremarkable, unless you happen to be an aficionado of travelogues, long discourse on mercantile trends, or the state of Varis's digestive health on any given day during his life. But, he does remark in passing on many contemporaneous issues, which are useful in providing corroboration or refutation of other histories and accounts of the same period.

'But one of his remarks has stuck with me over the years.' He scanned the page. 'Ah, there it is. Let me read it out loud, the dialect is somewhat antiquated and his spelling is atrocious. "In the evening, we came upon a village, by name, Hamtas on Jaguard, whereupon we were welcomed at an inn by name, The Restful Station. There did we encounter soldiers of the Empire, at their ease after a battle.

'"I remark upon this for two counts," – I am certain he means *reasons* here – "'the first, that they were not of the militia, but were legionaries from Queg that had been haste posted to this region, and the last, that they had struggled mightily against the Demon Brothers and their living dead."'

'Four hundred years ago, most of the Bitter Sea was still under control of the Empire of Great Kesh,' Pug remarked.

'What is truly interesting about this passage, Pug, is that

its timeline supports two other sources that we are aware of, one of which is in our possession.' He looked at the magician and his two companions with a satisfied smile. 'Varis wrote sixty five volumes over his lifetime, so I had to skim a couple before I could locate this passage.' He pointed to the page and said, 'The other source we possess on that struggle is a fairly standard tally of captured goods returned to Queg by the expedition Varis encountered. We know that he was surprised to find Imperial Legionaries in that town instead of local soldiers, and both accounts imply that something significant was being undertaken. Legionaries were only stationed in three garrisons around the Bitter Sea at that time: Durbin, Queg City, and Port Natal. They were not used elsewhere unless there was an uprising or some other menace of equal weight.

'If we look at what that expedition brought back with them, we discover an unusual list: besides a remarkably short inventory of precious metals, livestock and slaves, we also see a very long list of idols, books, and scrolls.'

Pug looked interested, but unsure of what Brother Victor was implying. 'It sounds as if they raided a library.'

The monk smiled. 'There were no libraries nearby, neither imperial, nor any maintained by the religious orders known to us at that time; no libraries existed west of Malac's Cross or north of Queg! Oh, there were perhaps some rooms full of books here and there, but nothing on a scale that would have required a detailed catalogue that the Empire was so famous for at that time.' There was a merry glint in his eyes as Brother Victor's smile broadened.

'What is it?' Pug said, unable to resist returning the man's smile.

'It's your Demon Brothers!'

'According to this inventory of booty, over a score of the volumes seized came from the "frateri demonicus", which is a very bad Quegan spelling for Demon Brothers.'

'The necromancers?' asked Pug.

'Not a common name by any measure,' said Brother Victor. 'And there's more.'

'More?' asked Magnus a moment before Jim echoed him.

'The title of one of the volumes . . . At that time, legionaries were not much better educated than the common Keshian Dog Soldiers of today. Their officers could read and were literate – a necessity for the giving and receiving of orders – but the common soldiers were not. This list must have been complied by a relatively uneducated officer, or possibly the task was given to a lower ranking soldier who was barely educated. In any event, the title they have recorded is *Libri Demonicus Amplus Tantus* and translated as "Really Big Demon Book."'

Amirantha laughed. 'I speak Quegan, and that's not a phrase I recognize.'

'It's four-hundred years old. I originally assumed that the scribe didn't understand that *amplus* and *tantus* have similar meanings – ample and large – but it now occurs to me that our less-than-scholarly-scribe was simply trying to describe two of the book's aspects: that it's a large volume, but also that it's important. "Tantus" can mean "of such great size", but "amplus" can be read as "of great importance", as well as meaning "ample". So, what you may wish to consult next is this very large, very important book concerning demons, which was written by a necromancer four-hundred years ago.'

'I don't suppose you have that volume here?' asked Amirantha.

'No,' said Brother Victor with a regretful expression. 'I wish we did. It sounds fascinating.'

'But you know where we might find it?' suggested Magnus.

The monk nodded. 'Indeed, if it still exists.'

'The Imperial library in Queg, perhaps?' suggested Magnus.

Pug said, 'If the book remained among the property seized by the legionaries, and if they didn't loot the library when recalled to Kesh during the abandonment of the north . . .' He tapped his chin in thought. 'It's possible. They might have taken the gold and other valuables south with them, but books and scrolls? Not as likely. It's as Brother Victor said, 'I must leave you now, as evening prayer is about to begin. I assume you do not need me to show you out?' His merry expression revealed that he already knew the answer.

'No,' said Pug. 'Thank you my old friend.'

'No, thank you for all you have given us. Too few people realize how much they owe you, Pug.

'Until we meet again,' he finished, turned and left the four visitors alone in the library office.

Magnus said, 'We have a new problem, Father.'

'I know,' said Pug. He turned to Jim and said, 'Queg is the one court in which we have no friends.'

Jim sighed as he anticipated what was coming next. 'I thought you had agents, or at least friends, everywhere?'

Pug gave him a tight smile. 'Queg is strategically unimportant. We manipulated some information during the invasion of the Emerald Queen, so they believed they were attacking a foreign treasure fleet; instead they ran into her armada, half the Imperial Keshian Fleet, and the Kingdom Navy. Not wishing to attack nations they were at peace with, they did their best to loot a few ships which instead of treasure held angry soldiers. It made them distrustful of information that doesn't come from reliable sources.

'To the point, they resisted all attempts to infiltrate their intelligence.'

Jim smiled ruefully. 'I know. I have had the same problem.'

'What about Kesh?' asked Magnus. 'Have they placed anyone within the Quegan Court who might prove useful?'

Jim slowly shook his head. 'No, they're just as frustrated by their small neighbour as the Kingdom is. If Queg didn't possess such a formidable navy, they'd have been reabsorbed by the Empire, or conquered by the Kingdom, a century ago. There aren't many resources on the island worth seizing, but they are a serious annoyance; while they may not be strategically important to you, Pug, controlling Queg would prove a significant advantage to Kesh or the Kingdom.'

'Which is why neither of them will let the other gain influence,' finished Magnus.

Amirantha said, 'Back to the point, if you don't have anyone at court to help with the search, how do you propose we discover if this tome exists there?' He smiled dryly. 'Are you just going to appear one day and ask to browse the shelves?'

Pug's expression became distant for a moment, and then he smiled slowly. 'That may be just the thing.'

'What?' asked Jim. 'I was certain that you were going to ask me to swim ashore, sneak into the library and steal the book.'

'No,' said Pug, looking amused at the suggestion. 'You're going to use your rank to get the Prince of Krondor to send you, with three advisors,' he indicated the three of them, 'on a scholarly delegation, with the intention of correcting distortions of the truth in Kingdom history – which will appeal to Quegan vanity when you explain that in the process their glorious past will be forever enshrined in our annals. You will then seek permission for your three scholars to spend a few leisurely days browsing the shelves of the Imperial Library.'

Jim's face went through a spectrum of emotions, from surprise, to doubt, to agreement, then delight. 'Play to their vanity!'

'Yes,' said Pug. 'Then, if we find out that they have the book, you can sneak into the library and steal it.'

Jim rolled his eyes. 'Can't we just study it there for a while?'

'No,' said Amirantha. 'We will need to examine it closely, and that could take weeks. If it's written in some ancient variant of the Keshian language, we'll need to find a scholar who can help us understand it.'

'And the Quegans may become interested in why we are focusing on one ancient, obscure text about demons when we were supposed to be looking at their histories,' finished Magnus.

Amirantha said, 'It would be helpful if you could convince the Star Elves to let their Demon Master return once we hold the book.' Shaking his head slightly as if he hated making the admission, he added, 'He knows much that I don't. I taught him a few tricks when he was on the island, but I think we'd work faster if Gulamendis was with us.'

Pug looked at Magnus. 'Have we heard any more from the taredhel?'

Magnus shook his head in the negative. 'Only through Tomas. He and his Queen are still in contact with the Regent Lord, but you know how elves are about taking their time.'

'All too well,' conceded Pug. 'Let's worry about getting the book first.' He looked at Jim. 'Can you do it?'

'Of course I can. The Prince is an eastern caretaker who doesn't have any sense of, or much care about politics. He's content to hunt, drink, chase serving girls and allow me to reassure him that all is well. Then he reports the assurances back to the King, that all is well in the west.

'I'll have my personal scribe draw up the messages to the Emperor of Queg and . . . will sign them. If you think it would help, I can use the royal seal to suggest that the documents come from the King, himself.'

'Forgery?' said Pug with newfound respect. 'Is there no end to your larcenous skills?'

'I have a few limits,' said Jim with no hint of modesty. 'It will take a couple of weeks, and the sooner begun, the sooner done.'

Pug said, 'Very well. Magnus get us to the island, please, and then take Jim to Krondor.'

As they assembled to transport to Sorcerer's Isle, Amirantha said, 'I wonder how that demon loving elf and his brother are doing.'

• CHAPTER SIX •

Survivors

*T*HE DEMONS ATTACKED.

Gulamendis drew back his hand; his brow furrowed in concentration as he watched his brother from the corner of his eye. Laromendis had conjured a battle demon illusion that was all talons and teeth, muscles like iron lay over skin hard like dragon scale. Ignoring the less threatening taredhel magicians, the three demons facing the brothers threw themselves upon the most obvious danger. Demon logic was simple: dispose of the most dangerous foe, then turn your attention to the lesser. Logic was not a prerequisite for the harrying demons, those whose job it was to seek out hidden prey and drive them to where the demon captains waited. All they saw was a rogue demon, not of their cadre, in front of them and never for one moment considered the improbability of the situation.

As long as the demons believed in Laromendis's conjuration, they were subject to damage from it, and it attacked them with frantic mayhem, slashing and biting, tearing and gouging. From bitter experience, Gulamendis knew the illusion would hold for only a moment or two longer, before the real demons recognized it for what it was. Laromendis had never smelled a demon nor experienced its magic aura, so those components were lacking in the conjuration, and as soon as the demons recognized the fraud, the two magicians would be assaulted.

Gulamendis held his wand at the ready. It was a treasure, gained by guile and subterfuge, part of the hoard the elves had brought from Andcardia to E'bar, the city they had constructed on the ancient planet the Star Elves called 'Home'.

The wand had been the only thing that had kept the two brothers alive over the last few days, a period beyond the expectation of the Regent Lord and other members of his Meet who had wished to see the two brothers dead sooner. Only Tandarae, the new loremaster of the taredhel was kindly disposed towards the Demon Master and Conjurer, but he wasn't in a strong enough bargaining position to keep them from being dispatched to the Hub World.

They were holed up in a relatively defensible position: a cul-de-sac of abandoned cottages in the city. They were taking full advantage of the one approach, and had created a series of trip-wire alarms and alerts so they could rest periodically. Their orders had been to remain there until recalled to Midkemia, but both knew that the summons was unlikely to come, so they had secured their position and only fought when the demons managed to catch sight or wind of them.

The three that now battled Laromendis's conjuration were

minor demons, any one of whom the brothers could have bested in a hand-to-hand fight should the need arise, but together, they were enough to give the elves pause in engaging them directly.

This was the third time they had used this ploy, the other two instances had taught them how to refine the illusion and ready themselves for the moment they would truly engage the demons in combat.

Gulamendis took his eyes from the struggle for a moment; his brother had to concentrate on the illusion, so it was up to the Demon Master to stay alert for unexpected intruders while they stood exposed in the open, on top of the rise that led to the highest cottage on the small street.

Behind the struggle, he saw something flicker in the distance, near the entrance to the portals. He hoped it was the other elves here, answering a recall that he and his brother had yet to hear.

The Hub World was where the portals – what the humans called *rifts* between the worlds – were clustered. In ancient times, for reasons that in retrospect now seemed the height of prudence, a Regent Lord had decreed that only one portal from each world would provide access to this otherwise nondescript world. It had been home to barely a thousand elves, just enough to ensure the portals were operating as they should.

The portal to Andcardia had been breeched a long time ago, and shut down. Only one had been maintained from Hub, to the world of Locre-Amar, and from there, back to E'bar. Once that portal was closed, there would be no access to Midkemia for the demons; at least no access the taredhel were aware of. Unless the Brothers could keep the demons who still roamed this world from reaching the last remaining rift – and also get to it before them – the two magic users would be stranded here forever, with the hungry demonic castaways.

And Gulamendis's knowledge of demons told him there were too many to give the brothers much hope of survival.

Then the conjuration failed and Gulamendis extended the wand. A sphere of silver light with pink and blue colours scintillating across its surface expanded around him; as soon as it touched the demons they shuddered, went rigid, and fell to the ground at Laromendis's feet. They remained in spasm, and the brothers knew they needed to act quickly.

At first they had simply used the wand against the demons, but a couple had recovered quickly, and that had taught the magic users to weaken them first, in order to extend the period they were stunned.

The brothers drew their large battle knives and began to cut the demon's throats as fast as possible. Gulamendis reminded himself that even though this method was not as dramatic or immediate as using his magical abilities, it sufficed for these circumstances. The demon's essences would return to their realm, but to the best of his knowledge, the portal to the demon realm had been sealed, and by the time these three were reborn, their problem of escape from this planet would long be decided.

It was over in a few moments. The two tall elves stood covered in dark demon blood, their eyes watering from the stench of carrion and sulphur. 'That bought us a few minutes,' said Laromendis.

His brother nodded. 'I sense some more to the south, but they're not coming closer yet. We should probably make our escape now.'

'Which way?' asked Laromendis.

Both were tall, nearly seven feet in height, but had similar proportions to the lesser elves. Their massive shoulders narrowed to trim waistlines above their powerful hips and legs. Neither was a warrior by trade or inclination, but both had been forced to learn to kill and had become adept at it. It helped that Gulamendis understood each demon's vulnerabilities and always communicated what he could to his brother.

'That way.' Gulamendis pointed to the northeast. 'There should be an alley leading to the broad street; the last portal should be there.'

'I thought it was the other way,' said Laromendis, pointing to the northwest.

His brother smiled. 'So does everyone else.'

'You have a plan?'

'Always,' said his brother jogging in the direction he'd indicated.

The small city that had been the home of those left to care for the portals was a simple place to navigate under normal circumstances; but an invasion by the Demon Legion was hardly normal.

They carefully made their way between buildings, stopping at every corner to make sure they were unobserved. There were a small number of demons that could hide well, becoming almost invisible, but Gulamendis's sensitivity to any demonic presence usually alerted them to their proximity.

They reached to the last stretch of open ground before the building that contained the entrance to the hub portal and Laromendis swore. 'Flyers!' Circling above it like vultures were half a dozen flying demons.

'Can you do anything?' said Gulamendis.

'I'm tired,' replied his brother, 'but I think I can manage a small diversion. Give me a moment to compose myself.'

The Conjurer closed his eyes, called upon his last reserves of power, and abruptly Gulamendis saw the illusion. It wasn't much as conjurations went, a slight scampering presence between two of the houses near one of the hovering demons, but it was enough to make the creature shriek and dive towards the imagined prey. The others were only a moment behind it, and they all flew off up the side street. 'Now!' said Laromendis.

The two elven magic users dashed for the entrance of the building Gulamendis had indicated and made it safely inside. They waited for their eyes to adjust to the gloom of the unlit hall, before they looked for any ground forces waiting inside.

'Now,' said Laromendis softly, 'where are we?'

His brother squatted with his back to the wall, and Laromendis followed suit. 'While I don't make it a habit to eavesdrop, I happened to be close enough to hear two Sentinels discussing the last recall. This building houses a single portal, one designed for the last of us to flee through. Assuming it was the recall we heard, every elf who was on this world went that way.' He pointed to a door.

They were exhausted, tired to their cores, but necessity made them rise. Gulamendis closed his eyes for a moment then said, 'No.'

His brother knew he meant no demon sign lay beyond the door and they moved towards it.

Gulamendis opened the door; they moved slowly for the illumination normally employed around a portal was missing. In the distance they saw a faint light, which became a line along the floor as they crossed a hall and reached another closed door.

The Demon Master paused again, to see if he could sense any demons, but when he felt nothing, he gripped the latch and pushed aside the heavy wood.

The room was a mess. Bodies littered the floor and the single platform which supported the two magically imbued wooden arms which framed the portal, were so blood spattered they looked as if they had been painted red. The stench was nearly overwhelming, despite the brothers' days of exposure to demon carcasses.

The portal was inactive.

Gulamendis said, 'Well, isn't this a surprise?'

His brother let out a long exasperated sigh and said, 'No, it's not. Those arrogant bastards in the Regent's Meet must think they have everything under control and we're no longer useful.'

'Well, if I were inclined to give them the benefit of the doubt, I would assume they just didn't try hard enough to make sure we'd get the recall in time. From the looks of things here, it was a quick and dirty fight,' said Gulamendis.

A sound behind caused them both to spin round, daggers and swords at the ready; but instead of a demon, they saw another elf, wearing the garb of a sentinel. 'I'm wounded,' he gasped as he clutched his left side with his left hand, leaning with his right against the edge of the doorway.

Laromendis motioned for his brother to care for the Sentinel and said, 'I'll see if he was followed.' He hurried down the hallway.

'Let me see,' said Gulamendis to the Sentinel. The brothers' upbringing on the frontier had given them both a fundamental education in field dressings. The wound was long and deep. He had already lost a lot of blood. 'Let me bind it,' said the Demon Master.

He cut the bottom of the Sentinel's tunic, then tore away a long length of cloth, fashioning a crude bandage. The elf lifted his arm above his head, he was obviously in pain, but seemed slightly more comfortable once the make-shift bandage was in place.

Laromendis returned and said, 'Nothing followed.' He looked at the Sentinel. 'They neglected to send you the recall, as well, I see.'

'There was no recall,' said the Sentinel. 'The demons swarmed the hub and some of us counter-attacked to hold them off while others tried to draw them away so the galasmancers could shut down the portals.' He pointed to blood and gore splattered across the walls. 'We all tried to reach this location, but I and two others were cut off. The rest of the Sentinels and one galasmancer were heading here to use this portal. My two companions perished on the way, but I continued on.' He paused. 'I really didn't think the portal would still be open. But . . .'

'You had to see,' finished Laromendis.

'I had to see,' agreed the Sentinel.

Gulamendis said, 'It appears that those who got here didn't make it through. That's what's left of them.'

'But they got the job done.' Catching his breath, the Sentinel said, 'My name is Sentinel Arosha.'

Gulamendis introduced himself and his brother then said, 'We're sorry to hear about the sudden evacuation; it's nice to know that this place was shut down before the recall out of necessity, and was nothing personal.'

The warrior looked confused by his statement, but Laromendis said, 'Never mind.' He glanced at the doorway into the huge room. 'We need think of something very quickly because eventually . . .' He looked at his brother.

'The flyers and most of the smaller demons won't trouble us unless we wander close to them, but the more powerful ones will sense we are here eventually.'

The warrior looked at him and said, 'You know about demons?'

'More than I care to reveal,' he said, 'but I think I know how we can avoid them, for a while longer.'

'If only we knew how to open this damn portal,' said Laromendis.

Gulamendis said, 'Something has occurred to me.'

'What?' asked his brother.

Gulamendis looked at the bodies on the floor and pointed to one dressed in a robe, and said, 'Arosha, is that the galasmancer?'

The Sentinel's knees weakened, and Laromendis helped him sit. 'Yes, and the others are the rest of my company of Sentinels.'

'Then they didn't have time to escape.'

'Obviously,' said Laromendis to his brother. 'Your point?'

Gulamendis went to the body of the fallen portal builder and pulled a demon corpse that covered him, he then turned over the blood drenched figure. The dead elf clutched a yellow stone in his hand, so firmly Gulamendis had to pry it from his fingers. Holding up the faintly pulsing stone, he said, 'He didn't destroy the portal! He only pulled the power crystal from it.' He pointed to the empty hole where the crystal should be placed. 'The portal should open if we put this back in here, and we can get home!' He reached down and pulled a small bag from the galasmancer's belt and quickly tied it to his own.

'It wouldn't do any good,' said Arosha. 'For the time being, anything that travels through a portal from this world will be killed the second it steps through.'

'Lovely,' muttered Laromendis. 'Now what?'

Gulamendis paused, then said, 'We go somewhere else.'

'Where?' asked his brother.

'Sorcerer's Isle,' said the Demon Master.

'How do you propose we do that?'

Gulamendis said, 'When I visited the island I was shown one of their rift gates. The wards there that act as a beacon.' He realized he was now at the very edge of his knowledge. Looking at the Sentinel he said, 'How much do you know about portals?'

The wounded elf smiled slightly. 'I've been watching galas-mancers play with those things long enough to have a fair idea how they work. But I don't know if I could find a portal that we didn't build.'

'Here's what I know,' said Gulamendis. 'According to the human, Pug, their rifts share an affinity; if a rift exists there and you then create a second rift, it tends to follow the first.'

'Tends to?' asked his brother in a sceptical tone.

'If you have a better idea, I would welcome it,' said the Demon Master. 'You can activate this gate?' Gulamendis asked the Sentinel.

'Yes,' said Arosha. 'That's the easy part. Setting a different destination other than the one already cast is the hard part. I think I've seen it done often enough to have a sense of how to do it, but only to reach other known portals, all now closed. If I open any of them from this end . . . They'll be guarded or worse.'

'What's worse?'

'The portal could be buried under rock, or at the bottom of a lake.' The Sentinel shrugged, though it made him wince. 'I can imagine what would happen if you stepped through into solid rock.'

Gulamendis said, 'Do you know the way to E'bar?'

The Sentinel said, 'It is already set for the new city.' He slowly rose and said, 'But as I said, if we activate the portal and step through, archers will fill us with arrows before we say a word.'

Gulamendis became thoughtful and then said, 'We change something.'

'Something?' asked his brother.

'What?' asked the Sentinel.

'Set it just past E'bar. If Pug is correct, a new rift should form, somewhere nearby.'

'How nearby?' asked the Conjurer.

The younger brother fixed Laromendis with an exasperated look and said, 'I will settle for anywhere on the same planet.'

'As long as we don't end up in the middle of the sea, or under a mountain . . .'

'Can you do it?' asked Gulamendis.

The Sentinel indicated that he needed help to reach the portal controls and the Conjurer put his arm around the wounded elf's waist. Laromendis shot his brother a concerned expression and with a slight shake of his head told him the Sentinel was in worse shape than he had first thought. He helped the guardsman stand before the controls, and felt blood drenching his arm where he held him.

Runes were set in a large platter before them, several glowing with a faint light. 'There's magic in the device, independent of the gate power.' He pointed to the crystal Gulamendis held and said, 'That will get the gate open.' He glanced around and said, 'Let me study this while you look for another stone. The galas-mancer should have it.'

'What type of stone?' asked Laromendis.

'It may be purple or blue.'

Laromendis did as he was asked and returned a moment later with a purple crystal half the size of the yellow one his brother still held. 'What is this?'

'It will close down this portal after we go. The gate will be useless and the demons will have to find another way to E'bar.'

'How does it work?' asked Laromendis.

With a slight smile, the pale Sentinel said, 'I pull out the yellow crystal, replace it with this one, hit any mark on the controls . . .'

'And then what?' asked Gulamendis.

'It explodes.'

Both brothers were mute.

The Sentinel said, 'We all know I'm already a dead man. I can barely stand. You'd better go now, or I won't be able to close the portal after you. Good fortune.'

Laromendis started to say something, but couldn't find the words, so he simply nodded.

The Sentinel placed the yellow crystal in a small depression cut in the surface of the control panel and it began to pulse with a stronger light. He struck all the runes but one, and held up his hand. 'I've put in the runes needed,' he started to sway, but gripped hard on the edge of the panel. 'Pick any rune save that one.'

Gulamendis didn't hesitate, he reached over, picked one randomly and pushed it. A faint hum was followed by a sudden increase in the pressure of the room, as if a huge influx of wind swept through it; then they heard a faint thumping sound. A grey void, colours shimmering across its surface like oil on water, appeared between the sides of the portal device.

'Go, quickly,' said the Sentinel, and the brothers hesitated for only a second, then stepped through. Certain death was their reward if they remained, so it made little difference if death also waited on the other side of the portal. But it also held the chance of salvation, and so they took it.

They were under water. They both experienced a moment of disorientation and used all of their focus and will power not to gasp in lungfuls of water. It was also very dark.

Fighting his panic, Laromendis realized they were not too deep, as he had learnt to judge water pressure while diving for shellfish as a youth. He blew out a small breath and felt the bubbles rise up his face. In the gloom he knew which way as up. He grabbed his brother's arm and pulled, and they both swam furiously to the surface.

They had been less than ten feet below the surface, but it had felt like one hundred. They broke above rolling combers and spat out mouthfuls of seawater.

Gasping for air, Gulamendis said, 'We aren't dead . . . Yet.'

Looking around, his brother said, 'We have time. I have no idea where we are.'

Gulamendis said, 'This isn't Home.'

'How do you know?'

'Demons. I can sense them.'

'How many?'

'A lot.'

The chop of the sea water would have been called relatively mild by a sailor, but that judgment was made from a boat. The peak to trough was roughly six feet, so they tried to time their exploration, looking in circles each time they crested the rising water.

'Lights!' said Laromendis.

'Where?' asked his brother as he slid into a trough and began to rise again.

'That way,' said Laromendis.

'I can't see where you're pointing. It's as dark as a cave.'

'You're right.' He swam closer to his brother and could barely make out his face. But it was faintly illuminated and Gulamendis turned to look for the light's source.

A single moon had risen high in the night sky, a slivered crescent obscured by a heavy curtain. 'Fog,' said Laromendis.

'Then we'd better make for those lights before they are obscured,' said Gulamendis. He felt his brother's hand on his shoulder and felt himself moving. He didn't need any more convincing and began to swim.

The brothers were not particularly powerful, but their people had greater strength and endurance than humans or even the lesser elves of Home. And both had spent years living close to an ocean, so could swim well. They had been forced to rely on what they could bring in from the sea more times than they cared to remember.

'Listen,' said Gulamendis as he paused.

'What?'

'I hear breakers.'

'Good. I'm starting to go numb and was desperately hoping we saw lights on land and not a passing ship.'

Saying nothing more, they set out towards the sound of breakers.

Minutes later the two exhausted, chilled elves heaved themselves out of the surf and trudged ashore in the dark. The beach was broad and welcoming, which they both counted as fortunate.

A sudden crash into jagged rocks would have almost ended this escape.

'Where do you think we are?' asked Laromendis.

'I have no idea, but with a little luck I might be able to find out. Even if this is one of the worlds taken by the Demon Legion, we might be able to come up with another means of reaching home.'

'You always were the one able to look on the bright side of things; it's ironic that you ended up spending so much time in dark caves as a child.'

His brother tried to chuckle, but couldn't quite find the energy. 'There!' he said suddenly, pointing to light dotting the side of the hill above them, before they were again consumed by the mist.

'Torches, I think,' whispered Laromendis. Without another word they started moving up the beach, moving cautiously in the darkness. Like all of their race, they possessed good night-vision, but they still needed some light with which to see, and the sliver of moon provided very little. The land was shrouded in a murky haze as they worked their way carefully along a path, possibly a game trail, that led away from the beach; movement was slow as it was littered with rocks and bramble.

Gulamendis kept his voice low and said, 'There are a lot of demons nearby.'

His brother whispered, 'We need to get further away from the beach. If there are demons around, we need to find a place to hide until we can work out what to do next. You were the one who told me some of those flyers can see in the dark.'

'Thanks for reminding me,' the Demon Master whispered in return. 'But not many of them are able to, and none of them like to fly in fog, it would be too easy to fly into something.'

They reached a sharp bend in the path and continued up the hillside. As they climbed higher, the fog thinned and a few minutes later they broke clear of it. The sky on the other side of the cliff was aglow, and they crouched instinctively fearful of being spotted by sentries.

Looking down, they could just see the game trail they had climbed vanish below them into a low lying bank of heavy mist. The heavy marine air that rolled in off the sea at sundown, would usually burn off by midmorning, but natural barriers like the cliff face could hold it in place for longer if it was thick, although the mist would never extend far inland.

Nearing the top of the bluff, they saw no sign of any other living thing, but they continued to move with exhausted caution. Neither of them had enough reserves left for a fight or a dash. Besides, where would they flee to?

The bluff swept away on both sides as they came to a cut at the top of the trail and found themselves on a plateau. Even without the fog, there was little light, the sliver of moon provided only faint illumination.

Scrub and a few scrawny trees dominated the landscape: a vague tangle of shadows and patterns of dark grey and black aided by the weak distant glow in the distance.

'Demons?' asked Laromendis quietly.

'No closer than they were,' answered his brother.

'I suggest we just sit and wait for dawn.'

Gulamendis squatted on the ground, then slowly stretched out his legs. After a moment, he said, 'No,' and rose quietly.

'No, what?' asked his brother, on the verge of sitting.

'You rest. I'll stay awake.'

'Why?' said Laromendis, despite the fact he didn't intend to argue over it.

'You have spent the last three days spinning illusions while I have only pointed a wand now and again. We both know I have no control over demons if their captains or lords are around, and even if I could command one, there are dozens running around us.

'You need rest more than I do, and if we need any talent tomorrow, it will be your skill at conjuration. I'll sleep tomorrow if we can find a safe place.'

'You have no idea how long we have until dawn. The sun may have set only an hour ago.'

'I have no idea how long night is on this world, either, but it doesn't matter. Sleep and I'll keep watch.'

Not wishing to argue any more, Laromendis put his head on his arm. It wasn't the first time he had been forced to sleep on the ground, and he welcomed the hard soil beneath him as if it were as soft as a feather mattress.

Despite his claims to the contrary, Gulamendis was as fatigued as his brother, but was determined to stay alert. His awareness of the demons made it far easier, and while he knew he flirted with exhaustion, he managed to fight it and stay awake.

The hours dragged by and the Demon Master shivered while his body heat slowly dried his clothing. He wondered how his brother had managed to fall so quickly into a slumber, then laughed silently at the question; had he the opportunity, he would also have been fast asleep on the ground in an instant.

He studied the night sky. He knew little about the skies of any world, it wasn't an area of interest, so the idea that he might recognize a constellation or any other astral sign and be able to discern their location from it was no more than an idle thought.

Moving and humming absently, to keep awake while his brother slept, he wondered at the strange course of events that had brought him here, and how they had in some strange way, brought him closer to Laromendis than they had ever been.

As children they had shared an interest in all things magical, and as initiates into the Circle of Light, they had shared their early training; but when the Regent's Meet had disbanded the Circle and, according to rumours, conspired to murder some of their more powerful members, the brothers had been separated for years.

They had later discovered that their paths might have crossed on several occasions during that time. They had even lived on opposite sides of the same island for the better part of a year without realizing, although – as his brother had wryly pointed out – Gulamendis had stayed in a cave high in the hills, while Laromendis had resided in the island's sole town, working as a labourer while the purging of the Circle had continued.

Only the Demon Legion's onslaught had staved off further persecution of the remaining members of the Circle. Gulamendis was certain that others still hid, but most had answered the call of their people, and had been welcomed back to Andcardia when the Regent's Meet granted them amnesty.

Amnesty for all but the Demon Masters. Fate had spared Gulamendis, for only days before he arrived at the Regent's court his brother had 'volunteered' for the mission to seek out a refuge for the taredhel should the demons overrun their capital. Because of Laromendis, Gulamendis had been kept in a cage but had been allowed to live; most of the Demon Masters hadn't been so fortunate.

The sky lightened and the black shapes resolved into greys and lighter greys. The Demon Master waited until he could see trees above them clearly enough to chance moving through them, and then he shook his brother awake.

Laromendis came around instantly, but it was clear he was still exhausted. He glanced about them and nodded. Without further communication the two elves moved into the woods.

The trees were scrawny and parched, and the brothers knew that finding fresh water might be a problem. The brush was dry and cracked when they stepped on it, so both moved slowly and with great care.

Finally they reached a small clearing where an extrusion of stone formed a ridge. They peered over the edge and Gulamendis whispered, 'Merciful ancestors!'

As far as the eye could see fires ranged, organized so that strict lines of flame defined areas of the camp. Many figures rested around the blazes and the Demon Master tugged at his brother's sleeve.

They moved back, away from the edge into the relative shelter of the trees. It had been these fires illuminating the sky the night before, the light had not come from one small fire nearby, the gloom had been pierced by hundreds of distant fires.

'It's the Legion,' whispered Gulamendis.

Laromendis said, 'Where are we?' As soon as he asked, he knew it was a stupid question, for his brother had no more knowledge of their whereabouts than he did.

They exchanged silent looks holding the same understanding: they were on the world being used by the Demon Legion as a staging ground. The demons below them were unlike any they had seen or fought before: armed, organized and resting before the invasion. About them lay a calm entirely unnatural for demons, it was frightening; and from their organization, the Legion would be moving soon.

Finally Gulamendis said, 'There is one good thing about this.'

'Really?' asked his brother, his eyes widening.

'If they're here, and if they plan to invade Home, it means they have a way to get there.'

'A Demon gate?'

'They must,' said the Demon Master. 'We just need to find it and get through it before they do.'

His brother shook his head. Words failed him.

• CHAPTER SEVEN •

Queg

*T*RUMPETS SOUNDED.

James Dasher Jamison, Baron of the Prince's Court, Envoy Extraordinary of the Kingdom of the Isles, occasional diplomat and full time spy turned to his companions; Pug, Magnus, and Amirantha were dressed as scholars, wearing light tan robes and sandals.

'One more time,' he said.

Pug smiled, but Magnus and Amirantha looked annoyed.

'One more time,' he repeated. 'These stories must be the first thing you think of should you be faced with unexpected questions.

Pug looked at his son and the Warlock, and said, 'I am Richard, a historian from the Royal Court of Rillanon. I have lived there for years.' Pug had spent enough time in the capital city over the last hundred years to easily describe most of the famous aspects of the 'Jewelled City,' and its recent politics had occupied all discussion between the four of them as they sailed from Krondor to Queg.

'I am his first student, Martin,' said Magnus. 'I have recently come to the capital and am still finding my way around.' Unlike his father, Magnus had spent relatively little time in Rillanon, so the identity chosen for him would serve that fact. 'I originally came from Yabon.' He knew that area very well.

Both father and son looked at Amirantha who said, 'I am Amirantha, a scholar from the distant city of Maharta. I have a royal patent from the Maharaja of Muboya, courtesy of General Kaspar, First Minister to the Maharaja, commissioning me to learn all I can about the nations of Triagia, and I am collecting histories toward that end.'

'Try to look a little more enthusiastic about it,' said Jim.

'Shouldn't we get up on deck?' asked Magnus.

Jim smiled. 'Quegan protocol dictates we keep them waiting for at least another five minutes, ten would be better. Quegans are an odd people: they favour self-aggrandizement, to the point that they consider even the Imperial Keshian Court "degenerate," and see themselves as the true inheritors of all things magnificent and imperial. They would seem silly if it wasn't for that irritatingly large navy they insist on sailing all over the Bitter Sea. That earns them a great deal of respect they otherwise wouldn't enjoy. Their position as something of a balance-shifter here in the west keeps them more or less at peace with their neighbours, but should the cause arise that unites the Free Cities, Kesh, and the Kingdom, we'd happily obliterate this island.' He said the last with a cheerful expression.

'But then you'd have another war over who got to keep the island,' said Amirantha with a wry expression.

'Oh, I'd be happy to let Pug and some of his compatriots just sink it.' He looked at the magician. 'You could manage that, couldn't you?'

Pug shook his head and deemed not to answer.

'What we have now is very little time. The Imperial Archivist is at our disposal, but for only three days. You must discover what we need to know in two, because if I am to break in and steal something, I need to plan how to do it the day before we leave.' He sighed. 'While I have little problem with robbing the Quegans, I do have a problem with needlessly starting a war, especially when soon we may need to fight a far more dire one. The Quegans are suspicious by nature, and you will be watched, so always remember there are eyes watching you and ears nearby, even if it doesn't seem that way. Once we leave this cabin, we will be living our roles as noble and scholars. If you have any questions, now is the time.'

No one did; they had rehearsed their various roles for the full seven days of sailing time from Krondor to Queg. The necessity of arriving publicly by ship had given them a great deal of time to perfect and review their plan.

'Well,' said Jim, standing, 'I think we've kept the Quegan nobles standing in the hot sun long enough. Let us go and be diplomatic.'

Pug and his two companions followed Jim up to the deck and found the sailors of the Kingdom Ship *Royal Dolphin* securing their vessel. A long gangway had been run out to the dock below and Jim paused dramatically at the top of it before starting his descent. Pug had not visited Queg in more than a century and his first sight brought amazement at how little had changed.

The City of Queg, capital of the island nation of the same name, was really made up of two cities. Below them lay the docks, the poor quarter, and every manner of industry given to dirt, blood, and filth: the tanners, dyers, slaughterhouses, fish markets and forges. The air hung heavy with smoke and soot, odours that assaulted the senses and noise to deafen.

The streets thronged with workers, traders and fishmongers. Few travellers came and went; Queg was not considered a hospitable nation.

The upper city rose upon the hills behind the harbour, and was dominated by the Emperor's palace. It shone brightly in the sun, for its walls had been faced with white marble over the years, and on clear days, this gleaming jewel of a building could be seen for miles out at sea. It was also, Pug thought, one of the finest examples of excesses and bad taste that could be found on Midkemia.

A delegation of Quegan officials waited for them on the dock, none of whom looked especially pleased at the duty before them, but all effecting broad smiles; their forced air of welcome that was less than persuasive. They wore the traditional white togas of office, each lined with a single band of colour that ran over the shoulder and along the hem. Those trimmed in red were city officials, while those in gold represented the Emperor. As only one person wore gold trim, Jim presented himself to him. 'I am Baron James, of the King's Court in Rillanon, and these are my companions.'

The official said, 'I am Lord Meridious, Chancellor of the Imperial Archives; I have been given the honour of hosting your visit.' He was a round-faced man, but broad of shoulder, heavy muscle was evident under his fat.

Jim shook the man's outstretched hand and said, 'I thank His Imperial Majesty for his courtesy and willingness to allow our scholars access to your archives. Especially in light of the abrupt delivery of the request.'

'It was rather odd,' agreed the Chancellor, 'but his Imperial Majesty is always anxious to keep harmonious relations with our neighbours and it seemed a small favour to ask.'

Jim turned and motioned to his three companions. He introduced Pug, Magnus and Amirantha. Seemingly overawed by the presence of the official's own majesty, all three magicians managed a fair imitation of a self-conscious bow.

'We have litters ready to bear you to the palace,' said the Chancellor.

Jim nodded and with a tilt of his head indicated that the others should follow. They walked along the docks between two lines of Quegan soldiers, four with herald horns which had been sounded when the ship had arrived. Now they stood motionless in the hot sun awaiting the order to return to barracks.

Reaching the quay, they found four litters waiting for them. The various city officials, who had not uttered a word, retired to their various offices and the Chancellor invited Jim to enter a litter. Pug shared another with Amirantha, and Magnus took the third.

The litter bearers were uniformly muscular young men, wearing only the heavy linen skirt of their trade, and heavy-soled cross gartered sandals. Their bodies gleamed with flower scented oils so their perspiration would not annoy their passengers. They picked up the litters and started off at a quick pace, while two soldiers marched ahead of them, clearing the citizens of Queg from their path.

Amirantha kept his voice low, and in neutral tones said, 'So, this is Queg?'

Pug smiled and nodded. He knew, as did Amirantha, that it was likely one or more of the bearers were listening, and they would almost certainly be a Quegan agent. 'Yes,' said Pug. 'Does your master know much of this place?'

'A little,' said Amirantha, going along with the pretence he represented the Maharaja of Muboya. 'One of my tasks was to learn as much about the Kingdom's neighbours as I could, as well as being tasked to study your nation. Queg was once part of Great Kesh, true?'

'Yes,' said Pug, assuming the Quegan agent listening would not pay close attention to a history lesson he knew as well as Pug did. 'A great revolt among the client states known as the Keshian Confederacy in the south of the Empire of Great Kesh, caused her to recall her legions from the north. They abandoned all of the lands to the west and south of Yabon. The Kingdom then pushed forward, out of Yabon into what is now the Far Coast, but the former Keshian cities on the shore of the Bitter Sea repulsed the Kingdom's invasion and formed the Free Cities.

'Queg was in a unique position; it had housed a garrison and the naval yards, but while the legions left, the navy refused to depart, as their families and lives where here. Kesh was kept busy fighting in the south, and by the time they had crushed the Confederacy rebellion, Queg had achieved independence and controlled the Bitter Sea.' He paused as if thinking. 'The people who lived here came from a relatively small province of the Empire, I believe it was called Itiac.' He knew better than that; they had in truth come from a province called Itaniac, but Pug wanted whoever listened in to believe he was no expert on the history of the island nation. 'I want to study some documents from that era and earlier, if possible, as our Kingdom history is full of holes and many misunderstandings.

'Our relationship with Queg has not always been as good as it should be, and as a result many erroneous notions about its history and people circulate widely in the Kingdom of the Isles. I will take pride in correcting those misunderstandings.'

'Well, it's all new to me,' said Amirantha, playing along. 'Whatever I learn will be useful for my reports. Perhaps my master will wish to send a trade delegation here; you say the Quegans build good ships?'

'Among the best,' said Pug, knowing that was a shade of the truth. The Quegans built fearsome war galleys, but they were coastal-clinging vessels not meant to be sailed further than a day or two off shore. They possessed nothing that could cross as vast an expanse as the Endless Sea, to the west of the Straits of Darkness and reach Novindus. Still, flattery always appealed to those who wanted to believe it sincere.

Amirantha and Pug chatted about nothing particularly significant as they observed the city through which they passed. The docks, disreputable inns and ignoble businesses gave way to a series of broad streets that housed more prosperous industries; many buildings stood several stories tall, their proprietor's families occupying the top floors. Beyond them stretched a green belt of parkland which marked the boundary between the lower and upper cities. On the rising hillside large homes with sprawling gardens and fountains gave way to even larger estates surrounded by high walls and sturdy gates. Most were guarded by soldiers wearing private livery, their uniforms competing with their neighbours in terms of ostentation. In contrast to the Imperial soldiers dispatched to meet them at the docks, some of the domestic guardsmen wore highly polished chest guards and helms of steel, painted in bright colours, while others went further, employing gold trim or ridiculous plumes of feathers or died horsehair. The guards looked stout enough to keep vagabonds and rabble from disturbing their masters, but one glance from Amirantha revealed what the Warlock truly thought of these fighting men.

Upward they travelled, until they reached the Imperial district: the buildings surrounding the Emperor's palace and offices. These apartments and villas were set aside for the functionaries and officers of the court, and all had been faced with white marble. 'Centuries ago, this part of the city was like the rest of it, made only of stone and wood, but years ago, an emperor – his name is lost to me now – attempted to restyle it to be the most beautiful city in the world. He started to bring in this white stone from a massive quarry in the south. Over the years the entire Imperial district has been finished to match.' He looked at Amirantha with an expression which made it clear that what he had to say next was for the benefit of their eavesdropper. 'It is said that Rodric the Fourth, known as the Mad King, was so envious of its beauty that he commanded Rillanon be likewise finished in white stone, but because he could find no fine white marble, he was forced to settle for an inferior riot of colours.' The truth, as Pug well knew, was exactly the opposite. The Imperial palace of Queg had always been encased in white marble, but it was only after Rodric of the Kingdom had begun the beautification of Rillanon – a task completed by his successor, King Lyam – that the Emperor Jumillis of Queg, had initiated his frenzied beautification of all of the Imperial district. The only reason he had stopped there was because the quarry had almost been exhausted; the remaining marble had been stored for repair, in case of weather and other damage.

Pug sat back silently for a moment remembering King Rodric whom he had met on his first visit to Rillanon; his contemplation brought on a dark and reflective mood upon him, a feeling he had managed to avoid since being sought out by Jim and Amirantha. Rodric had been a sorely troubled, but basically good man, driven mad by an illness no one could cure, and only lucid at the end of his life, when he had named his cousin Lyam his heir and saved the nation from a bloody civil war on the heels of twelve years of fighting with the Tsurani.

Such reminiscing made him think of everyone he had lost over the years: his old teacher, Kulgan, and Meecham, Kulgan's companion, Father Tully one of his first and wisest teachers. Princess Carline, whom he once thought he loved, and Laurie one of his closest friends, who had wed the Princess. Laurie had died too young and left Carline a widow for far too long. Lord Borric . . . He sighed and Amirantha looked at him with a questioning expression. Pug held up his hand to indicate it was of no importance, but the sinking feeling in the pit of his stomach remained. He had lost Katala, his first love, his first wife, to a wasting sickness no magic or art could cure. His first two children, William and Gamina, died the end of the war with the Emerald Queen's army. And now Miranda and his youngest child, Caleb, were gone too.

Pug pushed aside the feelings and chided himself for not conquering his black moods. He had known from the day he had made his bargain with the gods that this would be his fate, yet he still resented it.

The litters finally arrived at the entrance to the palace, saving Pug from more unhappy reflection. He glanced over and saw Amirantha studying him.

The three 'scholars' climbed out of the two litters and were immediately shown to their quarters, while Jim was escorted to a reception in the Emperor's Court. As part of his official retinue, they could have accompanied Jim had he insisted, but Pug had already decided there was work they could do, even from their closely guarded quarters.

Once they were alone, he nodded once to Magnus, who then sat on a chair in the corner of the room. Pug spoke to Amirantha and said, 'These Quegans seem like hospitable enough folks.'

Amirantha looked around the room, a large ante-chamber designed for entertaining and holding casual conversation; there were two doors in the walls to the right and left of the chamber's main entrance, and a large vaulted window opposite them. Amirantha said, 'Lovely view,' and Pug joined him.

'Yes,' said the magician as they looked down on one of the palace's many gardens. This one was dominated by a large pool in which several people were swimming or lounging.

Amirantha's eyebrows rose slightly when he realized the bathers were all nude, and he said, 'Ah, is that the custom here?'

Pug said, 'The Quegans are Keshian by ancestry. The Imperial Court of Great Kesh has a very hot climate, placed upon table-lands overlooking the Overn Deep in the heart of the empire. Their attitude towards dress is very different to those held by the Kingdom. We are a cold weather people most of the time and so dress accordingly.'

'I see,' said Amirantha. 'I pass no judgment. I just find it . . . interesting.'

'Ah,' said Pug with a smile. 'Don't let it become a distraction.'

'Unless the librarians are pretty young women wearing no clothing, Richard,' he said, using Pug's false name, 'I think I shall be fine.'

Pug laughed, but his eyes searched every inch of the room. They had assumed they'd be spied upon, but didn't know to what extent they would be monitored. It could be as simple as a listening post in a nearby-room, eavesdropping through a simple sound chamber, or through a tiny tube of metal hidden behind a tapestry or decorative plant, or they could well be employing a complex scrying spell, a possibility that Magnus now attempted to determine.

Pug looked at his son, who opened his eyes and shook his head once: they could detect no magic at play. 'I think I'll lay down for a while,' said Magnus as he stood up and moved to one of the nearby doors.

Pug nodded agreement and went to another. Opening the door, he found a small but well-appointed room containing a simple free standing closet, a clean bed under a window that looked down on a tiny flowerbed and across to another window, which was possibly an additional guest apartment from what Pug could tell. He saw no movement through the window and assumed that apartment was empty.

Pug closed the door and lay down, gathering his thoughts.

Since Miranda and Caleb's death, any amount of reflection plunged him into morbid introspection. He had fought many battles in his life; losing Nakor had begun the struggle, but the death of his wife and son had defeated him.

Still, there was more work to do and he had to pull himself out of a deep cauldron of self-pity and rage towards the gods that shackled him; he had made the bargain, he reminded himself again; he could have left this life after battling Jakan, the demon disguised as the Emerald Queen, but had elected to return and continue the struggle. The price he paid was to watch everyone he loved die.

He sat up. Something tickled the edge of his mind.

Standing, he hurried to the door leading into Amirantha's bedroom and quietly knocked. When the Warlock answered, Pug held up a warning finger before his lips, then motioned him to follow to Magnus's door. He knocked lightly again, and when his son appeared made a circling motion with his hand. Magnus nodded and motioned for them to enter.

Once in the room, Magnus positioned the two other magic users to stand close to him. He closed his eyes for a moment then said, 'We are shrouded. It is only a weak enchantment, more strength might alert anyone watching us.'

'We're being spied upon by magic, as well?' asked Amirantha.

Pug said, 'My son has skills even beyond mine. As you can sense demons he can sense the practice of magic, even to the point of understanding the spells and being able to counter them.' He looked at his son with pride in his eyes. 'It's a rare gift.'

'They are only using a poor scrying spell, easily defeated. But the longer I maintain the illusion that we're talking about which books to examine tomorrow, the more likely it is someone may discover my counter-spell. So, what is it?'

Pug said, 'Amirantha. I need to ask you something. We have spoken so much about what we know of demons and what we don't know, that occasionally a question gets set aside and we forget to revisit it.

'We have speculated much on what happened to Maarg on Shila, but we never returned to something you wished to discuss,' he said quickly to Amirantha. 'You were surprised at the demon captain Jakan seizing the Emerald Queen's body?'

'Demonic possession is very rare,' said Amirantha, speaking softly and quickly. 'And such cases have always been limited to a particular sort of creature. I think of them as spirits or ghosts as much as the demons we face. The idea of a powerful demon lord, one of the great captains, or one of equal strength possessing such an ability . . .' Amirantha shrugged. 'I really don't remember what I wanted to ask at the time. I am simply confused by it.'

'Why?' asked Magnus.

'It's not typical demon behaviour. Piecing together what you've told me, and what I learned from Gulamendis, I'm beginning to get a rough idea of demonic society, if it can be called that. Or rather, how things are done in the demon realm. It's chaotic by our standards, yet it has rules and boundaries. This demon possession by a powerful, magic-using demon just doesn't fit in with them.'

He looked around, frustrated, 'This really isn't a subject we can discuss in short, but it's good that you brought it up. If we don't find this tome we need, be alert for any other references to demon encounters or lore. It might provide us with additional insights.'

Pug nodded, 'We'll talk more when it's safe to do so.'

They parted company and Magnus dispelled the illusion he had conjured as the counter spell and they waited quietly in their rooms until they were summoned for supper with Jim.

The meal was sumptuous in true Quegan fashion. Four long tables had been established in a square, with just enough space left between the corners to allow servants to move inside the open area to bring fresh trays of food. Each guest was free to pick whatever morsel appealed to them or wave the servant past. Behind them moved more young men and women carrying large vessels of wine and a very light ale.

The servants were uniformly attired in a simple tunic that fell below the knees, cinched at the waist with a double cord. Pug thought of them as boys and girls as none looked older than their late teens or early twenties, and all were exceptionally attractive.

The nobles present were all minor palace functionaries. Only the Imperial Chancellor held a noteworthy rank; his attendance a concession to Jim's diplomatic rank. Normally a Kingdom Baron wouldn't be entitled to so lofty a host, especially when only on an academic mission with little political or military significance, but it was probable that the Quegans already suspected Jim of being more than he appeared. Jim's own spy network wasn't the only one operating in the Bitter Sea, and he had, over the years, no doubt attracted as much Quegan interest as he had from the Keshians.

Pug had been paired with a very attractive middle-aged woman named Livia, who reclined on one of the large settees employed by the Quegans for dining. She waved away a servant holding a tray of candied fruits and said, 'Too sweet. I must confess I prefer simple foods.'

She wore a traditional Quegan toga, which clung to her form well enough to promise a full healthy body beneath it. Her features were strong yet feminine; she had deep dark brown eyes, and a tiny touch of grey among her auburn hair, which she wore loose to her shoulders. While Pug had little interest in dalliances, he still found her attractive and interesting. She was introduced to him as a fellow academic, and the archivist who had been assigned to assist him and his companions the next day. Pug was certain that she'd prove helpful, and just as certain that she had been charged with reporting everything the three visiting academics did. What he didn't know was if she was an archivist playing at being a spy or a spy playing at being an archivist.

'Really?' said Pug in a non-committal tone as he selected a ripe pear lightly coated in honey and sprinkled with crushed almonds. He bit into it and said, 'Unusual, but very good.'

'You get bored,' she sighed. 'I'm not very good at this sort of thing. My parents were only minor nobles, ragged cousins of some very important people. I was not likely to marry well, so they secured me a position here in the palace.'

Unsure what to say, Pug merely nodded. Then he asked, 'Do you enjoy it?'

She seemed less than enthused by his question, but said, 'It can be interesting. Occasionally someone such as yourself arrives to disrupt the monotony.'

Pug smiled as if flattered. He was now certain she was a spy, sent to seduce him and discover if there was anything more to him than the story Baron James of the Prince's Court in Krondor had offered them. He glanced at where his son reclined, and saw that a somewhat younger, equally attractive woman had been seated next to him. Amirantha was paired with a very academic looking gentleman, and Pug held his grin in check. Amirantha had revealed himself to be something of a lady's man over the time Pug had known him, while Magnus . . .

Pug occasionally worried about his last surviving son. Magnus had been terribly hurt by a young woman when he was barely more than a boy, and had refrained from becoming involved with any woman since then. Pug knew he succumbed to his more fundamental needs – he was injured, not dead – but while he might enjoy the occasional company of a courtesan in Kesh or the odd visit to a good brothel in Roldem, Magnus had avoided more serious interest from several young female students at Sorcerer's Isle over the years. It would have worked out better for the Quegan intelligence apparatus had they placed the academic gentleman with Magnus and the pretty woman with Amirantha.

Pug turned his attention back to Livia and asked, 'Seriously, do you enjoy working in the archives?'

She shrugged. He had touched on something and wondered just how well she had been prepared for this visit. If she was a Quegan agent, she would have some knowledge of the archives, but would be far from expert.

She said, 'To be completely truthful, it bores me. Once in a while I come across something interesting to read and mind those hours less. My task is to write a one paragraph précis of the work, assign it a location within the archive, and ensure that my entry is copied into the main codex.' She fixed him with a calculating gaze. 'I could return to your quarters with you, if you'd like, to discuss some of the more esoteric volumes in the archives. Some are quite revealing.'

Pug held a smile in check, and merely inclined his head slightly, as if thinking about the offer.

'Unless you prefer to stay for the orgy?'

Pug's eyebrows lifted slightly. Of all the nations in this part of the world, he had visited Queg the least and had forgotten that some of their customs were radically different from those of the Kingdom or even Great Kesh. Now he remembered why all the servants were young and attractive. The after dinner orgy was a normal part of grand welcomes for foreign visitors and always a feature of certain holidays. He had no qualms about other people's moral behaviour on this level, but his own feelings demanded that intimacy be limited to a committed love.

Not having to feign his feelings, Pug softly said, 'I have just recently lost my wife.'

Livia's eyes widened. 'I'm sorry. Was it sudden?'

'Very,' said Pug. 'It will be a while before I'm . . .'

She reached out and touched his hand lightly. Her tone remained bright, but her expression was solicitous. 'If I can do anything, please.'

Pug admired her persistence. He sighed. 'Someday, I'd like to return and then, perhaps.' He slowly rose. 'Now if you'll excuse me, I think I shall retire before the festivities commence.'

'Of course.'

'I look forward to seeing you in the morning,' he said.

'Until then.'

Magnus and Amirantha both had noticed him stand and were watching. Pug nodded slightly at his two companions, indicating that they should leave as soon as possible. Jim was deep in conversation with a noble, but Pug knew he had missed nothing.

Pug reached his quarters and found wine, sweets, nuts and cheeses waiting for him. He sat heavily in a divan before the window; he hadn't eaten much at the supper, and wasn't particularly hungry now, but he did feel like a sip of wine. He picked up the carafe and then closed his eyes. He had learned a spell years before, which would cleanse the wine of any drug designed to incapacitate or poison. He doubted this was necessary if the evening's objective had been seduction, but caution was the byword on this journey.

A few minutes later Amirantha appeared. Laughing slightly, he said, 'You and Magnus get the pretty girls, but I get the scholar who wants to ply me with questions about Muboya!'

'Well, that is logical,' said Pug. 'Most people love to talk about their homes and the Quegans consider everyone beyond their island a potential enemy.'

'I told him plenty about it,' said the Warlock, sitting down in a chair on the other side of the room. 'Some of it was even true.'

Pug smiled broadly at that.

Magnus entered and with a raised eyebrow said, 'Orgy?'

'It's a local custom,' said his father.

'Maybe we should go back?' quipped Amirantha.

Both father and son looked at him with narrow gazes, one of the few expressions that made a resemblance between them evident. Magnus was tall and pale, while his father was short and dark, but their look was identical.

After half an hour of idle conversation, they decided to retire. As they stood to enter their respective rooms, Amirantha said, 'I wonder if Jim stayed.'

Pug smiled. 'As ranking noble, it would have been something of a political incident for him to leave.'

Amirantha sighed. 'I noticed him keep that very pretty serving girl at hand.' Shaking his head slightly, he said, 'It's heroic what that man does for his King.'

Pug chuckled and Magnus laughed as they both closed their doors.

CHAPTER EIGHT

Fortress

SANDREENA SIGNALLED.

The two Knights-Adamants reined in their horses. She had recruited Brother Farson as she prepared to leave Krondor, just as he had arrived in the city. Brother Jaliel, she had found in Durbin along the way. Her newfound rank gave them no option but to change their current plans and follow her.

She indicated they should stay while she slowly urged her horse on.

She had led them to a parched desert fortress, abandoned by Great Kesh's Empire centuries before. There was almost nothing that now resembled a fortification. A few large stones that were once part of a wall, the lonely foundation of a gate half-buried in dust, and a staircase leading down into a labyrinth of tunnels and storage rooms. So little was left above ground that anyone might ride past it at a short distance without noticing that the Empire had once thought this pass worth defending.

Sandreena's two knights had been told only what she needed them to know until they reached this point. Using the documents that Creegan left for her, she had followed an ancient trade route out of Durbin, south into the Jal-Pur, then southwest into some foothills. They would eventually rise in the west to become the Trollhome Mountains, but here they merely formed a landscape of tablelands and hills. Whatever the original name of this once proud fortress, it was now known to the desert men as The Tomb of the Hopeless. To its south lay a valley with an even less appealing name, The Valley of Lost Men.

Before leaving Krondor, Sandreena had studied all of the maps of this region that had been in the Order's possession, and not one had shown the fortress or the valley. She trusted that Creegan wouldn't have insisted she read the report if he hadn't wanted her to act on it, and she was equally certain that he expected her to do exactly what she was doing: taking matters into her own hands. There was no one in Krondor besides herself that could do so. She knew Creegan had a relationship with Pug and the others on Sorcerer's Isle, but in rushing off to Rillanon to become the Order's leader, he had neglected to leave her any hint about how to contact them. She suspected there were other Kingdom agents of the Conclave, like the man who had passed her the messages in Durbin, but she had no idea how to identify and contact any of them.

She remembered the young man who had fetched her from Ithra after she had almost died during her first encounter with the Demon Legion's agents; Zane was his name, yet she had no idea how to reach him. She felt frustrated that Creegan had put this burden on her alone, but she pushed down her concerns to deal with the matters at hand.

Farson and Jaliel were reliable, but neither of them had been named on Creegan's list, so there were some things she could not share with them. They knew only that they were needed for a special mission at the Father-Bishop's request and that secrecy was paramount.

They had left the city together at sunrise to ride into the desert, headed due east, and then turned south and circled around to meet the ancient caravan trail. Sandreena did not know if the Imperial Keshian Intelligence Corp was following them, but she was certain they knew her small party had left. When they failed to appear at the usual oasis in a few days, the Keshians might send someone out to track the three knights, but Sandreena hoped that by then, her business here would be finished and they would already be heading back to Krondor.

It was near sundown when they reached the edge of the ancient fortress. The report about the carnage that had taken place here had been written weeks before, but the scene before them now was no less grisly. The corpses were now bones, picked clean by scavengers, the drying heat and blowing sands. But enough of their connective tissue remained that a few skeletons still hung from the makeshift gibbets around the edge of the clearing. The piles of ash contained the contorted forms of those who had been burned alive, and bones riddled with arrows were strewn around the fortress ruins. Hundreds of people had been slaughtered.

Sandreena called out. 'You can come up now!'

The two other Knights rode into the ancient fortress and Jaliel said, 'Goddess! What manner of butchery is this?'

Farson looked at Sandreena and said, 'If you don't mind my saying, Sergeant, this is a little more unusual than any normal mission, secret or otherwise. Are we to know what is going on?'

'I'll tell you what I know,' she said. 'There is a very dangerous, evil man named Belasco, who consorts with dark powers; his followers did this.' She decided to omit the fact that most of the remains belonged to fanatics who had gone to their deaths willingly. It was an unnecessary detail for these two to do their duty.

'Sergeant,' said Farson. 'What happened here?'

'I only have a rough idea, but it appears that it's the work of a cult of death worshippers who have appeared around here.'

The two Knights exchanged glances, and Sandreena knew exactly what they were thinking. A death cult should be the province of the worshippers of Lims-Kragma or perhaps even, Sung the White, they were not usually a concern for the servants of Dala.

Sandreena said, 'Father-Bishop Creegan is worried that they may be abducting local villagers for their sacrifices.'

It was not a complete lie, for she could imagine that might be part of Creegan's concerns, but left her explanation at that. The Conclave of Shadows had made an alliance with the most important man in the martial order of the worshippers of Dala, perhaps because Pug didn't have anyone else to call upon. There were certainly few other people who had as much experience with demons as she did; she had destroyed more than her share.

'Are you both carrying wards?' she asked.

'Against what, Sergeant?' asked Jaliel.

'Necromancy, demons, and anything else you can think of?'

Both Knights patted their hip bags in which they carried their wards.

'Good,' she said. 'We have no idea what we're going to find down there.'

'Down where?' asked Farson.

She pointed south. 'Down there, in the Valley of Lost Men.'

Farson's expression communicated just how much he liked that idea, but he remained silent.

'We'll rest up for the night, then head down at dawn.'

The men secured their mounts without further comment and then began untacking them. Sandreena unloaded a small bag of grain, then took off her horse's saddle. The knights groomed the beasts and Sandreena took it upon herself to fill and fix nose-bags for all three horses. They knew that they would have to start their return journey within two days, else the horses would begin to starve. There had been no grazing or fodder to be found between their present location and Durbin, only arid table-lands, thorn-covered hills, and the odd dry desert plants that would bloom briefly after a rare rain, but otherwise remained dry and dormant. It was hard to believe that this area ever needed defending.

There was one obvious mystery that Creegan had failed to mention and its omission from the report he had given her surprised Sandreena; why in ancient times had Kesh built a fortress here in the first place? The Trollhome was, as the name implied, the residence of creatures best avoided. Mountain trolls were smarter than their lowland cousins, who were little more than animals, but the desert already provided an effective barrier against them. If she knew that the caravan route had originally only passed by this place, then perhaps then it would make more sense, but as far as she could judge from all the old maps she studied before leaving Krondor, the route ended in the valley below.

She mused over what might be down there; if it were an ancient gold mine or source of some other wealth, sense would dictate that the route ran east, eventually reaching the city of Nar Ayab, and then run on to the capital city of Kesh. She deduced that whatever they had been moving along the route, had travelled from Durbin to this location. Maybe, she speculated, this was the terminus rather than the start, and the trail was a quick supply route from the nearest Keshian city. Which would imply that the only reason for building this fortress would have been to keep whatever was down in that valley, in that valley.

She finished tending the horses and broke out her own rations, and said, 'Cold camp,' to her companions. They were both veteran Knights and a night without fire was nothing new to them. They understood there was a strong possibility that someone or something was out there watching them.

They ate in silence, and when they were done, Sandreena said, 'Jaliel, you have first watch, Farson takes the last.' They both nodded, but silently thanked her, for as leader she was taking the least desirable watch. She lay down using her saddle as a pillow and due to years of ingrained habit, fell asleep within minutes.

Dawn came hot and dry, which was no surprise, but brought an early wind. The wind was a blessing and a curse; it would stir up enough dust to prevent them from being seen should hidden sentries be posted along the trail into the Valley of Lost Men, but if it was too blinding, Sandreena and her companions risked losing the trail altogether and could find themselves taking a much faster route down to the rocks below.

AT THE GATES OF DARKNESS

Sandreena spoke loudly, to be heard over the rising wind.
'How many demons have you faced?'

Farson said, 'Two, Sergeant.'

Jaliel said, 'Seven, Sergeant.'

She said, 'Jaliel, you bring up the rear in case we get attacked
from behind.' To Farson, she said, 'Do not do anything unless
I tell you. Demons can be very tricky sometimes.' He nodded.
Both knights knew that she was right; she hadn't asked how
many demons they had defeated, because if they hadn't defeated
those they had faced, they wouldn't be alive.

Sandreena realized that Jaliel had faced two more than her
count, but the last had been particularly nasty and without
Amirantha's aid . . . She silently cursed herself for a fool at the
sudden stab of feelings. He was a miserable excuse for a man, a
charmer with no substance and his words were nothing but
honeyed lies. Still, he knew more about demons than any man
she had ever met, and right now she'd put aside her urge to
strangle him in exchange for his ability to control the monsters.

'Grab a tail,' she instructed.

Farson moved his horse close to her mount, approaching
from the side and guarding against an unexpected kick, and gripped
the warhorse's tale. The mare snorted, but she had been through
this drill before. Jaliel did likewise with Farson's horse, and the
three began a slow descent from the plateau into the Valley of
Lost Men. This formation ensured that no one wandered away
blindly, and missteps would be kept to a minimum.

The wind blew blinding clouds of dust at them; small stones,
pieces of plants, dried insect carcasses, and a powdery grit like
chalk or ash coated their skin and matted in their hair. Twice
they found large outcrops of rocks to shelter behind as the wind

increased in intensity and the howling in the air made even the well-trained horses paw the ground, nicker and snort. Sandreena patted the nose of her palfrey in reassurance, but she was hardly in a position to reassure anyone, even her mare. The impulse that had driven her to undertake this mission now seemed like an impossibly vain idea. But each time this doubt had risen, she had returned to the same conclusion; there was simply no one else in the order, save herself, Creegan and two other knights whose whereabouts unknown, who could follow up on what that mysterious Kingdom agent had reported, and she was the only one of them in a position to help.

Necromancy and demons were not usually intertwined. Demons took too much delight in devouring the living to leave enough useful remains for a necromancer to employ his arts. As demons always devoured whatever they killed, and quickly.

However, from her studies Sandreena knew there was a great deal of energy used in the dark arts, albeit black and evil, and necromancy was one of the most powerful. Perhaps someone was harnessing death magic to control demons? She left the thought unfinished; she really did not know if it was possible or what it implied, and wished again for five minutes to talk to Amirantha; before she'd strangle him. She became as aggravated with herself as she was with the Warlock: of all the times to start thinking about that bastard again!

The wind began to shift and then started falling away, but Sandreena knew the desert winds in these hot tablelands were unpredictable. However, for now, in the relative lull, free from the worst of the stinging sand, they would better be able to see trouble coming.

She motioned for the others to fall in and started down the

trail. The wind came in gusts and swirls, but she could see her way down clearly enough. The path was roughly equivalent in type to the one she had followed up to the fortress from Durbin: it was ancient, eroded by wind and the occasional flash flood, and rarely used. Yet, when the wind died down, there were moments she could see signs that the track had been recently used. A large number of horses and wagons had come this way, and by the look of the hoof marks, they had headed into the valley, but not out of it.

Sandreena wondered who was behind this, and what they were playing at. Durbin was a vermin hole on the Bitter Sea, where the governor made huge profits from looking the other way as smugglers moved contraband into or out of the Empire. It was endemic of Imperial Keshian behaviour, but no matter how many times the Empire sought to reform that office, the mixture of greed, opportunity and distance from the capital, that melded together in that miserable city, always asserted itself. Still, the number of wagons and men coming this way recently was high even by Durbin standards.

Sandreena estimated that there were at least one hundred dead people rotting in the ancient fortress, perhaps more; that amount of movement across the desert should have brought attention. Whoever was behind this incident had managed to prevent the Imperial guards reporting it, which meant that the governor or someone highly placed in his office had looked the other way, either due to bribery or fear . . . or both.

As they descended the winding trail, following long switchbacks that took them slowly down the mountain, the wind died. It was as if a curtain of blowing sand and dust was suddenly pulled aside.

'What is that?' demanded Farson.

'What, indeed?' said Sandreena as Jaliel moved forward and halted.

'Good Goddess!' He exclaimed.

A massive structure was being erected in the distant heart of the valley. The outline showed that it was a massive fortification of some type, encircling something, but from this distance detail was lost. Four towers were being built, one farther along in construction than the others, and it was clear they would arch over and touch over the centre of . . . whatever it was.

Farson said, 'I'm not an engineer, but my da built siege engines for the King, so I know a bit. Those towers . . .' he pointed, 'they can't do that; they can't arch over and touch.'

Softly Sandreena said, 'I won't mention it to them.'

'To whom?' asked Jaliel.

'Whoever's building that monstrosity.'

'I feel like we should be seeking cover,' said Farson.

Glancing around, Sandreena said, 'I will be happy to oblige you as soon as you show me some.'

They stood on an exposed mountainside. If there were sentries on the wall of the strange building, the three on the trail were still too distant to be noticed, but if they stood guard at the bottom of this long trail, or anywhere closer, they were only visible if anyone looked in their direction.

Sandreena pointed to a depression about a dozen yards below the trail. 'That's a stream bed when it rains here,' she said. She turned off the track and carefully led her horse down the loose rocks and scrub, weighing each step for treacherous footing. When she reached the gully, she saw that it quickly deepened.

Reaching the bottom, she halted. 'We'll leave the horses here and tonight get as close as we can to investigate.'

'Leave the horses, Sergeant?' asked Farson.

'There is no cover along the trail, those below can just sit there and start shooting arrows at you like swinging targets in the marshalling yard, as soon as they spot us.' She glanced up. 'We have three switchbacks above us and five or six more below.' She looked at the two knights. 'Farson, I want you to lead the horses back up to the top.' She pointed to a point directly above their hiding place. 'Wait up there. Untack them, clean them, water them and wait until sundown. Then tack them up again and be ready to ride at a moment's notice.' She sensed he was about to object, but cut off anything he might have said. 'You have the most critical duty. If we are not back by sunrise tomorrow, you assume we are dead. You must get back to Durbin and take the fastest route to Krondor, by ship if you can, or trade the three horses in for fresh mounts, and get to the Temple.'

She realized that only one man at the Temple was on Creegan's safe list. 'Find Brother Willoby, in Father-Bishop Creegan's office. Tell him what we've found. He'll know what to do.'

Brother Farson said, 'What *have* we found, Sergeant.' He pointed in the general direction of the distant construction. 'I don't even know if I can describe that, let alone divine it's purpose.'

'It is an invasion point,' said Sandreena. 'Can't you feel them?'

'Who?' asked Jaliel his dark brow knitted in concentration or worry.

'Demons,' said Sandreena. 'The place is crawling with them if my skin is any indication.'

Farson said, 'Sergeant, I'm a little on edge, but . . . I just don't feel it.'

'Me, neither,' agreed Jaliel.

Sandreena studied them both for a moment, then turned her attention back to the task at hand. 'You have your orders,' she said to Farson, and he nodded. He turned the animals around slowly; she knew he didn't relish the idea of leading three horses back up that trail.

She watched closely for any sign they might have been observed, while the returning Knight-Adamant tied her horse's reins to the saddle ring of Jaliel's, then that mount's reins to his own. 'See you tomorrow, Sergeant, Jaliel,' he said as he led the three horses back up the shallow gully and started the tedious climb back to the top of the ridge.

'Now what,' asked Jaliel quietly.

'We wait,' she answered, looking at the sky. 'Best if we rest now. You try to sleep. I'll stand watch.'

The more experienced of the two knights she had recruited nodded, not needing further urging. It was only morning and they might have a long day ahead of waiting, but years living in the wilderness had taught him to take rest when it was offered.

Left to her own thoughts, Sandreena crawled up to a boulder so she could rest her arm on it and then her chin on her arm and study the distant construction. Flickers of movement gave tantalizing hints of something going on, but she could make out no useful detail. She would have to be content to wait until darkness fell, which was a good nine hours or more away, and then creep down for a closer look. She offered a prayer to the Goddess, that they would remain undiscovered, because she had no illusions that they would be able to make it back to the top of that long switchback while being chased if they were on foot. Hiding was their only hope.

So she settled in, prayed, and waited for the sun to crawl across the sky, trying very hard to drive thoughts of Amirantha from her mind.

Night arrived slowly, but after the sun had set, Sandreena and Jaliel began to move carefully down the side of the mountain.

The failing light frustrated Sandreena: even as she got closer to the building, she could make out even less detail. Little Moon was the only one rising this early in the evening and the smallest of Midkemia's three moons provided scant illumination. Middle Moon wouldn't be seen until just before dawn and Large Moon wouldn't rise until well after dawn. Still, as their greatest need was stealth, she would rather deal with having to get closer now, than trying to approach the demons on a Three Moons Bright night.

Sandreena did notice that a small tower, barely two stories tall, had been erected near the base of the trail. Had they continued down earlier in the day, they would have been spotted by the sentry on duty. Sandreena used barely visible hand gestures to inform Jaliel they were going to circle even farther away from the trail.

The gulley down which they crept emptied out into a basin a hundred yards across, before running into a dry river bed that wound around the base of the hills. A fairly large river must have flowed through here in ages past, although Sandreena found it hard to imagine this area lush, or with rain enough to fill a brook, let alone a river. Yet the evidence of water erosion was under her feet, and currently hiding her from view as she and her companion crawled along the southern edge of the basin.

Both knights were battle tested and ready for any trouble, but both knew this was a reconnaissance mission not elective combat. Something this massive, in a place this far removed from any civilized authority, could only be the work of forces inimical to those authorities, which made it a matter of concern for the Temple as well. And the stench of demon was so strong here Sandreena knew those concerns were urgent.

She stood for a moment and studied the walls. Large flaming braziers hung from chains attached to tripods evenly spaced along the battlement, for it was indeed a fortress. But it was unlike any fortress Sandreena had ever encountered or heard of.

'What is this place?' whispered Jaliel.

'No place good,' answered Sandreena. 'We need to split up. I want you to go that way.' She pointed towards the southern-most end of the basin and moved her hand to indicate where he should make his way along the line that ran parallel to the walls. The entire structure appeared to be circular, but she would need to get closer, and have better light to be certain. The curve of the wall before her suggested it was a massive circle of stone with a gigantic gate in the middle.

She gripped him by the arm and whispered, 'Go; return here by midnight. If I'm not here, make your way to the top as best you can. If Farson has already left for Durbin, make your way to the Oasis at La-amat-atal, and wait for a caravan to get you safely to civilization. If you get there before he leaves, tell him what you see, and go with him to Krondor.'

'Yes, Sergeant,' he replied. 'You?'

'I'm going to circle in the other direction, and then I'm going to do my damnedest to be at the top of the trail before Farson leaves with my horse.'

He chuckled, and said, 'Goddess be with you, Sister.'

'And with you, my brother,' she replied.

He set off at once, moving surprisingly quietly for a man with armour and a shield strapped to his back. Sandreena waited for a moment, not wanting too much movement in this area, and when he was gone from her sight, set off up the side of the basin and onto the flat above. She crouched, though it was no easy feat with her shield on her back and her sword clutched in her right hand. She found a small stand of scrub brush between the lip of the basin and the watch tower. She prayed to the Goddess that whoever was stationed up there was watching for movement along the road and not for anyone coming from behind.

Occasionally, she turned and glanced at the far wall of the fortress, to try to discern some more detail: like who was on the wall and what they were doing, but it was still too far away. She came to an outcropping of rocks and knelt behind it, slowly raising herself up to observe the guardhouse. Then she sat down hard, barely able to believe her eyes. An elf stood guard in the guardhouse, and from his apparent size, she judged him to be one of the newly arrived Star Elves.

She sat down, her back to the rock, and felt completely confused. She sensed demon presence in huge numbers, yet an elf stood watch. Given their reputation for being able to see in dim light, she counted herself and Jaliel very fortunate to have made it down that gully undetected; had they stayed on the switchbacks, even at night, the elf would certainly have seen them half a mile away.

Now she knew she had to get closer to this structure and see if she could make any sense of what was occurring here. She waited until she saw the elf turn his back to watch the trail above, and she hurried across what felt like a vast open space, moving as silently as she could, until she found more rocks behind which to shelter. Holding her breath so she could hear any hint of alarm, she waited. Only the distant sounds of working from the fortress distilled the silence of the desert night. *Where was the wind when you needed it?* she thought, then off she went, moving around the perimeter, seeking a place that would allow her to get closer to the construction.

Sandreena crouched below some empty wagons; their traces were empty and there was no sign of the mules or horses that pulled them. She doubted those inside stabled their draft animals. They most likely just ate them. The venture had all the appearance of a one-way enterprise, with the final destination stretched out before her. She felt as if she might scream from frustration, but fear and caution combined to keep her focused and silent. There were so many questions plaguing her, but all she could do was creep around in shadows and continue to observe.

The massive gate was currently open, allowing Sandreena tantalizing glimpses inside. Her mind reeled at the image of dwarves, humans, elves, and even a troll, labouring under the watchful eye of demons. It looked as if they were using mortal beings as slave labour, something unimagined in the annals of all the demon lore she had been exposed to. Now more than ever she wished Amirantha was here, and not because he had broken her heart and she wanted to punish him; she needed him to make sense of the tableau before her.

A demon overseer hove into view. He paused, staring in her direction for a moment. She felt her heart jump and she held her breath. She had never faced a demon as formidable in appearance as this one. It had the head of a deformed ape, with two upswept ears, a grotesque parody of an elf's, and it wore a massive chest piece with a human skull set in the middle like a heraldic device. The monster's shoulders were covered with black steel spaulders that swept up and ended in gold tipped points. Its legs were covered in black armour, and it wore a circlet of gold with another skull set in the brow. The massive sword it carried in its right hand pulsed with an evil red light.

The demon sniffed the air, then after a moment turned away and shouted something to one of the humans. The human bowed and hurried off.

On top of the walls workers scrambled up wooden scaffolding to hoist large stones in order to raise the massive arching columns. Now that she was closer, Sandreena could see that the columns were being installed with great care and she could see their placement being watched closely. Two robed men studied the scene, and when the stones were in place, both began an incantation. The sound of their words was lost, but the feeling that descended upon her as she watched this part of the construction filled her with cold fear.

Something gigantic, impossible to decipher, and holding no good purpose was being fashioned here by demons, who oversaw a workforce of mortal workers and mages. None of this made any remote sense to her, and she knew her cause would be better served if she started back now, to make sure her report reached Father-Bishop Creegan. What she had seen could not wait for a messenger, even by fast ship or swift rider; she would rather make the voyage to Sorcerer's Island. Pug and his confederates had devices that could get her to Rillanon in days instead of weeks; the island was far closer to Durbin than Krondor, and a great deal closer than Rillanon. Besides, she thought in passing, the last place she had seen Amirantha had been on that cursed island.

Yet her curiosity tugged at her, for she wasn't sure she had seen enough. Perhaps more information could be gained.

As she mused, she heard footsteps approaching from behind, and by the time she had turned, the dwarf warrior was charging towards her. There was something in his eyes that warned her that she had no time to waste on discussion. He carried a short sword and swung it with deadly intent.

Sandreena managed to roll out of the way and get to her feet, slipping her shield off with a single motion and reversing it so she could slip her arm through the straps on the back; she had her sword up just in time to block the dwarf's following strike.

The shock that ran through her arm as she took that blow made her realize this was no untested swordsman she faced, but an experienced dwarven warrior who would offer no quarter. She had never faced one before, not even in a practice melee, their fortitude and prowess were renowned. She knew she could not wear him down; he could fight until she collapsed from fatigue and then dance on her grave. She certainly could not overpower him, and she doubted she could disable him. Her only hope was a quick kill.

Two strikes and the dwarf hesitated, and Sandreena noticed that his eyes were slightly unfocused, but she was nearly over-whelmed by an unexpected sensation. She had fought in more than a score of life or death battles, and three times that amount against men whom she was only trying to subdue. She had experienced every type of male body stench, and a few females, and thought nothing of it, but she had not anticipated that dwarves might stink like demons.

He aimed a skull-crushing overhand blow at her and over-extended slightly. In that moment, she noticed a talisman hanging from a leather cord around his neck. It was a foul thing with red glowing stones for eyes and was also where the demon stench was originating.

She danced away and rather than take his head from his shoulders – although she found the opening – she turned her blade and struck him with the flat of her sword on the side of his head. It was like hitting a tree bole and the shock that ran up her arm nearly numbed it to the shoulder.

The dwarf barely blinked and came straight at her. She hesitated only a moment, then leapt to her left, straight into the dwarf's next blow, but rather than take it anywhere vital, she couched under it, which was no mean feat against a foe barely taller than five feet, then came up behind him.

Before he could turn, she reached out and snatched at the leather thong holding the talisman in place. She ripped it from him and tossed it away.

It was as if she had struck him between the eyes with the hammer he was holding. He stumbled, half-turned, then fell backwards, landing on his rear. He sat in the dust, blinking as if blinded by brilliant lights, then let out a long sigh. His eyes finally focused on her and he said, 'What? Who are . . .?' He looked around, and Sandreena followed his gaze.

No one on the wall had witnessed their confrontation, but more workers were coming into view. Instead of leaping to his feet and alerting the others of an intruder, the dwarf crawled towards her, grabbed her by the leg and hissed, 'Get down, for the gods sake!'

Sandreena knelt, but kept her sword pointed at the dwarf. 'You going to keep trying to kill me?'

The dwarf looked confused. 'Kill you? Woman, I don't know who you are, but if you're not working for them—'—he pointed towards the fortress— '—then you're my new best friend.'

'Who are you?'

'I'm Keandar, son of Kendrin of Dorgin.'

She nodded, motioning for him to crawl with her back under the shelter of the wagon. Dorgin was the dwarven city closest to their current location, a tiny state on the border of Great Kesh and the Kingdom of the Isles.

'What is this place?'

'That's a long tale, one I would prefer to recount as far away from here as possible.' He glanced under the wagon and said, 'Some of my kin are in there, and I mean to get back to Dorgin, tell the king, and return with every war hammer we can raise.'

Sandreena knew it would take more than a small army of dwarves to deal with what was forming here, but she decided that debate could wait. 'Can you tell me what is going on in there?'

'Aye, some,' he said, 'but only a bit. I was used as a guard, mostly, though those of my people with skills, the engineers, smiths and mongers, and the stone masons, were given jobs inside. But we spoke a little while we ate, when we ate.'

'Come on,' she said, glancing at the position of the Little Moon. 'I have a horse and we can ride double, but it's some distance from here and we need to reach it by sunrise.'

'Sunrise?'

'Or one of my order will be taking it back to Durbin without me.'

'Ah,' said the dwarf. 'You're not alone?'

'No,' said Sandreena. 'There are two others.'

'Well, let's have a leisurely chat when we're miles from here. You lead, I'll follow.'

Sandreena nodded once and crouched, then scampered from the wagons to the first pile of rocks and began the long return to the gully that would take her past the guard house. When she reached it, she turned to Keandar and said, 'We need to slip past that guard.'

'Why not just go there and quickly kill him? It's only an elf.'

'We may have them after us when you don't return,' she said, 'but they'll send a larger hunting party if they find a dead sentry in that post.'

He sighed, as if he were disappointed, then said, 'Very well. They don't keep close track of us, mostly because of those things they make us wear. They sap our freewill and muddle our minds.'

'Tell me about it later,' said Sandreena, and Keandar nodded. To herself she muttered, 'If there is a later.'

Dawn found a very nervous Farson waiting in the designated spot, with all three horses tacked up and ready to ride. He had his sword out as Sandreena hove into view, and was about to strike when she called him by name.

'Sergeant?' he asked looking at the dwarf.

'This is Keandar of Dorgin. If anything happens and I fall, you must get him to Sorcerer's Island.'

Farson's eyes widened. 'Sorcerer's Island? Sergeant, no one goes to—'

'Sorcerer's Island.'

'But Krondor—'

Firmly, she said, 'Sorcerer's Island.' She looked around, then asked, 'Jaliel?'

Farson shook his head.

'We wait until the sun clears the horizon, then we leave without him.' She knew he was probably lost; had he been close, they would have encountered one another in the gully or on the upper trail even if he was coming from the other side of that fortification. Still, she honoured her word to him to wait.

The sun rose. When she could see it was full above the horizon, she said, 'Goddess watch over him.' Taking the reins of Jaliel's mount, she handed them to the dwarf. 'Do you need a leg up?'

The dwarf grinned. In the morning sun his hair and beard looked especially red and his eyes were a glinting blue. He was, like most of his race, barrel-chested and broad of shoulder, with powerful arms and thick legs. 'I'm short,' he replied, 'not a child.'

His vault into the saddle was impressive and he took the reins in hand like a practiced rider.

Farson and Sandreena mounted and she took one last look around, half-hoping to see Jaliel come into sight. Then, taking a deep breath, she said, 'Durbin!'

They turned their horses and rode to the north.

CHAPTER NINE

War

*G*ULAMENDIS LEAPT.

The lizard scuttled away, but not before the Demon Master seized it in a single motion and bashed it hard against the rocks. He hurried back to the cave where his brother waited. A small fire burned at the back and the Conjurer was huddled before it, trying to stay warm in the early morning chill.

The nights on this world were bitterly cold and the days scorching hot. The sun had just begun to rise on the seventh day of being stranded on this alien planet. They had found fresh water in a small stream running down the side of the hill and they had contrived to catch lizards and birds for sustenance; a bare subsistence, but despite being filthy, tired, and hungry, they were at least alive.

But they were more puzzled about the demons than when

they first arrived. Having rested for a day, they had then ventured out to look down upon the massive army twice. Both times they had proceeded cautiously and avoided detection. Something was stirring down in that valley, but they were uncertain what it was. Had this been an elven army, they might have guessed its behaviour, but demons organized in this fashion were outside their experience and knowledge.

The brothers barely spoke, they had talked over everything they knew about this situation over the first few days. They could not have ported into the demon realm, as had that been the case they would have perished in minutes. They might not be on the world they called Home, but they were in that same sphere of experience. Despite the less than hospitable surroundings, the air was breathable, the water drinkable, and the wildlife edible. Though one of the reptile species they had encountered had induced severe stomach cramps and other unpleasant reactions.

Gulamendis held out his hand as he reached the back of the cave where his brother waited.

'Lizard,' said Laromendis, dryly. 'How unexpected.'

His brother ignored the quip and started cleaning the small carcass with his battle knife. It was a clumsy tool, but a few days practice had given him the ability not to totally destroy their supper before it was cooked. After a roasting, it would provide less than a few ounces of meat and only a tiny bit of fat, but it would be enough to keep them alive for another day. They had slowly gained back enough strength to mount a single defence should they be discovered, but neither had the energy for prolonged combat.

So lying in wait was their current tactic, but both knew that option had a limited expectation for survival. They quickly devoured their meal and Gulamendis said, 'The thing I find most annoying about this at the moment, is the need to walk down to the stream every time I get thirsty.'

'Then don't get thirsty,' replied his brother. 'Or find us a damn jar or bucket or something to fetch water back.'

'I already suggested we use your boot . . .' said the Demon Master, in a weak attempt at humour.

His brother made a face indicating what he thought of that notion. 'How long can we sit here wondering?' asked the Conjurer.

'I don't know,' said his brother, on the border of exasperation. 'So much of this makes no sense to me.'

Laromendis had heard his brother's concerns before, from the first moment they had spied the demons over the rise, but asked, 'Perhaps if you outline it, one more time.'

'To what end?' asked Gulamendis, showing his frustration. 'Everything I know of demons must be wrong, or at least flawed. Both that human warlock, Amirantha, and I have lost the confidence to trust our conjurations. The rise of the Demon King made it certain we could not trust any creature we summoned to not turn on us; or to vanish back to their realm and report what they saw.

'Until we got here, our experience with the demons taught us that if they were not confined by magic they were out of control. On every other world the attacks on our people have taught us they were nothing but a horde of monsters, unrelenting, unforgiving, and without any sort of strategy save to assault, assault, assault.'

'We saw those captains on Andcardia,' reminded his brother. 'They were giving orders.'

'It looked like they were herding livestock, directing the flow of a stampede, not directing a coordinated attack.' He sighed. 'But that camp . . .' He shrugged in resignation. 'I can't explain it. I have no idea who is commanding them, but they are behaving unlike any group of demons I have ever heard of, let alone come in contact with.'

His brother said, 'I understand. You feel like someone has changed the governing laws of your art, without bothering to tell you.' Starting to rise, he said, 'Let's get something to drink and then decide if we want to watch the demons do nothing tonight.' As he started to rise, the ground suddenly heaved beneath them as a loud explosion echoed outside.

Laromendis was knocked on his rump while his brother said, 'What was that?'

Both looked up as dirt came showering down on them from the ceiling of the dark cave, barely illuminated by daylight coming through the entrance, fifty feet away. 'Get out!' shouted Gulamendis. 'This thing is collapsing.'

As the ground under their feet shook, they staggered to the entrance amidst a shower of dusty and loose rocks. Once outside they looked around, as Laromendis said, 'Earthquake?'

Another distant boom, followed by another lurch in the ground, and Gulamendis said, 'I don't think so.'

They quickly realized that the noise was coming from the other side of the ridge. Motioning for his brother to follow him, Gulamendis tried to half-climb, half-crawl up the shaking hillside. As they neared the crest they could hear the sounds of battle ringing in the distance, punctuated by more ground shaking explosions.

Peering over they could see only chaos.

Smoke and dust filled the air as thousands of demons were rolling out of their encampments to meet an onslaught of more demons.

'What is this?' asked Laromendis, not bothering to keep his voice down. Everywhere they looked demons were battling each other. The oddest aspect of this mad scene was the demons who were from the camp wore armour roughly uniform in fashion: dull silverfish breast armour and helms, some with spaulders or pauldrons, others without shoulder protection. Some possessed greaves or boots, while others – those with massive feet and claws – went barefoot. But it was easy to see that they fought under the same banner. That banner was raised high on top of a long pole in the centre of the camp, a massive black cloth with a red design upon it, impossible to see in detail at this distance.

The attackers were likewise attired in a haphazard fashion, but their armour was dark blue grey in colour and they flew no banner in the field. But they had clearly enjoyed the advantage in surprise and ferocity.

Even without arms, demons were lethally effective fighters; with weapons they were even more terrifying. The slaughter didn't pause: on every side demons went down in screams of pain, fountains of smoking blood, and body parts sailing through the air. It was butchery in every sense of the word.

Gulamendis replied, 'A demonic revolt, by the look of it.'

'There,' said the Conjurer, pointing across the valley to the ridge opposite the one they hid behind.

In the distance, Laromendis could see what had caught his brother's attention. On top of the ridge stood a massive figure, dwarfing those around him. It was still impossible to make out details at this distance, but it was clear that group on top of the distant ridge was orchestrating the assault on the demon horde encamped in the valley below.

Flyers rose up to meet those already overhead, and the two elves suddenly understood the source of the massive quakes and explosions. The invading flying demons carried large objects which they released above the ground forces below; when they struck the ground, a massive amount of energy was released, throwing a tower of earth, smoke, flame, and bits of destroyed demons into the air. The early assault must have included attacks on positions closer to where the brothers hid, for these impacts felt less severe.

From three gullies down, just outside the valley, a stream of attacking monstrosities flooded into the fray. They rolled into the encamped army, already caught up in the throes of panic, and the slaughter gained pace.

'What is going on?' asked Laromendis.

'Can you conjure enough cover for us to remain unseen if we need it?' asked his brother.

'Not for long.'

'If what I think is happening, is happening, we won't need it for long. Come we must hurry.'

The Demon Master headed off at a trot, staying just below the ridge and following it around the rim of the valley. Occasionally the ground shook, but the air assault ceased as the two opposing forces became entwined in hand-to-hand combat. Every so often, Gulamendis would peer over the edge then motion for his brother to follow.

They reached an outcropping of rocks, from which they could better observe what went on, and Laromendis asked, 'Do you recognize any of them?'

He nodded to the demons perched on the rim of the valley. Now they were close enough that Gulamendis could make out some details. The demon at the centre of the group was massive, perhaps twenty or twenty-five feet tall, with gigantic wings folded behind him. It might have been a flyer once, or the wings might just be there to affect a more impressive visage when unfolded, but the Demon Master doubted the creature could truly fly without magic. On either side of it waited demons of a type Gulamendis had never encountered before, black-skinned monstrosities that were, from the waist up, roughly half-human, and some sort of lizard creature below. Long tails dragged behind them and they were constantly watching in all directions.

'I think those two,' he said softly, pointing to the half-lizard demons, 'are guards or companions of some sort.' He made a small circular motion with his finger as he pointed. 'The rest are battle demons, but I've never seen them standing motionless, and never have seen them wearing armour and bearing arms.'

He knelt down and said, 'We're seeing something very new here.'

'What?'

'I'll tell you when we have a little more leisure time,' said Gulamendis. 'The big one is either the Demon King, Maarg, or someone who looks a great deal like the description Pug gave me.'

'Didn't Pug also tell you Maarg was found dead on some other world?'

'Well,' said Gulamendis, 'there's dead and then there's dead. I've been dispatching demons back to their own realm for years, and have even imagined I have destroyed a few, but I can't really say if they died or just went back where they came from in a messier fashion.' He glanced back over the rocks. 'If I'm right, we should find a way out of here down behind those monsters.'

'We'd better move, because this battle is going to be over soon, and I don't want to be here when the victors start looking around for more things to chew on.'

The Demon Master nodded. 'Be ready to make us look like rocks if needed.'

'I'll try,' answered his brother.

They moved slowly, checking their progress every ten yards or so, and then suddenly Gulamendis halted his brother. 'Something's not right.'

'What do you mean,' asked the Conjurer.

'I can sense demons all over this valley. It's like a throng shouting at me, but from ahead . . . Nothing.'

'Nothing?'

'If I close my eyes, there are no demons up on that ridge.'

Laromendis peeked over the rise and studied the scene for a moment, then said, 'That's odd.'

'What do you see?'

'Be silent; watch for a few minutes then tell me what you see.'

The two brothers ventured another look at the demons on the ridge, now less than a two hundred yards away. The Demon King stood with his arms crossed over his obscenely large stomach, his face a mask of delighted evil and he glared down on the struggle with burning red eyes. Suddenly, his hand shot up into the air and he motioned, urging his followers onward, but no more reinforcements were coming. 'Why is he signalling the attack when fight is almost done,' asked Laromendis.

'Because he's not signalling an attack. Come with me,' said

Gulamendis as he crouched and hurried along just below the circling rocks that shielded them from sight.

Keeping out of sight as best they could, they got closer than Laromendis felt comfortable with, then Gulamendis said quietly, 'Look, brother!'

They peered at the assembled demons and saw the Demon King signal the attack again. 'What?' then Laromendis closed his eyes. 'I'm a fool. It's all a conjuration.'

'A very good illusion, from what I can tell. It would fool anyone who can't sense demons, even you dear brother; and no one else is going to get close enough to see that this is all a trick of lights and magic.'

'But why—?'

'We can ponder that later,' said Gulamendis. 'We need to find the way home, or at least somewhere other than here. Why those demons were lured here to be slaughtered by their own kind is a matter for another time; right now we need to see if there's a gate of some sort down that side of the mountain.'

He hurried, unconcerned about being seen by the illusions nearby and Laromendis followed. The fatigue from days of privation were offset by the excitement of possibly finding a safe route off this desert planet, and they moved quickly.

As they passed the illusions, they found a wide trail, and realized it was freshly trampled by thousands of feet. 'Well, now we know the attacking army is real,' said Laromendis.

'Demons can't be fooled that long,' said his brother. 'I thought you'd have discovered that when they started ignoring your conjurations and started attacking us.'

'I thought perhaps in a melee, with blood and screaming demons on all sides, they might not have the facility to judge if there was enough demon stench in the air,' said the Conjurer as they quickly descended the trail, almost running.

'Point taken,' conceded his brother. 'Still, you're the conjurer. Could you create the illusion of an army on that scale?'

'No,' said Laromendis, his breath beginning to come hard. 'No one could. It would take a dozen as good as me. And then they couldn't sustain it for long. That's a great deal of magic being used. To achieve it to endure this long, at this level, it would take a hundred better than me.'

'Well, let's hope whoever's behind this monstrous betrayal is too occupied with whatever they are doing up there to notice the two of us slipping away.'

Suddenly the hair on their arms stood up and both slid to a halt, dust rising from their sliding feet.

'What's that?' asked Gulamendis.

'A barrier . . .' Laromendis reached out and drew his hand back. 'It doesn't hurt, but it's not a particularly pleasant feeling, either.'

'What is it?'

Pushing with his fingers, Laromendis said, 'I think it's—' He stepped forward and vanished from his brother's sight.

'Laro!' shouted the Demon Master.

Abruptly, a hand reached out of the air and grabbed him by the arm, yanking him forward.

'Where are we?' asked Gulamendis.

Wherever it was, it wasn't the desert world upon which they had stood only a moment before.

They stood in an empty marshalling yard of a massive black stone fortress. Walls thirty feet high rose up on all sides of an open area two hundred yards across and a hundred deep. Above them rose a keep unlike anything they had seen before. If the castle created by the Black Sorcerer had been designed to impose a warning on passing ships, the sight of this fortress would have simply scared the sailors to death.

In the sky above them hung a canopy of black clouds so thick it was impossible to tell the time of day, or if it was night. They were lit from below by the angry red light from a series of volcanoes that surrounded this place. Lightning exploded across the sky in the distance, and moments later was followed by peals of thunder that could be felt.

'Where are we?' repeated Gulamendis.

His brother grabbed his arm and pulled him into the relative shelter of the shadow of a corner tower. In the distance a large figure had walked out of the entrance of the vast fortress, across the yard; and even though it was three hundred feet away, they could see it was a massive battle demon, perhaps a dozen feet tall. It moved with purpose, but rather than attacking them, it travelled at an oblique angle to their position, intent upon some other business. Like those they had seen on the other world, it wore armour and carried a massive two-handed sword strapped across its back.

'Is this the demon realm?' asked Laromendis.

'It can't be,' answered his brother.

'Why not?'

'Because if it was the Fifth Circle, we would be almost certainly dead by now. Everything we know about the Fifth Circle says we would die within minutes if we weren't protected by strong magic.'

'Kosridi,' said Laromendis, referring to the tales they had learned about the human magician, Pug, and his allies travelling to the Second Circle.

'Yes,' said his brother.

'On the other hand,' said Laromendis, 'who is to say the laws within the Fifth Circle are the same as the Second?'

'I'll argue the theory later,' said Gulamendis. 'Despite that, I can't sense any demons.'

'Another illusion?'

Gulamendis slapped the wall of stone behind him and felt the palm of his hand sting. 'What do you think?'

Laromendis closed his eyes for a moment, touched the wall, then said, 'If it's a conjured fortress, whoever's responsible for it has the powers of a god.'

'Let's see if we can find a better place to hide, while we decide what to do next,' said Gulamendis.

Setting off along the base of the wall, staying as deep in the shadows as they could, the two seven foot elves who stood tried to make themselves as small and inconspicuous as possible.

'This may not be the demon realm,' said Laromendis, 'but the air is choking me.'

'It's the smoke and ash from the volcanoes,' whispered his brother.

'Who builds anything like this in a place like this?'

'I have no idea,' replied Gulamendis. 'Over there.' He pointed to a small building that appeared to have been constructed after the wall. It was a simple wooden structure, a shed or storage room.

They crept along. There had been no threat since they had spied the single demon crossing the marshalling yard, but they had no idea if they were nevertheless being observed from any one of the hundred or so windows in the keep above. It reared at least a dozen storeys above them, a massive malignant presence against the evil red and grey sky.

'Flyers!' said Gulamendis, pointing above the top of the keep.

A dozen black specks appeared in the red glow and then vanished, only to reappear a moment later, growing larger. 'They're coming this way,' said the Conjurer.

'Let's see what's in here,' said Gulamendis, opening the unlatched door.

Inside the hut sacks and boxes were arranged in a roughly organized fashion. When the door was closed, they were plunged into darkness.

The building was a rough construction, and there were cracks between the boards. The brothers peered through them and suddenly large winged demons descended into view, landing in the marshalling yard and assuming a rough formation: two lines of six.

'They are waiting for something,' said Gulamendis.

'What?'

'I don't know.'

'What do we do now?' asked Laromendis.

'Well, as going anywhere is out of the question, I suggest we just sit quietly here and watch, for now.'

Unable to think of anything else to say, Laromendis fell silent.

Hours passed, and nothing of significance occurred in the court-yard; after a while the sun rose high enough to be distinctive and give the inside of the hut faint illumination.

'What have we here?' said Laromendis, almost absently, as he pulled down a sack from a large shelf on the back wall. The bag fell open and red round fruit fell out. 'Apples!' he said.

Gulamendis didn't hesitate, he grabbed one of the orbs and bit in deeply. It was not the freshest he had ever tasted, but the cool, dry storage had preserved most of the fruits.

'What's in the other bags?' asked his brother as he bit down into his second apple. He began a haphazard examination, opening bags and using his heavy knife to pry off the tops of boxes and as he went, the brothers began to wonder.

The boxes and bags contained provisions and clothing. The clothing was human sized, too big for dwarves, too small for the taredhel, and certainly not of a fashion for the other elven tribes.

'What is this?' wondered Gulamendis.

'I don't know, but have some of this,' said his brother, tossing him a hunk of dried meat.

Gulamendis bit greedily into the jerky and began chewing. 'What is this place?'

'You know more about demons than anyone else I know; what do you think?'

'Demons eat everything. They suck life from the living, and then go after whatever's left.' He made an encompassing gesture and added, 'They don't store fruit, or dry meat. This is not demon food.'

'Then who does it belong to?'

'Let's eat, get some rest and then go and find out,' suggested Gulamendis.

Laromendis said, 'I don't have any better ideas. If no one disturbs our repose, we'll venture out after dark and discover what we can.'

'As you said, I don't have a better idea.'

They sat and began eating.

The day passed slowly. Twice they held themselves ready to fight as a company of demons marched by, but no one seemed to show much interest in the pantry. The two conjectures they arrived at, to explain the unexpected storage shed, were that the original builders of this monstrous fortress had been mortals and had been overrun by the Demon Legion, or that the demons had it built for reasons yet unclear. Given the size and look of the place, the latter seemed a more reasonable conclusion.

As the sky darkened once more, the massive fortress fell quiet, and finally Gulamendis said, 'We need to explore.'

'Why?' said his brother, anticipating his brother's answer. 'Very well,' he conceded before Gulamendis could voice his argument. 'I know, we can't stay here forever, even if there's enough food to last us months.'

His brother smiled and nodded, pointing over his shoulder in the general direction of the fortress. 'If there's any way off this world to one that will lead us back to Home, it is in there.'

'These are the times I wish we'd spent less time learning magic and more times learning how to sneak about unseen, like our forest cousins.'

'It's a difficult choice,' said Gulamendis. 'We can skulk about, or you can enchant us to look like something else, but then we'd reek of magic to anyone sensitive to it.'

'What's your best guess, Demon Master?'

'With this bunch, I have no idea,' he admitted. 'They don't act like any demons I have ever encountered.' He fell silent for a moment, then said, 'Neither those camped in the valley, nor those attacking them, remotely resemble the monsters we faced on Andcardia.

'It's as if we're encountering an entirely new breed of demon.'

'What of their look?' Laromendis asked.

Gulamendis shrugged. 'Before all this, I thought myself familiar with demons, but in the last few days I have seen more creatures which are new to me than I have my entire life. Demons always tend to a type: battle demons are large and powerful, but they can look like bulls or lizards or bulls and lizards, or lions or . . .' He shrugged. 'Flyers tend to be small, but we saw some very large nasty ones on Hub. I've seen demons in magician's robes.' He sighed. 'I wish we had that human warlock around to talk with; he knew a great deal, as did his friends, Pug and Magnus.'

'If we get Home, let's go visit them,' suggested his brother, dryly, 'but until we do, we should turn our attentions to the matter at hand; illusions or skulking?'

'Skulking,' said Gulamendis. 'Save your energies for other conjurations.'

'Skulking it is,' said Laromendis, carefully opening the door.

The marshalling yard to their left was empty and the shortest distance to the side of the massive keep was directly across from them. 'If someone's watching from one of those windows above, we will be seen,' said Laromendis softly.

'It's dark,' said his brother. 'If we hurry . . .'

Not waiting another moment, Laromendis dashed from the large storage shed and his brother followed, pausing only to close the door behind them, before setting off at a full run. It was not a vast distance, less than fifty yards, but they felt as if they were exposed on every side for the longest time.

Hugging the keep wall, they waited, listening for any sounds of alarm. When none was forthcoming, Gulamendis said, 'Now what?'

'That way,' said his brother, pointing to the rear of the keep.

'Why that way?'

'Would you rather try to walk in the main entrance?'

'Point taken,' conceded the Demon Master and the two elves moved towards the rear of the keep.

Reaching a tower, they moved around its base until they were looking at a large rear yard, half the size of the marshalling yard. Laromendis whispered. 'I see steps leading down to a basement door, and a broad flight of steps leading up beyond that.'

'Down,' said Gulamendis. 'Let's sneak in through the basement'.

'Have you wondered why there are no guards?'

'I presume they're all too busy obliterating other demons wherever it was we were before we came through the portal.'

'One can hope, but I still find it odd that we've only seen that one battle demon and those two small patrols,' Laromendis observed.

'Count it a blessing and move on!' hissed his brother.

They made a dash for the steps leading down and found themselves before two large doors. The latch was unsecured and Laromendis gently pulled the nearest door open just enough to peer through. 'It's a long, dark stairway,' Laromendis whispered.

'Is there anyone there?'

'Not that I can see.' The Conjurer slipped through the door, with his brother following.

'This is the height of madness,' said the Demon Master.

'If I push you back to the wall, do not move. I'm going to make us look like part of the stone.'

As plans went, it wasn't a particularly brilliant one, but Gulamendis didn't have a better one so he said nothing.

They moved down a very long staircase that took them deep into the basement of the keep. It finally ended in a large chamber, and Gulamendis judged they were at least three storeys below the surface. The chamber had four doors, the one through which they had just stepped, two other open doorways with stairs leading up, and a barred, heavy wooden one opposite them.

'That one,' whispered Laromendis.

His brother gave him a tiny push from behind, signalling his agreement, and they quickly crossed the open room. The door had a small, barred window, and they peered through it. 'It's a dungeon!' said Gulamendis.

Through the small window they could see a long hallway: floor-to-ceiling bars separated cells on the right. Evenly spaced on the other side, stood three large, heavy wooden doors like the one through which they stared.

In the barred cells, they could see captives: humans, dwarves, and elves. The last were lesser kin to the taredhel, being of similar stature, but smaller than the two brothers. 'What is this?' whispered Laromendis.

'Demons don't take prisoners,' whispered Gulamendis back.

'What now?'

'I have no idea.'

In an inexplicable dungeon, beneath an impossible keep, on a world unknown to them the day before, created by beings also unknown to them, the two elven brothers stood motionless, crippled by the fact they had no idea of what to do next.

CHAPTER TEN

Demon Lore

*J*IM GROANED.

The festivities had ended far too late for him to be welcoming the dawn, yet Pug, Magnus, and Amirantha had come into his room at first light, pulled aside the draperies and insisted he awake.

'Water,' Jim croaked.

Amirantha picked up an earthen pitcher on the night table next to the huge bed Jim occupied and filled a mug with water. He handed it to the noble who took it and drank deeply. Then Magnus noticed that a large lump in the bed next to Jim was moving. Magnus poked his father with his elbow and pointed, and Amirantha followed the gesture.

'Ah,' said Pug. 'We will wait in the antechamber until you are more composed,' said Pug.

'Thank you,' Jim said, his voice still gravelly from the previous night's debauchery.

Once outside they retired to a divan against the wall and sat. Pug said, 'I should have brought along a powder for this sort of thing.'

'Which one?' asked Magnus.

Lowering his voice, Pug said, 'Years ago, before I met your mother, I occasionally indulged in a little too much wine. A healing priest from the Order of Killian had this powder that one mixes with water to banish the effects of such nights; it was very effective, and, it turned out, easy to make. There was no magic involved; just the right mix of herbs and tree bark . . .'

The door opened and a very attractive young woman slipped out quietly. Her hair and eyes were dark and she wore the garb of a servant, though she was barefoot at the moment. With a slight smile she barely nodded at the three men and hurried across the room, to the hall door.

'Wonder where she left her boots?' asked Amirantha. 'Or if she even remembers where she left her boots?' he amended as he laughed.

Magnus seemed less than amused. 'We have some serious work here for the next few days,' he said.

Amirantha put his hand on the white haired magician's shoulder and said, 'You sound disapproving. If Jim wishes to pass the day with a pounding head and turning stomach, that's his prerogative. We had a good night's rest and once we've eaten, we'll be off to do our work. The state of his health isn't a matter for concern today, is it?'

Magnus shook his head and said, 'Sorry. I worry too much.'

'Takes after his mother,' said Pug, and Amirantha was struck by the fact that Pug had made the first reference to his late wife that didn't contain a note of sadness. He hoped it was a sign that the magician's black moods were behind him. Too much depended on Pug's leadership in the coming fight.

A few minutes later, Jim appeared, looking far more composed than any of them had expected. He smiled and said, 'We should dine,' and led them to the door leading out of the apartment he occupied.

As if anticipating his need, a servant waited to guide them to a small alcove overlooking one of the seemingly endless gardens within the palace. Rather than lying on a divan to eat, they sat upon large cushions around a low table. A variety of foods were provided, several Kingdom dishes like fried cake and savoury sausage, as well as the more traditional sweet Quegan delicacies. To everyone's delight, a large pot of steaming Keshian coffee sat alongside a pot of boiling water and an infuser containing one of the more exotic teas from Novindus.

Jim ate like a man who had been starved for a week, and when he noticed the others staring at him, he said, 'I worked up an appetite last night.'

'Apparently so,' said Magnus with a slight smile.

'You scholars can slight the Emperor's generosity if you wish, and I don't denigrate your reasons, but it would have been an insult had I left the festivities too early last night.'

'We noticed,' said Amirantha. 'She was very pretty.'

'Very smart, too,' said Jim. 'I managed to get out of the orgy by cornering a particularly attractive server, which given the differences in our cultures, my pretty host assumed had something to do with Kingdom modesty.'

Pug began to smile. 'She was a spy.'

'Of course, and if I get back this way any time soon, I'm going to do my best to turn her.' As if to himself he said, 'Though if she won't turn, I'll have to kill her, which would simply be a waste.' Looking at his three companions he said, 'I was certain the Quegan intelligence service would have several agents watching us.'

'The young woman seated with me?' asked Pug.

'No,' said Jim. 'She is the youngest daughter of a very minor noble who if the Emperor can't marry off to some minor functionary,' he waved his hand at Pug, 'will have to marry off to some distant cousin, and this Emperor would rather save himself even that modest dowry.' Looking at Amirantha, he said, 'That voluble fellow who bent your ear last night, now he is one of their best men. I doubt you even know how much you told him.'

'Only the truth,' said Amirantha. 'The questions he asked about my homeland were obvious, but it was equally obvious after a while that I knew little he would find useful. He asked about the Maharaja's army, and I said it was big. I had no idea how big, which is true, it's just big.'

Jim grinned, and took a drink of coffee. 'You have the makings of a good spy, Amirantha.'

'I gamble,' said Amirantha. 'I assume that anyone asking that many questions could read a lie, so I find small truths work well in those situations.'

'Ah,' said Jim. 'We must play cards sometime.'

'What are we doing today?' asked Magnus, knowing the rough plan, but not the details.

Jim chewed a mouthful of juicy melon, then swallowed. 'I meet with functionaries until midday, at which time I dine with a few minor nobles – the Emperor and anyone of rank are done with me now – and then I'll come find you in the archives.

'You three will go about your business and someone will see to your midday meal. After we dine tonight, we'll discuss the next day's work.'

They all understood that he meant stealing the Great Book of Demons should they locate it, but no one spoke of it.

When they had finished eating, servants came to escort them to their different destinations.

Pug, Magnus, and Amirantha were led through a series of long hallways and across several large galleries and gardens until they started down a long tunnel which headed into a portion of the palace excavated from the very soil under the foundations.

They emerged into sunlight, and could see they were now on the far side of the rolling hills that supported the palace, looking down at a far less populated portion of the city. The ample houses and estates were still nearby, but below them the jumble of merchant and poor houses had thinned out. Instead, they could see an ancient wall beyond which the rolling hills, on top of the tablelands, were dotted with farms.

They trudged down the long road to another building with a long and low façade and a dozen large windows, most of its bulk had been constructed out of the hillside. 'Gentlemen,' said the servant. 'We are here.'

He turned and left, and the three magic users exchanged glances.

'We are here,' echoed Amirantha mirthfully.

Pug smiled, nodded and indicated they should enter.

Once inside, Pug saw a long hall and off to the left a gallery illuminated by the sunlight streaming in from the tall windows.

Two long tables trisected the room, and around them were arranged chairs. Opposite the windows were the end-caps of half a dozen shelves, each with books arrayed spines out.

A woman sat waiting; seeing the three men enter, she rose and crossed over to them wearing a smile on her face. 'Richard, how nice.'

'Livia,' she said Pug, bowing slightly. 'I believe you met my companions.'

'Yes,' she said, 'albeit briefly. Martin, Amirantha. It's a pleasure to see you once more.'

Amirantha's expression broadened. 'As it is mine,' he replied. 'I was sorry I didn't have the opportunity to speak with you last night. Perhaps . . .?' He let the question hang.

She glanced at Pug as if gauging his reaction, then said, 'Perhaps. Now, what may I do to help you?'

Pug said, 'Martin and I have been commissioned by the King of Isles and the Prince of Krondor to investigate certain discrepancies in our relative histories, especially between accounts of the period after Kesh's withdrawal from the region, but prior to the Kingdom's expansion westward through Yabon.'

'I think I know where to start you off,' said Livia. Looking at Amirantha, she said, 'And you?'

'I have a different charge, from my master, the Maharaja. At this point, I would be interested in any subjects of a mystical nature.'

'Mystical?' she said, as if not quite understanding.

'Our faiths are much the same as yours, but there are some differences. Our gods have different names, and slightly different aspects.'

'How odd,' she commented. Then realizing she sounded judgmental she quickly amended that by saying, 'I mean, it's odd that there are differences, not that your view is odd.'

'I took your meaning,' said Amirantha with a broad smile. 'It might help my understanding if you could show me anything on non-faith tales of magic, of spirits, ghosts, and demons, let us say. Sometimes the tales of the villages and towns give us more insight into the beliefs of a people than the official records of the government or temples.'

'I'll see what I can do,' she replied. Turning to Magnus and Pug she said, 'Let me get you two situated, then we,' she smiled at Amirantha, 'will start looking for folk stories and legends.'

Amirantha conveyed he was amenable to this with a nod, and for a reason he couldn't quite put his finger on, found himself annoyed.

They moved off down the hall, towards the rear of the archives.

Amirantha stood with his mouth closed only by conscious will. The term 'jaw dropping' entered his mind as he looked at a mountain of tomes, books, scrolls and codices. There was one table in the far corner of the room, and no chair.

Livia said, 'I'm sorry, but for the sort of thing you're looking to find, this is the most likely spot.' She gently touched his arm, which he found both reassuring and distracting. 'My people, as you will no doubt discover, are predisposed to be interested in three, no make that four, issues: Glory, both military and commercial, comprise two of the four. The third is self-aggrandizement, for I will confess we are a vain society. Lastly, pleasures of the flesh, which you would have discovered had you remained at the banquet last night.'

Amirantha tried to appear disinterested. 'I've been to orgies before, Livia.'

'As have I, and like you I left before it began, but what I'm trying to say is, if it's not wealth, war, vanity, or lust, it's in there.' She pointed to the massive pile of writings.

'So what you're saying is that Richard and Martin,' he used Pug and Magnus's false names, 'are likely to find only officially blessed histories where they are researching?'

'No, they will look among the only histories not fed to the fire. However, there may be something in this mess that could provide them with a clue or two about what really happened in years past. However, for your research, any discussions of folk tales, myths, superstitions, or reports of encounters with the gods – not sanctioned by the temples, of course – are in there.' She again pointed to the mass.

Amirantha was silent for a moment, then said, 'I have three requests.'

'What may I do to accommodate you?' she said with a clear double meaning as she studied the handsome Warlock.

He smiled his most charming smile and said, 'First, could you arrange to have a pot of hot water and some tea brought to that table over there? I will not risk spilling anything on these old volumes, but I do like to refresh myself from time to time.'

'Of course. What else?' she asked, touching his arm again.

'Could I have a ladder?' He inclined his head towards the mass and said, 'It would be better for whatever is in there if I took the volumes off from the top down. A small ladder, ten feet tall or so, should serve.'

She laughed, and he found the sound of it delightful. 'Of course. I'll have that sent along at once.'

'Could you also provide me with a servant, to haul books aside if I don't wish to look at them, and have him bring along some writing implements and paper or parchment as I wish to take notes.'

'Of course,' she said, though he noticed her manner was cooling.

Understanding that a moment was slipping away, he added, 'Perhaps I should have said four things. Would you dine with me tonight? Assuming Lord James doesn't insist on the three of us dining with him, of course?'

She hesitated a moment, not wishing to appear too anxious, and said, 'If your sponsor doesn't require your presence, I would enjoy supper with you.'

She turned and looked over her shoulder in a playful fashion, 'I'll have the tea, ladder and servant sent to you immediately.' Her smile could only be called seductive as she added, 'And I'll come back later to see if there is anything else you need.'

'Thank you,' said Amirantha, enjoying watching her walk away. The long Quegan toga might run from shoulder to floor, but it hugged her curves in a most tantalizing fashion.

Taking his mind off the lovely woman, he turned and began to consider the prodigious task before him. Sighing, he reached out and took a book at random from the pile. He opened it and found it to be written in a language alien to him. Glancing around to make sure he was unobserved, he then took from his belt pouch a small item Pug had given him before they arrived in Queg. He did as he had been taught and, holding the trinket to his forehead, incanted a short phrase, then put it away. When he opened his eyes, the letters on the page seemed to swim then come together in words he could read.

He muttered to himself, 'I should have met these people a hundred years ago!'

Now able to read this ancient Quegan text, he began to read softly aloud. 'On the matter of the stars and their locations in the heaven by seasons . . .' He read another page, then put aside the amateur astronomy text and looked around. To no one he said, 'You know what you want is at the bottom of that pile, don't you?'

'Sir?' came a voice from behind.

'Oh,' said Amirantha seeing two servants in the doorway. One held a tray with a pot and infuser, cup and canister of tea, the other a short ladder. 'Never mind.' He pointed to the stocky man with the ladder and said, 'Put that over there, climb to the top, and gently pull down the top most book.' To the other he said, 'Put that on the table please.' As the servant moved to do as he was instructed, Amirantha said, 'And find me a chair for that table. Thank you.' He turned his attention to the man climbing the ladder and the massive job before him.

The day wore on, and Amirantha drank two pots of tea. Other than having to relieve himself three times before lunch, his morning was uneventful; there was nothing remarkable about his findings. He had chanced across a few things, a treatise on higher consciousness and the gods, which he found more compelling for its blind leaps of faith than he did for its hypothesis; but it had been composed in precise and elegant language, and he found himself admiring it despite its irrelevance to his current search.

There was one interesting account of a very bad famine, more family chronicles than he imagined possible; the Quegans were a self-aggrandizing people. Even modestly successful merchants had commissioned family histories – most of which were more fancy than fact, he surmised. One particularly vivid, but improbable tale concerned a merchant from the Kingdom city of Krondor who had contrived to build a fortune out of thin air, or so he claimed.

There were a couple of other interesting finds, beyond quaint curiosities; a book of dark spells, which had more truth in them than the author understood. He put it aside for Pug or Magnus.

Another work was a chronicle of a struggle between two temples, neither of which he recognized. The magic he used to read foreign languages did not make the understanding of proper nouns any easier. Someone named Rah-ma-to was named, and his only insight into that puzzle was context. It might be a local god, a local name for one of the gods he already knew, or he could have been a farmer, for all Amirantha knew. Still, it touched on myth and magic, so he set it aside, too.

Other volumes contained similar curiosities, but nothing akin to the information he was seeking. He wondered if Pug and Magnus were having any more luck.

The midday meal was announced by the arrival of Livia. The charming Quegan woman seemed amused by the sight of Amirantha on his knees stacking books. 'Are you finding anything useful?'

He pointed to a dozen volumes stacked on the table next to the empty tea pot and said, 'Those look promising.' He exaggerated, but he wanted to make this look like a worthwhile undertaking to bolster his need to return.

'I've come to take you to the archivists' quarters, where a repast has been provided.'

He rose and found his knees slightly stiff. Feigning more discomfort than he felt he said, 'I need to walk a bit more I think. Too many days of sitting and I'm turning into an old man.'

She smiled as she slipped her arm through his. Amirantha had dealt with flirtatious women all his life, and from her familiar gesture, knew he had been judged and found appropriate enough to warrant further scrutiny. He considered the odd aspects of this culture, that a woman this attractive and bright might consider a foreign scholar of modest means a suitable substitute for a man of rank; then he remembered women of her age might see their child-bearing years coming to a close, and reconsidered; she might be ready to marry the first man who asked her.

He sighed and weighed his need for pleasure against the possible injury to her.

'What?' she asked.

'I'm sorry,' he replied.

'You sighed, and rather heavily.'

He smiled. 'Oh, it's just that the amount of material yet to be considered is daunting,' he lied. He would dismiss the servant after lunch. The pile was manageable enough now for him to sort through alone and now that he was becoming used to the manner in which the Quegans recorded their personal histories, business records and the other sea of useless, he should be able to get through the bulk of it by supper.

'Perhaps you might stay longer?'

He smiled as he looked at her and saw that his instincts in this were almost certainly correct; this woman needed to find a husband and start a family. With a pang he realized that he didn't find the idea repellent, just impossible.

He shook his head. 'As I understand it, the agreement between your Emperor and the King of Isles is for three days, no longer. As I am but a companion to the official researchers . . .' He shrugged.

'I might talk to someone?' she ventured.

'I live a very long way from here,' he said neutrally, but she took his meaning.

She fixed him with a narrow gaze and pulled away ever so slightly. 'You have a wife?'

'No, nothing like that,' he said. 'My work consumes me.'

'Ah,' she said as if that explained everything.

They remained silent until they reached the room set aside for their meal. A modest lunch by Quegan standards, but a small feast by anyone else's, was waiting for them. A moment after Amirantha had been shown through the door, Pug and Magnus arrived. Livia withdrew with their escort, leaving the three of them alone.

'Find anything interesting?' asked Pug as he picked up a stoneware plate and a long two pronged fork and began putting cheese, meat, and fruit on his plate.

'Nothing worth becoming excited over,' answered the Warlock. He pointed to a large pitcher of water then another with wine and his expression was questioning.

'Water, please,' said Magnus. 'Wine with lunch and I'm asleep all afternoon.'

Pug nodded, and Amirantha said, 'Three goblets of water it is.'

They assumed they were being listened to so they spoke in a fairly noncommittal fashion. They chatted and Amirantha finished his meal and said, 'So, anything noteworthy revealing itself?'

They knew he was asking if they had found any clue that might help him in his search through the massive pile of books.

Magnus said, 'Quite a bit, it's clear that Kingdom records of the region are spotty at best.'

That was a code phrase telling Amirantha they had found nothing that would aide his search.

After the meal, servants escorted them to their respective study areas and Amirantha felt mild disappointment that Livia did not make an appearance. He cursed himself for his appetites and willingness to construct reasons to do what he wanted, rather than what he should. Since meeting Pug and his companions, many things had profoundly changed his view of the world in which he lived: the scope of the dangers they faced, the commitment and bravery of those confronting those dangers, and their generosity and selflessness. But one thing continued to leave him constantly unsettled and troubled, and he had once thought it something of minor importance.

His encounter with Sandreena and Creegan had reopened old wounds, wounds he would not have even admitted to, before that encounter.

To those, like Brandos, who knew him well, he was usually unapologetic about his womanizing behaviour.' He stopped for a moment and tried to focus on the pile of books yet to be examined, but his mind was on the young Knight-Adamant from Krondor.

As a young man, like many young men do, he had loved easily, or at least he had told himself it was love. But his life being what it was, they never endured. By the time he found Brandos as a boy scrabbling around the city streets, he had learnt not to let his heart get involved. Women were creatures of comfort, to be taken and then left behind, lest one become attached and again face loss.

What he feared was that he had cared a great deal more for Sandreena than he had admitted; that the time they had spent together, in the oddly named little village north of Krondor, had forged something deeper than convenient physical intimacy. He hated how he felt.

He forced aside his morbid introspection and cursed himself for a sentimental old fool trapped in a young man's body, and set about working on the volumes before him.

An hour into the afternoon, Amirantha began to sense something. He held a book in his hand and glanced at the title, then put it aside. He picked up the next and again felt the oddly familiar, yet nameless tingling. He cast aside that book and picked up two more. As he dug deeper into the pile, the sensation became more familiar, and more immediate.

It was demon.

He pushed his way down, ignoring the damage he might be doing to ancient books – many of which were on the verge of falling apart – as he felt the pull grow even more compelling.

His hand touched something and he recoiled as if experiencing a shock.

Trying to work as quickly as possible, yet not damage the object of his attention, he got the cover of the work clear. Once he could see the volume clearly, his flesh crawled.

This volume was rife with demonic magic.

He reached in and gripped it; the alien sense of demon magic assaulted him again, but this time he was ready for it. He lifted the large volume off those below it and carried it over to the table. He put it down gently and studied it for a moment before he touched it again.

He was almost certain the cover was made of skin; human,

elf, or some other, he was unsure, but this book was definitely bound by something that was once living and aware.

He opened the cover and let the magic spell Pug had given him serve him. The language may have been ancient and obscure, but he read it as easily as he did the first language he had learned as a boy.

Whispering aloud, he read the title page. 'Greater Demon Lore.'

Slowly he turned the first page and began to read.

After a few minutes his legs grew shaky and his stomach began to knot, but he sat in the chair and kept reading, resisting the urge to run from the room screaming.

From the moment they gathered at the end of the day to dine, it was evident to the others that Amirantha had something to tell them, but was keeping silent lest they be overheard. When at last they were alone, Pug gave Magnus a questioning look, the younger magician nodded once, closed his eyes for a moment, then said, 'We have a few minutes; the magic they're using to spy upon us is poorly done, but if I counter it too much, someone may notice.'

'What did you find?' Jim asked Amirantha.

'What we came for,' he answered. 'It is the Greater Demon Lore, and more.'

'More?' asked Pug. 'What is in it?'

'Everything there is to know about demons,' he said with barely contained excitement. 'I consider myself a practiced warlock, demons are my specialty; but I know nothing!' He sat back. 'I haven't finished it yet, but I have read enough to know that something incredible is underway.'

Pug glanced at Magnus. 'Another minute, no more.'

Amirantha said, 'We can talk in detail later,' he glanced at Jim. 'After you steal the book.'

Jim shrugged, as if that would be a trivial issue. The library was not the Imperial Treasury, he could be in and out in minutes with the volume secreted within his baggage. As a diplomat, he would be spared any search of his personal items, and once at sea, the three magicians could pour over it to their hearts content.

Amirantha said, 'There is so much to consider.' He paused, knowing they would have to keep silent soon. 'The demons are so much more than we thought.' He fell silent. 'Much more,' he repeated, then Magnus raised his hand and loudly said, 'I found a recounting of the sea battle of Questor's View, in the Fifteenth Year of the Reign of Rodney the Third.' Forcing a mild laugh, he added, 'This account is quite different to the one we found in the Royal Library at Krondor.'

Talk turned to mundane academia with a few comments made about the hospitality of the Quegans, all flattering; each of the men quickly falling into their role of innocent guest.

Jim considered the perfect time to leave his quarters without waking whoever was with him; he knew the Quegans would ensure he shared his bed with an agent. If he encountered no one along the short road from the palace to the library, he could get to the library, get the book – once Amirantha gave him a precise description – and return in less than a half hour, perhaps as little as a quarter.

Pug and Magnus shared the same thought: just what had Amirantha found in that book?

And Amirantha sat silently, unsure that he had even begun to understand what he had uncovered, and wondering if he was able to make sense of it. For if this book wasn't the total fabrication of a deluded mind, it changed everything he had ever thought he knew about demons and what his people called the Fifth Hell.

Amirantha placed the huge volume down on the table. Jim quipped, 'Stealing it wasn't a problem. Getting it back without falling over was.'

The tome was a foot and a half along the spine and contained about fifty or sixty pages of heavy vellum. It easily weighed fifty pounds; not a difficult load to carry, but impossible to hide. Luckily, as Jim observed, if the Quegans suspected he might skulk around during the night, they would expect him to attempt to pilfer state secrets or imperial treasure, not forgotten books.

They had left Queg less than an hour before, and once clear of the harbour and any observation, mundane or magic, Magnus had transported them to his father's study on top of the tower at Sorcerer's Isle.

Amirantha looked as fascinated as a child opening a gift from Father Winter at the Midwinter's Festival. He pointed at the book and said, 'It should take me only a day or two to determine if what is written is remotely true. If so . . .' He looked at Pug. 'My newfound friend, the elf Gulamendis, and I both came to our skills the hard way, through trial and error. We are among the few who survived that education, Pug, for I suspect a few lads and lasses who tried to conjure their first demon ended up with painful, deadly results.

'With this,' he poked his finger at it for emphasis, 'I would be twice the master of demon lore that I am now.'

Pug said, 'This sounds impressive.'

'You sound very enthusiastic,' observed Jim.

Magnus shot him a sideways glance and then asked the Warlock. 'Who wrote it?'

'I see no author name,' replied Amirantha. 'It may be stated somewhere; I only read a fourth of it before Livia returned to call it a night.

'There are—' He caught his breath. 'I don't know where to begin.' He paused again, then said, 'My perception of the demon realm, what we call the Fifth Circle of Hell, was that it's a place of chaos, constantly shifting and violent, where the strong rise and take command.' He let his voice drop. 'But it's so much more than that.'

'They have hierarchies.' He held up his hand and could see he had both magician's undivided attention; even Jim listened closely. 'I, like you, thought that the demon king, was simply the strongest, the one who had achieved his rank through combat, murder, terror, or alliances with those seeking his protection . . .' He sighed.

'What is it?' asked Magnus.

'Those demons are a slave class,' said Amirantha.

'Slave class?'

'Like Keshian Dog Soldiers, trained killers, crazed, vicious, only good for one thing: fighting war.

'Even the imps are little more than criminals in their society.'

'Criminals?' asked Jim, now obviously interested.

'They have a society,' answered Amirantha. 'They have builders— Where was that hall you describe on the other side of the rift where Macros died fighting Maarg?' he asked Pug.

Pug blinked as if he had never thought to question it. 'I saw it so briefly.'

'Yet you described it to me when you told me of Macros's,' said Amirantha.

'I thought it was some other world,' he shrugged.

'One the demons had already conquered?' said Magnus.

Amirantha said, 'I'll have to spend a few days studying this.' He looked at Pug. 'May I take it to my quarters?'

'Of course,' said Pug.

Amirantha put his hands on the book, but instead of picking it up, he opened it to the very last page. The page was folded, and as he unfolded it, the others could see that it had been tipped into the volume, and a four foot by three foot piece of heavy vellum was revealed.

'What is that?' asked Jim.

Almost grinning, the Warlock said, 'Unless I'm mistaken, My Lord James Dasher Jamison, this is a map of hell!'

CHAPTER ELEVEN

Escape

*T*HE BROTHERS STOOD MOTIONLESS.
      Laromendis used all of his skill to conceal their presence
in the basement as a pair of demons escorted a handful of prisoners out of the cells. Only Gulamendis's demon sensitivity had
alerted them in time. The quip he had made moments before
became reality as they stood flat against the wall while the
Conjurer made it look as if they were part of it.

   The time passed torturously slow yet eventually the door to
the cell block was closed and the prisoners marched away. They
had been a mixed group: four dwarves, two humans and two
elves. All were silent, sullen, yet had not looked particularly
fearful.

   When the room was empty, Laromendis let the illusion fade.
'What was that?'

'I couldn't understand the language,' said his brother. 'The demons are not speaking any language I recognize.'

Since coming to this alien castle on this unknown world, they had been confronted with one conundrum after another. The frustration that had first gripped Gulamendis when he encountered the demon encampment on the previous world, that had raised to a maddening degree when he witnessed the assault by the rival demon faction, was now close to delivering him into a rage at not knowing what was occurring, 'We need information,' he said.

'Where do you suppose we get it?'

'I think our only choice is to go in there and talk to some of the prisoners.'

'Are you mad?' asked Laromendis.

'Why? Do you think they might give us up to their masters?'

'If they think it will curry favour, they might!' argued the Conjurer.

'What do you suggest, then?'

'I think we should try to find out more on our own. Let us get out of here and see what else we can discover.' He sighed. 'If we find no clear way home, or at least gain a better sense of this place, we can always come back.' He glanced around and said, 'Besides, I'd rather strike up a conversation in there with our distant cousins when we're less likely to be surprised by guards.'

Gulamendis inclined his head as he thought, then said, 'Agreed. We might better be served to do it while the humans and dwarves sleep. We can certainly count on our kin to not betray us.'

'You have a better opinion of our people than I do, brother,' said Laromendis. 'Come on, and stay close. If I have to conjure another illusion quickly, it will only be a small one.'

'I shall be your shadow,' said his brother softly.

'Which way?' asked Laromendis.

'Across or behind? Let's go forward.'

They set off softly, moving carefully up the stairway that had been on their right hand when they first entered the dungeon.

'Any other suggestions?' whispered Gulamendis.

'Keep still,' hissed his brother.

They had reached the top of the stairs and found themselves in a vast armoury. At the far end, a group of demons were endeavouring to fit armour to what were apparently new recruits. They communicated with them in grunts and other guttural sounds, showing them how to fasten the new chest-plates and helms. They were so intent on their task, that they failed to notice the two elves who walked into the hall.

Gulamendis backed into the hallway as his brother tugged on his tunic. When they were back in the shadows, they turned and hurried down the stairs. When they were near the level of the entrance to the dungeon, they knelt and peered into the room; seeing no movement they hurried across and paused. 'That way,' said Laromendis.

'This time a little slower, brother.'

'Agreed.'

They crept up the stairs.

Most of this huge keep was empty. The elves judged that there must have been room enough for a thousand or more soldiers to be garrisoned in the now empty barracks scattered throughout the massive structure. It was clear from its design that the occupying forces would be ideally placed to reach their defensive positions in the shortest time possible, rather than housing them in a single large barracks, as was common practice in most fortifications. It was also clear that this gigantic keep had been constructed ages before, but that its scale was wrong for demons. The halls and galleries were too large for the smallest of them, and yet far too small for the greater demons. Something between a dwarf and tall elf had lived here in the past.

Moreover, the demon occupation was obviously a recent one. Vast areas of the place were empty and covered in dust. One tower to the front of the main keep showed signs of occupancy, but all of the others were abandoned.

They climbed one out of curiosity, to see if a higher vantage might give them a better sense of where they were. When they reached the top room, they found the door locked. 'Do we try to break it?' asked Laromendis.

'We might as well risk one of the knives,' said Gulamendis. 'If we run into demons, these two blades will not count for much.'

'I still have the wand,' he said, patting his tunic.

'That might buy us a few minutes,' said the Demon Master, 'but I'd rather not put that to the test. If an alarm is raised . . .'

Laromendis said, 'How do you propose attacking this door.'

His brother smiled. 'By stealth,' he answered.

'No, seriously, what are you thinking?'

'Hinges,' said Gulamendis taking his blade edge to the top of the bottom hinge. It resisted, but after wiggling the blade, he managed to get it under the head of the hinge bolt, and when it came up slightly, he gripped it with powerful fingers and pulled. 'Got it!' he said softly.

The second hinge took longer, but after several frustrating

attempts, it finally yielded to the brothers, leaving Gulamendis with bruised knuckles and a dull knife-edge. The door protested as they pushed on the hinges, but gave way and moved forward slightly. 'The latch, it must be one of the long metal types,' said Laromendis.

'Let me see if I can squeeze through and free it from the other side.' They pushed and wiggled the door back as far as it would go, and the Demon Master squeezed through. Once he was on the other side, he said, 'Step away, I need to push the door back a little.' He did so, then Laromendis heard a door latch free up and suddenly the door began to wobble and fall back.

His brother caught it and said, 'I could use some help, this thing is heavy!'

Laromendis reached out and grappled with the hinge edge of the door and helped his brother swing it out of the way. Then they stopped and examined the inside of the locked room.

'What is this place?' whispered Laromendis.

The late afternoon sun illuminated the room just enough for both the brothers to see that it had once been a study. There were books and tomes against one wall, and a writing desk with a dried up inkwell and ancient quills; rolls of brittle parchment lay scattered on the surface.

'My skin is itching,' said Gulamendis. 'Whoever resided here, practiced dark arts.'

'Is that why the demons didn't open the door?'

'Probably just too lazy,' said Gulamendis. 'They tend to take the path of least resistance.'

Laromendis picked up a paper and said, 'Whoever penned this left in a hurry. It's unfinished.'

'But he expected to return,' said Gulamendis. 'He locked the door behind him.'

'A mystery,' said his brother. Pointing to the window he said, 'Let's take a look outside.'

The window was a vaulted affair, with a large cushioned window seat. They could both stand on it and peer through the dirty glass. 'Can we open this? I can't see a thing,' said Laromendis.

'It has a latch,' answered his brother.

Gulamendis jumped down and his brother followed. The Demon Master tried the latch and found it reluctant, but slowly released it. He pulled on the window and found the hinges just as difficult. 'No one has used this room in a very long time.'

Laromendis said, 'Does any of that look familiar to you?'

Gulamendis looked and saw a foreboding mountain range in the distance. The low light on the left told him he was looking southward as the sun set behind the dark clouds. After a moment, Gulamendis said, 'No, nothing.'

'Can you see the fire peaks?' he asked, indicating the distant volcanoes.

'Of course,' said Gulamendis. 'Why?'

'See how that one massive one rises up on the right, while those other two look like smaller twins to the left?'

'Yes,' said the Demon Master. 'Does it mean something to you?'

'The Fire Twins.'

'Could it be?'

'If you were miles to the south, looking northward . . .' said Laromendis.

'From the battlements of Can-ducar!'

'The twins would be on the right and the Fire Queen on the left!'

'How did we not know about this ancient fortress?' asked Gulamendis.

'We never got this far,' answered the Conjurer. 'Can-ducar was the northernmost fortification on Telesan when the demons appeared.' He said, 'We never occupied much of the world because of this foul smoke and ash. The only reason we sent anyone here was to mine metals.'

'Do you think that's why the demons have dwarven prisoners?'

'Possibly,' said Laromendis.

'Well,' said his brother. 'We have some idea where they came from, at least.'

'Do we?'

Feeling defeat, the Demon Master said, 'No. I mean, we know that portal in the wall by the gate leads to the world where we saw the demon battle, and we know they didn't come from this place originally.'

Laromendis sat down in the gloom of the fading afternoon light. 'We dare not light anything, even if we could find tinder and flint, in case it is seen, so we must wait until tomorrow to find out if anything here is of use.'

Gulamendis stood. 'Help me get the door back on its hinges, just in case this is the one day they decide to investigate the top of the tower. Then one of us should go back to the storage shed and fill a sack with food.'

'I'll go,' said Laromendis. 'You were always the better scholar. See what you can make of this with what little light is left.'

Laromendis left, closing the door behind him; Gulamendis latched it shut. He looked at the many volumes on the shelves, wondering where to start, then found his gaze pulled to a large leather-bound book. He reached up and when his fingertips touched it, he jerked his hand back. 'Demon,' he whispered. 'Could this be?' He pulled the book down and opened it. At once his vision swam and he recognized the writing as the arcane runic symbols of demon control. 'Oh, my,' he whispered as he sat down and began to read.

A short time later his brother returned with a sack full of food and said, 'It's a good thing we vacated that shed. When I got there some dwarves were leaving with food for the prisoners.'

'Why didn't they find us last night?'

Laromendis shrugged and tossed an apple to his brother. 'Perhaps they don't feed their prisoners every day.' He started eating an apple and after a juicy bite, asked, 'Find anything?'

'Yes,' said his brother. 'I think I may have found several important things.'

'Such as?'

'Where the Demon gate is that lets them into this realm.'

'Really?' he seemed impressed. 'What else?'

'Who or what may be at the heart of this madness.'

Laromendis let out a slow sigh. 'It's almost too dark to read. Finish that tomorrow.' Elves were capable of seeing in the darkest of nights, when only starlight was the source, but without any kind of light, reading ancient ink on parchment was beyond even their gifts.

'One other thing,' said Gulamendis.

'What?'

With a broad smile he said, 'I think I have found a way for us to get to Home.'

*　*　*

Night dragged on and Laromendis repeated what he had just been told to be sure he understood it. 'So, this lair was the study of a human magician, by the name of Makras—'

'Macros.'

'Macros; and he was an advisor to the local ruler.'

'The King of Des.'

'The King of Des. And Macros discovered a portal, built by some unknown people in ages past.'

'Yes.'

Laromendis said, 'So while experimenting with this device, he opened it.'

'Yes, to the world . . . Well, I will have to reread that part when the light returns.'

Laromendis sat silently in the darkness, then he said, 'I'll skip over the other parts. This portal is not the one we came through to get here?'

'No, for he described its location as a nearby vale; if we assume he meant near where he was writing, and that he was writing in this room.'

'Well, let us say we can find this portal. How are we to operate it?'

'That is why I said "I think" I have found a way home, instead of "I know". If we can control it, I suggest we make for Home—.' Laromendis was about to object, but Gulamendis cut him off. '—Not for E'bar, but for Sorcerer's Island.'

'How?'

'I spent enough time near the portal on the island to . . . Well, *I think* I can contrive to get us there.'

Laromendis was determined not to let his brother's hopes rise too fast. 'And what do we use to power it?'

Gulamendis held up a small bag and even though his brother could barely see him in the gloom, he sensed his smile. 'I took these from the dead galasmancer.'

'Crystals?'

'Crystals.'

Laromendis said, 'As I don't have a better idea, can I suggest we leave now, taking the volume with us, and read it somewhere far from here at first light?'

Gulamendis was loath to leave behind such a treasure-trove of ancient human magic, but saw the wisdom in getting out of this place when activity was at its lowest point. He lifted the volume, nodded once and opened the door.

Moving slowly, but purposefully down the circular stairs of the tower, they reached its base and looked down the long hallway that would eventually lead them to the stairs back down to the dungeon, and then up to the yard. They made their way past silent doors and empty rooms, and when they were once again in the dungeon, Gulamendis risked a hurried peek through the door to the cells. The prisoners were all asleep, huddled together for warmth. There were no guards.

They moved on as silently as possible to the low door that opened onto the courtyard, Laromendis opened it a crack and peeked through. The three steps to the surface were clear and no one else was in sight.

They crept along the wall, staying against it as much as possible, despite the extra cover of darkness; loath to take even the slightest risk with the slim chance at freedom before them.

A quick stop in the storage shed had them loaded with provisions. They were only stymied for a short while when they reached the gate and found it bolted. Remembering that they had come in through the portal straight into the marshalling yard, they realized that they hadn't thought of how to get through the gate. Logic dictated there was more than one way out, and a hurried examination of the wall led them to a postern gate behind the keep. It was unguarded, so they opened it and went outside.

'We need to start going south,' said Gulamendis.

'Towards the volcanoes and the battlefield?' asked his brother.

'Yes,' said Gulamendis.

With a slight nod of his head to indicate acceptance, the Conjurer indicated that his brother should lead the way. The two elves ventured into a very dark night, neither of them certain of where they where headed, but both aware they left nothing good behind them.

Dawn found Gulamendis and Laromendis sitting under the shelter of an overhang, their eyes smarting from the acidic smoke which hung on the hillside like a cloud of suffering. The three volcanoes were belching smoke and ash into the sky on a regular basis. As Laromendis had wryly observed, it would be just their luck to reach their destination as one of the three erupted and destroyed the portal. He was sure that fate's cruel irony would have them burned alive within the portal, or have them watch as their last hope of escape went up in flames. He was inclined to think the second a more painful outcome.

His brother had merely given him a withering look and said nothing. As soon as he could, Gulamendis began reading the volume he had purloined from the ancient keep. Finally he said, 'As I understand it, these people, called the Edhara, were just beginning to experiment with portals. They had created the one we are seeking in a cave – that I hope is not too far from here – and had already discovered a few relatively benign worlds. Then the demons found them.'

'Found them?'

'Remember what Pug said about the nature of rifts?'

'Not really,' said his brother. 'I think that was a conversation you had while I was talking to that odd creature from that world whose name I can't pronounce; the fellow with the blue skin and those things coming out of his neck; he could make the most stunning illusions . . .'

'From you, my not-so-modest brother, that is high praise,' said Gulamendis.

'I'll grant him his due; he was very good.'

'Pug told me rifts have a loadstone quality: as loadstones draw iron to them, rifts tend to draw other rifts. So if you have an established portal from one world to the next, there's a better than average chance that anyone casting about for a random destination will connect to a world that already has a portal on it.'

'I wonder if that's why the galasmancer created Hub?'

His brother shrugged. 'As the Regent's Meet didn't see fit to consult with me on the matter, I can only speculate.' His finger stabbed a page. 'It's written more hastily from here to the end, and reads much like the reports we received when our people first encountered the demons: massive chaotic assaults, no quarter asked or given, wave after wave of demon of every stripe.'

'Obviously something is different,' said Laromendis. 'Those demons we saw being slaughtered, and those in the keep to the north are not like any we've seen before.'

'This is where this gets interesting,' said Gulamendis. 'Let me read, "And then to our lord Hijilia came a herald of the demon kind, under a banner of truce, offering terms".'

'A truce?' Thinking of the dozens of worlds overrun by the Demon Legion and the millions of taredhel left dead on those worlds, he muttered, 'We never had such an offer.'

'The Edhara didn't accept their terms, vowing to fight to the end. The author of this chronicle wrote this as if it was his last testament, and jammed in every detail he thought was important.

'The reason I think we might contrive to use the portal in the cave to get away is because that was what the rulers of the Edhara were planning to do. It's not clear if they managed to get away in time, or if they even reached the portal.

'The point is, if we manage to get out of here, and if we can reach Sorcerer's Island, and then E'bar, we will have something of vital importance to tell the Regent's Meet.'

Laromendis was silent for a moment, then said, 'You mean we need to tell Tandarae?'

Gulamendis was silent and then said, 'It always comes back to that, doesn't it?'

'The Meeting can not continue on the course it has been on for the last three hundred years, brother. The Circle of Light must be reformed, and all offices regarding magic need to be restored to it. Spending just a few months with those humans on Sorcerer's Island tells me that this is true; if you spoke to Magnus or Pug about their own history and learned of Pug's first attempt, the Academy at Stardock . . .' He took a breath. 'Very well, let's get back first.'

Gulamendis said, 'I think we can be there today if we leave now.'

'In daylight?'

'Do you see anyone else around here?'

'No, but a few months ago a really massive battle took place only a few miles south of here,' reminded the Conjurer.

'I doubt it's still in progress,' said the Demon Master. 'Which would explain why there's only a small garrison left in that huge fortress, and why we were able to come and go as we pleased. They've gone somewhere else.'

Laromendis stood up. 'The thing that's annoying me most,' he said, 'is that there are still too many mysteries. I'm a simple elf at heart; I make things appear out of thin air, and people give me things: food, gold, their daughter's virtue, a nice robe . . .'

'You have always thought like a brigand, and you are a brigand at heart.' He smiled. 'Still, you're my brother and my brigand, and I shall always stand with you.'

For the first time in days Laromendis felt like returning his brother's smile. He clapped him on the shoulder and said, 'As it should be. You may choose to consort with the foulest of beings, but I shall be at your side to the end.'

'Let us go.'

As they walked to the south, Laromendis said, 'There's a question I've been meaning to ask you for some time now.'

'Yes?'

'Remember when that human girl, Sandreena said all those things about Amirantha?'

Gulamendis laughed. 'How could I forget?'

'Do you remember the part about a creature he summoned, named Dalthea? She appeared as a female of extraordinary beauty as I recall.'

'A demon who looked like a beautiful human woman; Yes,

I remember. He conjured a succubus and modified her to look beyond compare.'

'Imagine conjuring a totally obedient beautiful female elf? Do you know that trick?'

For the first time in almost a century, Gulamendis, hit his brother on the arm.

It was midday and the two brothers were closer to the volcanoes. The air was heavy with the stench of burning ash and their eyes stung even more from the low hanging smoke: there was almost no wind. It masked them from casual observation, but also made their lungs and eyes hurt.

The landscape was now a rugged sea of basalt rock, large sheets of light grey and black shadow were interrupted by jagged outcroppings of up-thrust stone. At times their weight would crack the rock below as they stepped on the relatively thin skin of a lava bubble, which released a cloud of noxious, sulphurous gas. Gulamendis even dropped part way into one gas dome and his brother had to help free him. The edges of the rock were sharp and they had to move slowly to avoid injury at almost every step.

'Who would want to conquer this miserable place?' asked the Demon Master.

'We did, for a while,' said Laromendis. 'We needed the crystals that come out of these volcanoes; there are also huge deposits of metals on this world.' He glanced around, as if gaining his bearings. 'I spent a little time here when I was exploring for the Regent's Meet, and the mines to the south, on the other side of the abandoned fortress . . . Well, I can only say they were impressive; we found copper, silver, iron, gold . . .' He took a deep breath, then coughed. 'How much further?'

Gulamendis paused to read out of the journal to ensure he was not making any mistakes. 'If I understand this correctly, we must climb that ridge over there,' he pointed to the south, and Laromendis could see it about a mile away, and the long flow of basalt that had created a relatively smooth ramp leading up to it. 'The cave is somewhere on the other side.'

They moved slowly and an hour later made it to the top of the ridge. As they surveyed the landscape, Laromendis said, 'Gods and fathers!'

Before them spread mile after mile of more twisted and broken rock. In the distance they could see gas plumes and steam vents, and they knew they were seeing the outer boundary of volcanic activity. Since coming to this world, the taredhel had witnessed two eruptions, neither of which had been violent enough to threaten the fortification in the south, but large enough to deter exploration in this region. The brothers speculated that the taredhel explorers would have found the human fortress to the north, had the volcanoes not stirred. Of course once the demons had reached this world, it lay behind their lines.

'Where now?' asked Laromendis.

'Somewhere out there?' said Gulamendis.

'Can you be more precise?'

'No,' said his brother, as he started walking down the side of the solid lava flow.

CHAPTER TWELVE

Allies

SANDREENA GALLOPED FORWARD.
Farson and Kendra urged their lagging mounts to keep up as they started down the final hillside into Durbin. Dust blinded those without shelter as another hot wind blew hard out of the desert. Sandreena had set an unrelenting pace, pushing the poor animals to the limits of their strength, knowing that the three fine warhorses would only be fit for the knackers yard when this ride was over; they would never again be fit for battle.

Still, she judged it a necessary sacrifice, just as she judged Jaliel's loss necessary. Each night she prayed to the Goddess for protection, and hoped that Jaliel had been fortunate enough to become a captive not a corpse. With the Goddess's mercy, he and the other slaves there might be freed if the mystery she had discovered in the Valley of Lost Men could be further unravelled.

Durbin was the most dangerous city on the Bitter Sea by a measure. It was the titular seat of Imperial Keshian government in the Jal-Pur desert and the Bitter Sea, and was effectively a law unto itself. Occasionally, an Imperial edict would be handed down from the Emperor's Court in Kesh instructing reform, but strength of arms, gold, and power remained the only real means of safe passage in the city.

Three ragged riders entering at a gallop would hardly elicit a second glance from the city watch and anyone else studying the party only considered them as potential prey.

Sandreena drew the most attention, for despite the dark circles of fatigue under her eyes, the road dirt, sweat and filthy hair, her face was still beautiful. However, her arms and surcoat warned that whatever profit the slave pens might offer, it would be hard won. Any Knight-Adamant of the Order of the Shield of the Weak would offer far more than she received in a melee. The other knight and the dwarf were equally dismissed as not worth the trouble, and so the three proceeded through the city untroubled.

Sandreena pulled up her mount before a stable near the docks and found the owner. A quick round of haggling got her enough gold to buy a boat. No captain in Durbin would take people to Sorcerer's Isle, no matter what the price, so she knew they were on their own.

A quick stop in an inn for food and they took possession of their craft. The boat was small, less than twenty feet in length, and if they encountered bad weather, they would drown. Even so Sandreena mustered up her meagre sailing skills, said a prayer to the Goddess, and they departed.

Sandreena had one advantage at sea, she knew how to read

the stars, and she had no doubt she could find Sorcerer's Isle. She dead reckoned going north by northeast, during their first day, and would adjust that when night fell. Both Farson and Kendra were ignorant of boats and got a swift instruction in what she needed them to do. It would be cramped and uncomfortable and there would be no privacy, but by now they were used to one another.

Little was said. None them had slept for the last two days, they were all exhausted and Sandreena had gleaned all she could from Kendra with questions while they had rested on the road. The new information, added to what she had seen, made Sandreena aware just how far this discovery was beyond her ability to judge. Nothing made any sense, and right now she felt a driving need to bring order from this chaos.

Once aboard, Sandreena had ordered Farson to rest as best he could; Kendra needed no urging to cross his arms, drop chin to chest, and lose himself in sleep. Sandreena knew she must somehow keep awake until nightfall and then wake Farson, and give him two clear guides in the heaven to steer by, only then would she give herself permission to rest. Her main concern now was the marauders that harassed these sea lanes. By sailing straight for Sorcerer's Isle she hoped to quickly leave the coastal routes behind, with their attendant risk of pirates. Three armed warriors in a city with plenty of defensible positions was one thing. Three armed warriors in a small boat come upon by a full company of armed men at sea was quite another. Sandreena knew that should pirates heave into view, she and her companions would be bound for Durbin and the slave pens.

Sandreena stayed awake by sheer strength of will, and when

finally the sun set and the stars rose, she nudged Farson. With a nod of her head she indicated they should let the dwarf sleep, though from what she could see, waking him might prove difficult.

She quickly gave Farson a brief lesson on steering the little craft. With a single boom sail and no jib, it only took her a few minutes to demonstrate the simple task of running abreast a following wind. She made it clear that if something proved too difficult for him, he should wake her at once. He nodded, and she pointed to a star rising directly ahead. 'That will be your point of reference, that large slightly blue star. If you keep the prow pointed directly at it, you'll eventually come north and we'll be sailing west of where we want to be. So in about three hours you'll see three small stars rise at about the same place. They form a tiny triangle, point down. Put the bow of the boat between where they rise until the blue star is over there.' She pointed off to her left. 'Once it's past the highest point in the sky . . .' She yawned uncontrollably, then blinked. 'If it starts to go down . . .' She lay down, closing her eyes, and said, 'Steer between the blue star and the three until the blue star starts to sink, then aim straight at the three. You'll zig and zag, but we'll get there. Wake me when the eastern sky starts to brighten. I'll need a quick look at the sky to see . . . how . . . far . . .' She fell asleep.

Fortune, or the Goddess, smiled on them. For three days they had fair winds and Farson didn't sail them too far off course at night. Kendra had proven useful once he had overcome his aversion to sailing; deep water and boats were not something his people found appealing. Still, once he had learned the basic mechanics of sailing the small craft, he seemed almost to enjoy it.

Their food was gone and the water running low when the sharp-eyed dwarf said, 'I see land!'

Sandreena motioned for Farson to take over the tiller, and moved to stand behind the dwarf, putting one hand on the mast, and peering ahead. A few minutes later she saw a smudge on the horizon and said, 'That will be Sorcerer's Isle.' She glanced behind her and saw a storm approaching. 'Just in time, it seems. I think we're going to be getting foul weather soon.'

No one spoke as the smudge in the distance resolved itself into a dark spot, which in turn became a distant island. By the time the sky above them began to darken, they could make out cliffs and a castle on the eastern edge. 'There's a beach to the west of that point,' Sandreena said, and Farson nodded.

Sandreena said, 'Beach landings can be tricky, so plan on getting wet.' She had had them strip off their armour as soon as they had cleared Durbin harbour, so she wasn't worried about either of her companions drowning a hundred yards off shore, then she thought to ask, 'Kendra, do you swim?'

'Not a stroke,' he said. 'Never had much need to learn.'

'I'll try to keep from swamping the boat.'

'That would be appreciated, Sandreena,' said the dwarf calmly.

She took the tiller from Farson and said, 'When I tell you, move to the back.'

She deftly moved the small boat so it pointed straight at the little beach and when she felt the swell rising beneath the hull, she shouted to Farson, 'Take down the sail!'

He did as ordered and Sandreena saw the canvas fall loosely just as a comber broke behind the boat, hurling them towards the beach. 'Back!' she shouted, and they moved a few feet to the rear, tilting the bow up so it wouldn't plant in the sand. 'Get ready to jump and pull us in.' She waited. 'Jump!'

The dwarf and Knight-Adamant leapt over the side into thigh high water for Farson, which was chest high for Kendra, and four powerful arms hauled the boat safely into the sand. Sandreena let out a long sigh of relief. She had trusted in the Goddess to bring them safely here, but she had never been completely free of doubt. 'Get your armour,' she instructed as she picked up her gear.

On the beach they quickly rearmed themselves and when all were ready, Sandreena led them up the small path that ran from the castle until it reached the top of the bluffs, where it split, one path heading into the heart of the island, the other towards the beach.

No one hailed them; there was no sign that their landing had even been observed, yet Sandreena knew Pug was aware she approached, or if he was not home, then whoever he'd left in charge. She was tired to her bones, but energized by at last reaching her goal.

When she entered the courtyard to the ancient looking castle, she found a familiar face. She had met young magician, Jason, on her previous visit to the island. 'Sandreena,' he said with a warm smile. 'I am to see to your needs.'

'These two need food, clean clothing, and rest,' she replied, introducing Farson and Kendra. 'I need to speak to Pug at once.'

He inclined his head and with a wave of his hand summoned another young man who had been standing at the door of the keep. He took Kendra and Farson and led them into the keep while Jason said, 'Are you certain you wouldn't rather rest first, too? If you don't mind me saying so, you look a little in need of it.'

She smiled. 'I look like I need a lot of it, you mean.' She shook her head. 'No, talk now, rest after.'

He turned and said, 'Very well. Follow me, please.' He led her into the keep and then across the main floor where she could see Samantha hard at work over a massive kettle of stew. The plump woman smiled, hurried over and threw her arms around Sandreena's neck, almost knocking her over.

Sandreena was so tired she could barely laugh, but she hugged her old friend back and said, 'I take it this means Brandos is still here?'

'Yes,' said Samantha. 'And Amirantha.'

'Good,' said Sandreena, to Samantha's obvious surprise.

'Good?'

'He may be a bastard, but we need his knowledge. I've got to go. I'll catch up with you later.' They hugged once more and Sandreena found Jason waiting. He led her through a door and up a winding staircase to a tower. 'Through there,' he said.

Sandreena opened the door, expecting to see Pug and perhaps Magnus and Amirantha waiting, but instead the room was now empty. 'What?' she asked.

'Step through that portal,' said Jason from behind.

That's when she noticed the tiny ripple in the air, like a heat shimmer. She nodded and walked into it.

Suddenly she was somewhere else. The room was huge, well furnished, and there were two dozen people sitting around a semi-circle of benches. Facing that semi-circle was a table behind which Pug, Magnus, and Amirantha waited.

'Sandreena,' said Pug, standing to welcome her. 'We had word you were approaching the island.'

She nodded, suddenly wishing she had taken up Jason's offer, for she was filthy, smelled of horse, sea-salt, and sweat, and now stood in the midst of what was obviously a very important meeting. Pug motioned for her to take a seat at the end of the table next to Magnus and she complied.

Pug said, 'That is all that we have for you now. Please go back to your designated tasks, but be ready. The call may come any moment.'

The score or more of people who sat in the semi-circle stood, and several of them winked out of sight instantly. A couple of others vanished moments later, while the others filed out one at a time through another invisible portal. Finally, Sandreena was left alone with Magnus, Pug and Amirantha.

'You have something to tell us?' asked Pug.

Sandreena nodded. 'Creegan has gone to Rillanon, expecting to be named Grand Master of the Order. He left me in charge in Krondor and then left me with this report—'—she looked at Pug with suspicion— '—which I'll warrant you've read.'

'A copy,' said Pug.

'There was no one else I could trust to investigate, so I went myself.'

'What did you find?' asked Pug.

'Very few answers. Many more questions. I'll tell you in detail, but first I need to know, did I just walk into a meeting of the Conclave?'

Pug nodded slowly. 'The end of a meeting.'

'There are more of you than I thought.'

'There are more of us than we want people to know, even our friends in some cases. But it was necessary to call them here.' Pug stood up.

'To brief them?' asked Sandreena, rising as well.

'No, to instruct them,' said Pug. 'Those you saw are the leaders of groups we have hidden all over the world. But we must begin to marshal our resources.'

'Marshal?' asked Sandreena, fatigue making her mind sluggish and uncertain of what she was hearing.

'We're going to war,' Amirantha said. 'And it's going to be the bloodiest, nastiest fight this world has ever seen.'

Sandreena sat back down.

'It should be near here,' said Gulamendis.

'How do you know?' asked Laromendis.

'The author recorded the travel time. I know how long it takes the average human to ride a horse.'

'What if he was on foot?'

Gulamendis threw his brother a withering look. 'He mentions riding. I assume, given the abandoned stables back at the keep, it means riding horses.'

His brother conceded. 'Go on.'

'I compensated for that, factored in how much this landscape has changed, and how long it would take us to walk the same distance.' He made an encompassing arc with his hand. 'We should find it somewhere around here.'

'What exactly are we looking for?' asked his brother.

'A portal.' He sounded far less convinced than he had the last time he answered his brother's question.

'You do remember that the one at the fortress was invisible?' asked Laromendis.

The Demon Master pondered it for a moment, then said, 'You're the master of the unseen. Do you have any means to discern invisible things?'

'If I know what I'm looking for, perhaps.'

'A portal?'

Laromendis looked embarrassed as he realized that he should have thought of using his skills in this way. 'It would help if I knew the general area.'

Gulamendis indicated their immediate surroundings with a wave of his hand. 'If I read this book correctly, the portal should be close by. It appears that they built it far enough away from the fortress so that if something dire occurred, they would not endanger their ruler and his court.

'This blasted countryside has been ravaged by those volcanoes, so scorching a few more hectares of land would hardly be a problem.'

'Then where would you logically place it?'

'Somewhere close to an ancient road that once ran below our feet.' He pointed to a non-volcanic hilltop close by. 'That may be the only remaining landmark from before the recent eruptions, but if that's the hill mentioned in this journal . . .' He looked around. 'We should be close. You would put a portal by the road, someplace flat, a spot easy to observe from a safe distance . . .' He pointed. 'Like over there.'

Laromendis nodded and walked up an incline and then down a steeper one to a flat area dotted with a few loose rocks. He closed his eyes and extended both hands outward and downward. After a minute he said, 'No. Nothing.'

Gulamendis said, 'Well, we might as well be methodical about this.' He turned and looked for another observable location and pointed, then led his brother to examine it.

They found the portal three hours later. It wasn't invisible. Instead, it had been knocked flat by some geological shudder in past years. It had a large base very similar to those used by the taredhel, with two slender bowed arms sweeping upward. They had to be careful getting it upright again, as there was no means to repair any damage they might inadvertently cause.

Laromendis said, 'Do you think you can make this thing work?'

'I don't know,' answered his brother honestly. 'I can only try.' He consulted the book several times, then said, 'Look for a recess in the base.'

Laromendis did so and said, 'There's a very tightly fitted cover.' He poked and prodded, and eventually the lid slid to the side. A faint humming filled the air. Inside they saw a glowing yellow crystal.

'It's still working?'

'I don't know,' said Laromendis. 'You're the one who read the journal.'

'We've both been through those portals a dozen times.'

'Yes,' said the Conjurer, 'but neither of us has programmed one.'

'I did,' said the Demon Master dryly.

'And almost drowned us both.'

Gulamendis knelt and inspected the base, then the two arching wands of wood that formed the boundary of the portal. 'I feel energy, but it's very faint.'

'Do you see controls?'

'Here, I think,' Gulamendis answered. 'Feel here.' He pointed at a spot on one of the uprights.

Laromendis did and said, 'I feel a depression . . . wait, there are a series of them.'

'Try turning your hand sidewise.'

'Fingers!' said Laromendis with delight. 'You put your fingers in there.'

'And one for the thumb, I am certain.'

'Why?' asked his brother.

The Demon Master said, 'Because few of the demon hosts have four fingers and a thumb, and most of those that do have long talons that would prevent their fingers from fitting.'

'Or they just designed it that way because that's how they created artifacts.'

'Or there is that,' agreed Gulamendis.

Laromendis moved his fingers around in the impressions and said, 'I don't know how this works.'

'There's nothing in the journal about how this device operates. Lots of discussion covering what happened when they used it, but nothing as to how it's controlled.'

'There are no markings, no devices, nothing to tell you if you've selected the proper alignment.' Laromendis looked defeated.

Suddenly Gulamendis said, 'Think about where you want to go.'

'Think?'

'You're the Master Conjurer. Conjure it in your mind the place where the dragon landed us on Sorcerer's Isle.'

Having no better idea, Laromendis closed his eyes and envisioned that location as best he could. Suddenly a shot of energy ran up his arm, causing him to jerk his hand away. 'Ow!'

'What?' asked Gulamendis.

Shaking his hands a little, his brother answered, 'Nothing. Just a little – unexpected shock. As if I had touched metal on a very dry day.' Tentatively, he returned his fingers to the spots and said, 'It's not so bad if you expect it.' Closing his eyes, he again tried to concentrate on Sorcerer's Isle.

After a full minute he took his hand away and said, 'No, something's not right.'

'What?'

'If I knew, I'd be a galasmancer, not a conjurer.'

Gulamendis sat, opened the journal and began turning pages. 'This is probably futile, but let me see if there's something I've missed.'

His brother sat down a short distance away, content to wait and rest. While they had endured little physical exertion since escaping the battle with the demons, the stress and lack of sleep had taken its toll. Laromendis wished he could sit on something more comfortable than a rough patch of basalt. He ran his fingers over the finely grained dark grey rock and then inspected the edges. On the tips of the stone was a powdery dust and it glimmered with tiny fragments of crystal. He let his eyes wander over the landscape, noticing a glint of light here and there as the afternoon sun reflected off exposed outcroppings of crystal or rhyolitic glass. He could see a vein of obsidian running through the rock face not too far from his uncomfortable perch. Ages ago, water had started to seep through an interstice in the rocks, and at some point in time a portion of the hillside had slid away, exposing a record of this region's geological history. The mineral riches of this violent place had drawn the taredhel here. He wondered if the demons had come for the same reasons, or if they had merely come because their enemies were here.

There were so many things Laromendis didn't understand. From any perspective the war with the demons had been lost the moment it started, for the only magicians with demon lore had been the members of the Circle of Light. Only the few who had avoided the destruction of the Circle centuries before or those who, like his brother, had gleaned their knowledge in isolation, had survived to come to the aid of their people. Not for the first time Laromendis was visited by a deep, bitter resentment over the Regent's Meet and their policies.

Perhaps Loremaster Tandarae was sincere, and some progress could be made, or perhaps it would only take violence to change things. As fatigue washed through his soul, Laromendis closed his eyes for a moment, as he realized his thoughts were academic unless his brother could come up with a way home.

He turned his mind to wondering what they would do if Gulamendis couldn't activate this portal. Would there be any possible way home in the old taredhel fortress, many miles to the south? Even if there was a working portal, would it take them back to Hub? And if they got to E'bar, would death be awaiting them as they stepped through the portal? For the first time in years, he felt defeated.

'I have it,' his brother said softly.

Laromendis sat up straight and said, 'What?'

'I know why the portal isn't working.'

'Why?'

Rather than saying anything, Gulamendis scrambled a few feet to the base of the device and opened it to reveal the crystal. He removed the stone, then opened the small bag on his belt and took out one of the crystals he had taken off the dead galasmancer on Hub. He inserted it into the receptacle and closed the latch. Looking at Laromendis, he said, 'Now try.'

Laromendis came to his feet, put his fingertips in the depressions and was instantly overwhelmed by images. He closed his eyes and said softly, 'I see things.'

Gulamendis said, 'That shock you received was designed to let anyone operating the device know that the crystal lacked sufficient energy to make the device work.'

Laromendis took his fingertips away and laughed. 'Of course. There are no symbols, no markings, nothing . . .' He took a deep breath, closed his eyes and saw tumbling landscapes. 'I feel as if I'm flying over worlds,' he said softly. 'Desert, mountains, oceans . . .'

'Try to steer it. Like a ship at sea.'

'I'll try.' Laromendis first started by imagining he was halting and suddenly the image around him was motionless, as if he hung a few feet above the ground. He saw a meadow, with trees that almost looked familiar but were still enough different to inform him that this was not a world he knew. He willed his mind to the vale near the burned out shell of Villa Beata on Sorcerer's Isle, where he had been reunited with his brother.

There was resistance, as if the device did not wish to go somewhere not already known to it, or so far away, but then he felt a wrench and was suddenly speeding among the stars. He felt an almost overwhelming sense of vertigo and his stomach knotted, but he kept his grip on the device and his eyes closed. He saw a world hurtling at him, then abruptly it seemed as if he was instead falling towards it; he could see a vast ocean, two great landmasses and a sea, with islands at its centre! Then he was heading straight for a small island, northwest of the coast, and he willed himself to slow down.

Fearing to open his eyes, he softly said, 'I think I've found it.'

His brother spoke in hushed tones. 'Open the portal, Laro.'

He willed the portal to open, imagining a way between the worlds, and felt a shock run up his arm, not a sharp warning, but a physical vibration as the air made a loud whooshing sound and sizzled with energy. He opened his eyes.

'You did it,' Gulamendis said softly.

Laromendis said, 'This is amazing. This portal device is better than our own, many times over. Better even than those of the humans from what I've seen.'

'Their builders were humans,' reminded his brother.

'I mean the humans on Home.'

'Home,' said Gulamendis. With a look of profound relief, he said, 'Let's go home.'

He stepped through and Laromendis followed.

They walked out upon another world and for a moment were startled by the change in air pressure; they had come from high mountains straight down to sea level and their sensitive elven ears protested. The smells were different, too, changing instantly from the acrid stench of the volcanic blasted lands to the salty air of this green island.

And there was also the matter of a dozen determined looking magicians forming a half-circle before them, with Pug at the middle.

Gulamendis held up his hands, palms out. 'It's us, Pug.'

Pug motioned for the magicians to step back. Turning to the two elven brothers, he said, 'How did you do that?'

'We found a portal, ah, rift device on another world and knew if we turned up in E'bar, we'd be—'

'Explain that later,' said Pug. 'I want to know how you got the rift to open?'

Gulamendis looked at his brother, indicating he should answer.

'I just told it to bring us here.'

'And it did?' said Pug in amazement.

'Yes, is that so odd?'

'Very,' said Pug, looking concerned. 'I have placed wards on this island since the last attack, which is why I knew you were coming. We were alerted only a second or two before the rift punched through our defences. We located the source and were here as you emerged.'

'Defences?' asked Laromendis.

'You should not have been able to get through my barriers without magic of incalculable power.'

The two elves glanced at one another and Laromendis said, 'I know the portal, I mean rift gate, was better than what our builders have created, but I didn't think it was that much better.'

Pug put out his hand as if reaching for the rift through which they had stepped and then, looking concerned, let his arm fall. 'Nothing. It closed a moment after you stepped through. Where did you come from?'

Gulamendis gave a brief description of their travels and said, 'If we can deal with the demons and get safely back to Hub, I can get you to Can-ducar on the world of Telesan, and from there I can find that portal again.'

'That will have to wait, but I will take you up on that offer. That design explains why a lot of things have happened over the years that shouldn't have, especially attacks on this island that overcome my defences.'

'Could we go somewhere and sit down?' asked Gulamendis. 'We are both rather tired.'

'Yes,' said Pug with a forced smile. 'Forgive me.' He motioned to the other magicians, 'We'll meet you back at the keep.' He put his hands on the shoulders of the two elves and suddenly they were in Pug's private study in the tower.

Laromendis said, 'This is a prodigious conjuration, Pug. I'm impressed.'

Pug smiled. 'You are good at your craft. I have two rooms occupying two different locations and anyone who steps through the door without knowing how to control entrances comes here. My office, and I do work here, is in a different location.'

Laromendis glanced out the window. 'The view?'

'Another illusion, reflecting what you would see if you were looking out of the tower.'

'Again, impressive.' He glanced around. 'The other room, the one you enter if you do know what you're doing?'

'That is for another time. Please, sit.'

The two exhausted elves did so, and Pug said, 'I can see from your appearance that you've been through a lot recently. I expect you'd prefer a hot bath, meal, and bed before any long interrogation, so I'll keep this brief and we can delve into all we need to know from one another tomorrow.'

'That would be welcome, Pug,' said Gulamendis. 'But I feel compelled to report two things; first, I think we've found something never encountered before. On the abandoned world of Telesan we discovered an ancient human fortress, but the demons have occupied the fortress and are keeping prisoners.'

Pug remained motionless, then nodded once and said, 'I see.'

'I don't know if you do,' said the Demon Master. 'Demons don't take prisoners. They eat everything they can and move on. It's as if they've somehow changed from what I've always known them to be.'

'Isn't that a conclusion you and Amirantha reached after your pet demons betrayed you to Dahun and Belasco?'

Gulamendis said, 'That was . . . yes, we did, but that was us being confounded at how their behaviour changed. This is evidence that their nature has changed. They're becoming more like us.'

Pug again nodded. His dark eyes studied both elves for a moment, then he said, 'You said there were two things?'

'They seem to be at war with themselves.' He described the attack by one army of demons upon another, the illusion of Maarg, and surprising organization of the operation.

When Gulamendis was finished, it was his brother who said, 'Right before we abandoned Andcardia, we began to notice some demons in the field did not simply throw themselves at our defences, but seemed to be instructing other demons, organizing them in a rough fashion, sending them in waves against specific areas of defenders. I didn't think too much of it at the time, because it wasn't my job to think about it, and I was preoccupied with running for my life . . .

'However, what we saw on Telesan was far beyond that. There were demons organized into units, camped as humans or elves would camp, with officers, pickets, and even what I took to be a command tent; the attacker came down the hill in multiple columns, coordinated by some unseen overseer, since the demons we thought to be in command were simply illusions.' He sat back, obviously bordering on exhaustion.

Pug was silent for a long time, then said, 'We have much to discuss. But it can wait until you're recovered from your ordeal.'

Gulamendis handed the journal he was carrying to Pug and said, 'You might find this interesting. I know I did, and I don't understand half the things he wrote.'

'Who?'

'The author, Makras, I think?' He sighed. 'I don't really know. He had a little tower, in which there were many books and scrolls, and he kept copious notes and journals. This was the one I found conveniently on the work desk, else I might not have noticed the information that got us to the portal we used to come here.'

'Very fortuitous,' Pug observed. 'Please, if you don't mind, find your own way downstairs to the common room and feed yourselves. Brandos's wife, Samantha, has taken charge of the kitchen. She should have food for you. Then Jason will find you a place to sleep. I'll have water heated for a bath.' He stood, then said, 'Though where we'll find clothing to fit you . . .?'

'We'll get by,' said Laromendis. 'We can wear these a while longer if we must.'

'Perhaps some fresh robes while your clothing is washed?' suggested Pug. 'In any event, please eat and rest, and tomorrow we have much more to discuss.'

The two elves left his study and Pug looked at the book handed to him by the Demon Master. He didn't even need to open it to know who authored this work. He recognized the symbol on the binding. But to satisfy himself, he opened it and saw the glyph on the first page. 'Macros,' he said softly.

Pug let out a long sigh. Had Macros lived on that world and

advised some alien ruler, or was this another false lead left for him by the Trickster God?

'Kalkin!' Pug shouted. 'Is this your handiwork?'

Silence was his only reply.

CHAPTER THIRTEEN

Ancient Histories

*P*UG HELD UP HIS HANDS.

The others in the room fell silent as he said, 'We have three issues before us. What the elven brothers have brought us is important and worth further investigation,' he nodded at the considerably cleaner pair of taredhel magic users. 'It also supports our recent observations of changes in the Demon Legion's behaviour.

'The book that Amirantha found,' he continued, pointing to a massive volume lying on the table before him, 'is still being examined, and may give us a far more fundamental understanding of our enemy's nature and purpose.'

He paused, then said, 'But what is most imperative, what demands our first consideration is the information that has come to us from Lord James and Sandreena.' He nodded towards Jim Dasher, who had chosen to stand in a far corner, and then towards the Knight-Sergeant, who sat on the other side of Magnus at the table, just to his father's right.

'This construction in Kesh, in the Valley of Lost Men, is something I plan to investigate personally. It's nature and purpose must be determined within a few days.

'Kendra, the dwarf who came here with Sandreena, was only able to help us understand some of what is taking place down there. He was a hunter, herdsman and warrior, and was made a sentry and given a patrol. The smiths, engineers, miners, among his people were taken away to aid the invaders in building the device.'

From deep in the shadowed corner a voice said, 'It's a trap.'

Those at the table turned to see Lord James step into the light as he said, 'It was far too easy for us to find that trail of slaughter. The more I think on that, the more I believe that they did not care that they were seen, or that they wanted to be seen.'

Sandreena studied the way he moved. He could well have been the Kingdom agent dressed as a Jal-Pur desertman, who had handed her the message for Creegan. There was something about him that put her on edge, but she couldn't quite decide what it was. It was unlikely that she'd seen him before, she had so little contact with the nobility, that had she met him she would certainly remember where and when.

Pug said, 'From what Sandreena reported, it's guarded.'

Sandreena's attention was pulled back to the situation before them and she said, 'Lord James may be right. I had little trouble getting close and it was only fatigue and carelessness that allowed Kendra to discover me. Had I not removed the magic token that kept him under control, I would have killed him; he's sturdy enough and a skilled fighter, but they're not feeding their prisoners well or resting them, and so he was weak.

'They are undertaking something on a tremendous scale, Pug, for a lure to a trap.' She reiterated what she had seen for those who weren't aware of what she had reported to Pug earlier in the week.

It was Gulamendis who spoke next. 'I don't know if it's a trap, but it's certainly something neither Amirantha nor myself can reconcile with what we know of demon behaviour. It's far too patient. This device Sandreena describes has been under construction for at least a year, probably two, given the amount of stone in those walls and the number of workers involved.

'Our own geomancers could do it in a fifth of the time; Sandreena, did you see any sign of magicians constructing anything?'

'No,' she replied. 'Three of the four arching towers are finished, and the forth was half-built. They were hauling stones up with a gigantic hoist on top of a series of huge wooden platforms. The workers looked as if they were ready to drop from exhaustion.'

Pug said, 'Jim, I appreciate your impulse towards caution, and I promise that my own experience with demons tends to put my instincts in harmony with your own, but this occurrence is clearly demon controlled, and so we must go down there and put an end to it.'

'May I suggest one more reconnaissance before you launch an assault? I can provide sufficient distraction for the Keshian court to not pay attention to an army of ten thousand mercenaries, but it would benefit our cause if we didn't get them all obliterated and have to inform Kesh that an infernal invasion is underway on their sovereign territory and, that the Demon Legion is heading straight for them.'

'Then we'll make sure that doesn't happen,' said Pug. 'I will go with Magnus to look over this site.' He looked at Amirantha and Gulamendis. 'I would really find it useful if you two would accompany us.'

'Of course,' said Amirantha, and after considering the request, Gulamendis nodded as well.

Laromendis said, 'We need to send word to the Regent Lord, as well.' He did not look happy at that prospect, and Pug thought it best to ask him about this later, in private.

Pug said, 'Given the time, we shall leave after the evening's supper. Sandreena,' he said, turning to the Sergeant-Adamant, 'would you care to accompany us?'

Amirantha barely managed to hide his surprise at the request, but said nothing.

'Certainly. If there's any way I can find out what happened to Knight-Adamant Jaliel, I will take it.'

'Our first responsibility will be to further evaluate the situation.' To the others in the room he said, 'Continue your duties, but stay alert.' He motioned for a young magician to come to him, and when he was close, Pug said, 'Send word to Lord Kaspar and ask him to join us, too. Tell him we'll have him back inside his palace before anyone notices he's gone. Thank you.' The magician nodded that he understood and departed.

'Let us adjourn; we shall send word when we have completed our reconnaissance.'

The meeting broke up and Sandreena rose quickly from the table, wanting to put some distance between her and Amirantha;

she found being with him in the name of duty acceptable, if barely, but would avoid his company if she had the option.

Besides, she was intrigued by the Kingdom nobleman who lurked in the corner of the room, and decided it was as valid an excuse to get away from the Warlock as any she could contrive. She would be forced to confer with Amirantha on matters of demon lore and, more importantly how to eradicate them.

She caught up with Jim at the door and said, 'Excuse me, sir, but have we met before?'

With a slight smile, he nodded. 'On the docks in Durbin. I was the agent who gave you the package.'

'Ah, yes,' she said. 'Still, I have some other meeting in mind. In Durbin I could not see your face, just your eyes . . .' She squinted slightly. 'There was something about your eyes.'

'Well, then, a formal introduction: I'm James, Court Baron in Krondor, aid to the Prince, servant of His Majesty the King, and,' he lowered his voice, 'member of the Conclave of Shadows.'

She glanced around. 'Apparently I am as well.'

'I heard about Creegan hurrying off to become Grand Master of your order.' He motioned for her to walk with him. The meeting room was in the basement of the castle opposite the pantry and kitchen, and he led her up the stairs to the central keep's great hall. Here tables had been set up and a large fire was burning against the need to feed the thirty key members of the Conclave. 'Walk with me outside,' asked Jim.

Sandreena said, 'I could use some fresh air.'

They stepped outside the central keep and found the marshalling yard relatively empty. Whatever activity the Conclave was undertaking, it was doing a masterful job disguising it, to guard against the possibility they were under scrutiny.

'You and Amirantha?' He looked her in the eye. 'Is something going on between you?'

'It's personal.'

Jim took a slow, deep breath and looked away. He said, 'I was going to have this talk with you tomorrow; I've already discussed it with Creegan and Pug. But now is as good a time as any.'

She caught a glimpse of his profile as he stared into the sky, and for reasons she couldn't name she felt herself tense and her hand moved towards her mace. Suddenly his hand seized her wrist, his thumb digging into a nerve, paralysing her arm for a moment. She instinctively twisted away, breaking his hold, but the damage was done. She could not get a decent grip on her mace with her right hand.

She switched it to her left. 'What did you do that for?' she demanded as she got into a defensive position.

'Your training,' he said backing away. 'I didn't want to take the chance that you'd leave my brains all over the sand before I had the opportunity to explain a few things to you.'

'Such as?' she asked.

'Let's start with the first problem between us, though it is the least important. You've been trying to remember where we have met before, correct?'

'Yes,' she said, still on guard. The numbness in her right hand was wearing off and she tossed her mace deftly from left to right.

'I sold you to the Keshians.'

Her eyes widened. 'You're Quick Jimmy!'

'Jimmy Hand, Jim Dasher, yes.'

He could tell that she was using all of her self-control not to lash out at him right then. Slowly she put her mace back on her belt. 'I will kill you later, if I must,' she said softly, almost a hiss of warning. 'Why? Don't tell me this was some part of a great plan you and Creegan had for me. I was a whore.'

'Creegan had nothing to do with it. He didn't even know you existed,' countered Jim, crossing his arms over his chest. 'And it had nothing to do with the Conclave at that time, at least not directly. I wanted you in bed with that merchant, and we planned to contact you after a month or so, and offer you your freedom if you worked for us for a while.'

'Freedom . . .?' She paused to consider his words. 'You wanted me to spy on him!'

'Yes. He was well connected to members of the Keshian Intelligence Corp, but he also had dealings with Kesh's criminal empires. The man was a smuggler as well as a trader.' Unfolding his arms, Jim put his right hand on his chest and said, 'I am also the Upright Man of Krondor, and I needed my competition from Kesh neutralized.

'As fortune would have it, even though you didn't reach Kesh and instead joined the Order of the Shield of the Weak, I found other means to achieve my end.' He looked at her with a narrowing gaze. Her expression was one of open shock. 'You know what this means?'

'The Upright Man . . .' She weighed the mace in her hand. 'It means I don't leave this island alive if I don't agree to something.'

He grinned. 'Creegan said the Goddess had better plans for you, and I will not dispute them. You are far too intelligent to wither away in some Keshian lord's bed, or simply retire on the gold we would have given you.

'No, you are destined for greater things, Sandreena.' He took a folded parchment out of his belt and handed it to her.

She took it and saw the seal of her order pressed into heavy wax. She cracked it and unfolded the message. She read it a second time before she softly said, 'He can't be serious?'

Jim was forced to laugh at her response. 'He predicted your exact words. He knows you well, Sandreena. Or should I say, Mother-Bishop Sandreena.'

'Me, in charge of the Order in the West?'

'You already are. As you no doubt realize, the Conclave have not recruited many agents within the various temples. In several of the temples, we have none: Sung, Astalon, and Lims-Kragma being the most difficult. It's their absolutist mind-set, I think. I am as practical a man as you'll meet, and even I feel divided in my loyalties at times, between the Kingdom and the Conclave.'

'Then why compromise?' she asked.

'Because while I love my homeland, Pug is trying to save the world; it will be hard to argue for the Kingdom's interest if the entire planet is conquered by demons.'

She took a deep breath and said, 'What if I don't want to be Mother-Bishop?'

'Well, you were wrong about not leaving here alive. Instead you'll wake up on a beach somewhere near Land's End with a vivid memory of your boat overturning in rough water and you not reaching Sorcerer's Isle. You'll decide that rather than trying again, you should return to Krondor and seek out help there.

'After that, you'll continue as Sergeant-Adamant of the Order while waiting for Creegan to send a new Bishop to run things in the west, and so . . .' He shrugged. 'Creegan will find another.'

'Another?'

'You're not the only talented youngster in the Order, Sandreena. You just happen to be in the right place at the right time, and, well, you're very talented. Amirantha practically sings your praises on the matter of dispatching demons.' Jim narrowed his gaze as if appraising her. 'You have always been one of the most striking women I've ever seen; there was a reason you commanded the highest price in the brothel. You've kept the core of that beauty despite the hard training, and pounds of muscle you've put on, but I'll tell you this much: he sees more in you than most men do.'

Her expression turned dark. 'He has a pitiful way of showing me.'

'Ah,' said Jim with a single slow nod. 'Now I understand; he sees more than he admits to himself. Very well, that's between you and Amirantha. Now, are you taking the commission or not?'

She looked one more time at the folded message then said, 'Of course I am. If I don't, I'll never get to look for Jaliel.'

Without another word, she turned and walked back to the keep. Jim stood outside, enjoying the cool breeze off the ocean and the relative calm. He knew there wouldn't be peace after today.

Taking a deep breath, he shook his head over how things had turned out, and he chuckled at how well Creegan understood his protégé, then he slowly returned to the keep, trying to savour the fresh air before plunging back into the intrigues and murderous needs of the Conclave.

Pug asked, 'Why can't you go?'

Laromendis said, 'My brother and I are not well regarded by our people.' He sat back in one of the two chairs before Pug's desk. The other should have been occupied by his brother, but

Gulamendis was somewhere with Amirantha pouring over a volume on demon lore. 'To understand, you'd have to have some knowledge of our history.'

'I know a little,' said Pug, 'from Tomas.'

Laromendis nodded. 'Yes, his memories from the Valheru, Dragon Lords . . .' The elf's forehead furrowed in an expression of worry. 'There are many things that I still fail to understand, and that particular miracle is one of them, but what he remembers is only what one being saw. It is not the only perspective.'

Pug indicated that the elf should continue.

'I will spare you the long story of our struggles and just say that at the height of our power, the taredhel had become greater than any elf living on Midkemia could imagine. We were rulers of worlds, Pug.

'But with such a change in our nature came a price, arrogance. Few of my race would admit to it, but having spent some time on this world, scouting and encountering—' He took a steadying breath. 'Before I returned to Andcardia with word that I had found Midkemia, I killed a cleric of your race. I captured him, and after I had obtained all the useful information I could, simply disposed of him to ensure no one would know I had been there. Travellers who have ventured too close to E'bar have also been murdered. I know the Regent Lord has ordered raids against farms and villages in the Free Cities, and allowed the blame to fall on our cousins, the moredhel.'

Pug said, 'This is disturbing news. Why are you telling me this if you know this will indispose me towards helping your people?'

'Because within the taredhel there are those who do not agree with this course of action. Before I was born all mystical matters

– those that your priests, magicians, healers, are concerned with here – were independent of civil authority.

'Your friend Tomas is wed to the woman who we view as the unbroken connection to our roots as elves primarily responsible for the cultivation and care of the holy groves, what we call The Stars. But real power for our people has resided with the Regent's Meet and the Circle of Light.

'When our people first encountered the demons, the Regent's Meet made a law that all of the members of the Circle of Light must subject themselves to the rule of the Regent's Meeting or suffer the consequences, which were imprisonment or death, the later being the more usual consequence.'

'For what reason?'

'Power. Pure, naked power. The Regent has traditionally been forbidden to take the title of King, because there always was a faint hope among the taredhel that we would someday return here and reclaim the world.' Laromendis sighed and shook his head slowly, as if in regret. 'We never expected a world like this. We thought we'd find one in ruins, or perhaps in a primeval state, or even one occupied only by other elves, where we would easily assume our rightful place as their rulers.

'We even imagined a world where the Valheru were still in residence, and we were prepared to fight them for our freedom. We have evolved. You've seen the other elves of this world, Pug, and you know that we are larger, stronger, faster, and more ruthless. Our magic eclipses that of the Spellweavers of Elvandar.

'In short, the Regent doesn't want allies; he wants subjects. And he is least likely to hear my voice on the subject.'

'You were a member of the Circle?'

'Barely. My brother and I are young compared to the others

of the Circle. I was a member for less than ten years, Gulamendis not at all; Demon Masters are not well regarded, even among the most accepting of our people.'

'Amirantha suffered the same regard,' said Pug. 'Or should I say lack of regard.'

Laromendis said, 'He is the first human my brother has developed some affection towards; it's quite remarkable. As I said, we are an arrogant people.' He sighed, then said, 'I do not particularly care for your race, Pug, but I do not hold you in disdain. If I were to admit my shortcoming here, it is that I don't feel much kinship with anyone besides my brother. Perhaps that is due to our upbringing, but I feel much the same way towards the other elven races on Midkemia.

'But to return to our original subject, I believe anyone you choose to speak to the Regent will have difficulty.' He narrowed his gaze. 'The only person I can name who might persuade him to mitigate his position regarding alliances is Lord Tomas.'

'Why?' asked Pug, now intrigued.

'The Regent honours the Queen, but he doesn't respect her. The eledhel are seen as rustics, simple, lacking the sophistication of the Eldar. The other Eldar, the ones who did not become the taredhel, are viewed with even greater distrust.' He made a small motion of dismissal with his head, Pug knew he meant the moredhel, glamredhel, and others were not even worth discussing. 'But the Regent cannot completely rid himself of our heritage. He fears Lord Tomas. As much as he would like to displace him and the Queen and proclaim himself King of all Edhel, he doesn't dare think about the consequence of trying. You don't need to see Tomas on the back of a dragon, to know that he is Valheru when he stands in his armour.' Laromendis nodded slowly. 'Yes, have Lord Tomas speak with the Regent Lord, and perhaps then some good may come of it.'

Pug was silent, then said, 'Thank you, Laromendis. Both for the suggestion and your frankness. The truth is the few of your people I've met, besides yourself and your brother, strike me as being just as you have described.'

'I have another name for you,' said Laromendis standing, as he knew this discussion was coming to a close. 'Tandarae, the newly appointed Loremaster. He understands there are powerful beings on this world and that having them as friends is a better choice than trying to conquer them. Were there a million of us, the war would already have begun, I fear, but we have perhaps ten thousand or so who now cling to the legacy of the stars. It's both a sad time and a time for opportunity, Pug. Tandarae; keep his name in mind if you ever have cause to speak with anyone in the Regent's Meet, it would have to be with discretion, but he's the one.'

Pug nodded. 'I will remember. Thank you.'

Laromendis left, and Pug sighed. He had much to do, but it seemed that a quick visit to Elvandar was now at the top of his list.

Amirantha was astonished by elf's insight and observational skills. Gulamendis had quickly digested all that Amirantha had come to understand from the tome they had removed from Queg, and had drawn conclusions from the material that had left him doubting his own intelligence; they were obvious once they were pointed out. The elf was slightly arrogant at times, but was for the most part respectful of the work Amirantha had done and had complemented him on a particular insight on more than one occasion. Amirantha could ~~have~~ become increasingly annoyed with the elf's attitude or accept it for what it was; he chose the latter, because he was forced to admit that his own behaviour mirrored that of the Demon Master more closely than anyone else he had ever met.

He left Gulamendis alone, taking a break from the work, as the Warlock had given everything he had to give, and was tired of reading, discussing, and wondering. He simply needed a few moments outside, in the fresh air, away from worry and concern.

That sense of freedom vanished a moment later when Sandreena's voice cut through the air: 'Amirantha! I need a word.'

As he turned to watch her approach, two things struck him simultaneously: the first was that she still took his breath away, despite her martial apparel. He knew all too well how she looked without the armour, tunic and trousers. The second was that he knew she would want more than one word. He recognized that expression.

Deciding it was time to say little and listen, he said, 'Of course, Sandreena. What is it?'

She paused, gauging his expression and manner, deciding what to say next, then she blurted, 'I've been made Mother-Bishop of the Order in the west.'

He inclined his head slightly, smiled and said, 'Congratulations. Deserved without a doubt and I know you will excel in your new post.'

She blinked, revealing that whatever she had expected him to say, that wasn't it. Then suddenly she reached across and back-handed him across the face, knocking him to the ground.

Amirantha sat stunned for a moment, then reached up and

put his hand to his now throbbing right cheek. Finally he said, 'I wish you'd stop hitting me.'

Her eyes shining with emotion, she hissed, 'Just be glad you're needed; otherwise I'd have no compunction about killing you!' With that she turned and hurried off, back to the keep.

Walking back to the keep she passed Brandos, who took one look at Sandreena's determined stride and then another at Amirantha sitting on the ground and broke into a broad grin. Coming to stand over his old friend, he reached down and helped him to his feet. 'You'd better do something to help that girl get over you, or she's going to kill you.'

'Any suggestions?' asked Amirantha, wiggling his jaw and hearing it pop in and out.

'Kill her first or marry her, are the only two that come to mind.'

'Marry? She'd rather marry a demon. Not to mention she's just been promoted to Mother-Bishop.'

'No wonder she's so cranky,' observed Brandos. 'Well, I guess marriage is out of the question. Unless you think you'd like temple life?'

Amirantha gave him a look that would wither fresh flowers. 'You wanted something?'

'Yes. Pug sent me to fetch you. Gulamendis seems to have found something in that book you stole . . . retrieved from Queg.'

Amirantha put aside his annoyance, and confusion over Sandreena and followed his friend. Brandos led him to the entrance to the tower, and said, 'Let me know if it's anything interesting.'

'Things have hardly been boring around here lately,' said Amirantha moving quickly up the stairs.

Reaching Pug's private study, he knocked once and heard Pug say, 'Come in.'

Amirantha entered and found the magician sitting at his desk with Gulamendis seated in a chair opposite him. Amirantha said, 'You sent for me?'

'Yes,' said Pug. 'Gulamendis has interpreted a few of the passages that seemed to have caused you some problems, and we have, if he's correct, a very different situation than we anticipated.'

'Really?' said the Warlock, sitting in the empty chair next to the elf.

'Yes,' said Pug. 'I'll let him explain how he arrived at these conclusions, but in short, it seems that things in the demon realm are not how we imagined them to be.'

'I thought we understood that Belasco subverted our demons when Villa Beata was sacked.'

Pug visibly tensed at mention of the destruction of his home, where his wife died.

'Sorry,' Amirantha said softly. 'No disrespect intended. What has changed?'

It was Gulamendis who spoke. 'I want to go over this with you in detail, Amirantha, but unless I have been misled, my brother and I witnessed part of a very nasty civil war in the demon realm.'

'Civil war?'

'We know Maarg is dead, but someone is keeping alive the notion that he's still around, still in command. But he's not. Pug saw his corpse on the world of Shila, and the demon king we saw on Telesan was an illusion. Even if his essence returned to the demon realm, it will be some time before he could rise to power again, if ever.

'That leaves us with two questions: who's pretending to be Maarg, and why?'

'Three,' said Amirantha. 'Who are they fighting?'

'Four,' amended Pug. 'What has any of this to do with Midkemia?'

The three sat back, thoughtful as they realized that for every question they had answered since the Demon Legion started threatening Midkemia, they now had two new ones.

CHAPTER FOURTEEN

Slaughter

PUG SIGNALLED.
Magnus followed Gulamendis's instructions and suddenly they found themselves standing in a vast chamber. The Oracle of Aal rose above them, her magnificent dragon form made all the more impressive by the multifaceted jewels adorning her body, the result of a magical fusion that took place during a battle with a Dreadlord over a century before.

'You come uninvited, Pug,' said the Oracle, though her tone was neutral; it was a statement, not an accusation.

'I face the unknown, Lady,' answered Pug. 'A great danger approaches, and I would know what you can tell me.'

The Oracle was silent for a while, as if weighing the question, then spoke: 'There are too many futures, most of them dire, some ending life as we know it. Too many nexuses of possibility.'

'Is there anything you can tell me to enhance the possibility of avoiding the most dire of consequences?'

'Two waves: the one you see and the one behind it. You remember, from your youth.'

Pug was startled. No one knew of that moment; he was almost certain he had never spoken of it. It had happened on the day he had first spoken with his old teacher, Kulgan. He had been knocked over by a wave on the beach and as he was attempting to rise, a second one had swept him under. 'I remember,' he said. 'It was a lesson I've remembered all my life.'

'You must seek out the hidden wave. The wave before you is designed to distract, to bleed your resources and scatter your focus.'

'Can you tell me any more?'

'Shadows hide deeper shadows. There is a void from which no light emerges, and into which none may see. Those who seek to destroy all you love lurk within.' The massive figure then said, 'Seek more knowledge before you act, for once begun, this conflict can only end in complete victory or utter defeat.'

Magnus said, 'It's not the first time we've been faced with that option.'

The Oracle said, 'Wave after wave, young magician, that you must realize. This struggle started before you were born, before your father was born, before even I was born. It is not yet apparent, but all is connected. Be cautious, be wise, seek more intelligence is my counsel.'

The dragon's massive head slowly lowered to the floor and the men and women who had been standing in the shadows – the Oracle's companions – moved forward to meet any need she might have.

Pug nodded to his son and suddenly they were back in his study.

Magnus asked, 'Father, did that help?'

'Somewhat,' answered Pug. 'Before we run down to Kesh to look at Sandreena's big hole in the ground, I think we need to retrace the elven brothers's route, and find that lost castle.'

'What do we seek there?'

'Knowledge, as always. There are dwarven, human and elven prisoners there, so we should free them. And there's also a room full of books I wish to bring here.'

'Books?' said Magnus. 'What sort of books?'

'We won't know until we fetch them.'

'Why are they important.'

With a wry grin, Pug said, 'Because it appears that the fortress was another small den of your grandfather's.'

Magnus visibly sagged. 'Macros.'

Pug reached over and pulled a book off the shelf, handing it to his son. 'Look at the mark on the first page.'

Magnus opened the volume. 'It's grandfather's glyph.' For a painful moment, Pug looked lost and he said, 'I just wish I knew what your mother would say right now.'

'Something scathing, no doubt,' said Magnus and he laughed.

Suddenly Pug laughed too. 'No doubt.' It was the first time either of them had been able to laugh since Miranda's death and they looked at one another. They needed to put the past behind, for the coming struggle was fast approaching, and they needed to be at their best. Pug pushed aside a rising fear: when will I lose my son? He had never resigned himself to the bitter price that gods were exacting for his return, but that didn't mean it would happen now, or even soon.

'I think we need to find Gulamendis and start back to that world with the volcanoes.'

'Who else?'

'Amirantha and Sandreena; we need all the demon knowledge we can bring to this, and Brandos, because we could use a good sword and he's faced his share of the creatures.'

Magnus said, 'When do we leave?'

'As soon as you gather them all here. No time like the present.'

Magnus nodded and hurried out of the tower. Pug sat in his chair, lost in his thoughts. Fear over his last child's fate threatened to rise, but instead of succumbing to it, he forced his mind to dissect the Oracle's riddle: the hidden wave; an enemy hiding in a lightless void. He could feel his mind almost comprehend something, but as always with the Oracle the mix of simple fact and metaphor often confused things. He focused on her predictions as he waited for the others.

It took some time, but they eventually discovered the source of the brothers' last rift. Pug had spent the better part of an hour searching the clearing on Sorcerer's Isle in which they had appeared, using his powers to seek out any lingering effects of the magic. It was a faint trail, but with calculations and patience he finally decided he could reach the point of origin.

'Everyone, stand back,' he instructed. 'Magnus be ready to get us out of here if needed.' Rifts could be very unstable and destructive, and while no living man knew more about their nature than Pug, he was still cautious when constructing one to a new location.

Pug closed his eyes for a moment, then with a quick incantation he formed the rift.

He was pulled forward a step, as if seized by a massive invisible hand, then fell back, as if that same hand pushed him away. Brandos steadied him, keeping the sorcerer from falling on his backside.

'That was unexpected,' said Pug.

'What was, father?'

He looked at Magnus and said, 'That rift was formed with a great deal more energy than I intended. It was as if someone was helping me construct it.' He turned to the others and said, 'Best be ready for anything when we step through.'

Pug led the way. When the others came through they found him examining the gate used by the elven brothers. Brandos and Sandreena coughed as the air was thick with smoke and its acid stung their eyes and noses. 'There must have been a recent eruption,' observed Gulamendis. 'It wasn't this bad when we left.'

Magnus came to stand beside his father and instantly understood what held his father's attention. 'I've never seen its like.'

'Neither have I. Look at this.' He pointed to the impressions where fingers were to be placed.

Magnus put his fingers there, closed his eyes, then they opened wide as if he had been surprised. 'Those controls . . .'

'Masterful,' said Pug. 'If this is one of your grandfather's designs, it surpasses anything I've been able to construct. If it's someone else . . .'

'Who?' said Magnus quietly.

Amirantha said, 'The wind is rising!'

Pug looked around. It was impossible to tell exactly what time of day it was, as ash and smoke formed a canopy in the sky. The air was thick with stench from the distant volcanoes, and ash covered everything in sight. 'Yes,' he said, 'I think you're right; there's been an eruption recently.'

'None of this ash was here when we left,' Gulamendis said. Glancing around, he said, 'At least the darkness will help mask our approach.'

The ground rumbled as if to accent his observation and a hot tower of flame appeared above one of the distant cones. 'I wonder how long this has been going on,' said Amirantha.

'Ages, no doubt,' said Pug. 'These volcanic regions can go through very calm periods then suddenly become active again.' He pointed to the sloping ground. 'The lava flow fans out at the bottom of the cone and forms these relatively flat surfaces.' He then pointed to the distant eruption, 'But a big explosion can lift this and drop it . . .' He shrugged. 'I want to take that gate back with us, if we can.' He turned to Gulamendis. 'But first, which way to the fortress?'

Pointing north, he said, 'That way. About half a day's walk.'

'We'll get there a little faster than that.' He motioned for them to stand close. Sandreena and Brandos stood beside Magnus, while Amirantha and Gulamendis stood beside Pug. They all joined hands and suddenly they stood on a ridge a mile north of their previous position. 'Don't let go,' Pug said, and another jump took them to a plateau. They could see the fortress rising in the distance. 'What's the best way in?' asked Pug.

'We came out of the main gate,' said Gulamendis. 'It has a small door to let people in and out without opening the big gates fully. There was no one in the yard; we just opened it, walked through, and closed it behind us. It may still be unlatched.'

Pug nodded and said, 'I think over there,' and at once they appeared on a slope opposite the main gate. If anyone was on the wall or in the tower, the chances of being seen were high, although Pug was confident he and Magnus could deal with anything likely to emerge from the half-abandoned fortress.

No alarm was raised, nor was there any movement on the walls as they crossed the open area before the gate. Pug stopped for a moment and knelt. He poked at what appeared to be a fibrous plant, knocked down by falling rock and ash. 'This plant was nearly four feet tall.' He stood. 'No one has cleared this area for a while. You always deprive an attacking foe even the most modest cover.'

Gulamendis said, 'I suspect this place was abandoned years ago and only reoccupied by the demons recently. Parts of the keep we passed through had layers of dust on the floor.'

'Any tracks?' asked Magnus.

'We just didn't worry about them,' said Gulamendis. 'We judged that if no one has used the rooms for years, they were unlikely to start using them immediately, and that if anyone did explore them . . .' He shrugged. 'We planned on being far from here by then.'

Pug said, 'Logical.'

They walked to the door within the massive gates and Pug pushed it open. 'Apparently they had no idea you visited.'

They slipped through the gate, staying within the deep shadows along the walls. Moving quickly, Gulamendis led them into the corner then over to the side of the shed. He glanced around. There was no hint of life.

He led them to the stairway leading down to the door into the basement and found the door refused to open. He pushed, but despite his strength, it simply wouldn't budge. Magnus whispered, 'Let me.'

The younger magician moved to stand before the door and held up his hand. With a short motion and a single word, the door moved in balky fits and starts until it was open enough for them to see what had blocked it.

'Bodies,' whispered Magnus.

The stench of decomposing flesh rose and even Brandos swallowed hard.

Sandreena said, 'What happened here?'

'We won't know until we get inside,' said Pug. He spoke in a normal volume, without displaying any concern about being overheard. 'I think the demons have quit this place and decided not to take the prisoners with them.'

Magnus waved his hand again and the door flew off its hinges and into the room. The large chamber that led to the dungeon was littered with corpses: human, elves, and dwarves all piled on top of one another. It was clear a good number of them had been trying to reach this door, and were cut down from behind. The wounds were mixed: some smooth cuts, from sword or knife blade, others torn and ragged as if made by fang or claw.

Once they had cleared a way through the pile of bodies, Pug knelt and inspected them more closely. 'I recognize some of the clothing,' he said softly. 'I think this dwarf here is from Dorgin, perhaps a companion of Kendra's. That pattern in the weave of the tunic is common there. But these elves . . .'

Gulamendis said, 'They are unknown to me, but until we found Home . . . Midkemia, we knew only the taredhel.'

'I don't think they're from Midkemia,' said Pug. He felt the torn shirt of a dead elf and said, 'I do not recognize this material. It's not silk or linen, but it's so light.' He stood and said, 'Too many mysteries. Too many distractions. Where is the tower?' he asked.

'That way,' pointed Gulamendis.

Sandreena and Brandos had seen their fair share of battlefields, yet both appeared pale and shaken by the carnage and were glad to leave the room.

The light was faint and at the end of the hall, Magnus raised his hand to create a bright blue-white glow that illuminated their surroundings more efficiently than a lantern. They reached the bottom of the tower stairs and moved quickly to the top.

The door was still unlatched and once they moved inside, Pug said, 'I can feel it.'

'Grandfather?' asked Magnus.

'Yes, though how long ago . . .' He shrugged. Reaching up, he pulled a book off the shelf at random and glanced at it. 'I have a copy of this in my library.'

Magnus came to his side and said, 'I will gather anything that I don't recognize.' He started with the volumes on the desk and quickly tossed duplicates of those already on Sorcerer's Isle, to the floor.

Soon Pug had a small stack of books set aside. He was taking one off a low shelf when a massive upheaval in the ground below the keep threw them to the floor. Dust between ancient stones rained down on them and the stones of the tower seemed to undulate for nearly half a minute. When it subsided, Brandos looked out the window and said, 'Look!'

In the distance the biggest of the three volcanoes was shuddering, sending a shockwave rolling through the rocks and soil beneath them, causing the keep to shake. Then they felt an explosion of titanic proportion, a massive gust of brilliant hot lava plumed a funnel of white steam straight into the sky like the god's own teakettle boiling. Rock, ash, and liquefied stone spewed from the mountain at astonishing speed. Pug said, 'In about one minute a wave of poisonous air, hot enough to broil the skin from your bones, will hit us. Grab those books!' Everyone grabbed an armful of books. 'Stand close!' he instructed.

As the sound of the wind rose to an ear-splitting shriek, there was a sudden, rounder pulse of air in the room and a grey void appeared less than six inches in front of Brandos's nose. Without a word the old fighter leaped into it, and others followed, Pug pushing his son through; and suddenly they were back on Sorcerer's Isle. The transport through the hasty rift landed them hard on the ground, and Amirantha, Sandreena, and Gulamendis all lost their footing and fell. The others staggered a bit.

Pug let the books he held fall from his arms and turned. A wave of his hand dismissed the rift just as a pulse of super heated steaming air came through, and he immediately erected a shield that redirected the scalding wet air around them.

Everyone could feel the heat suddenly dissipate, but it gave them a queasy feeling at how close they had come to being boiled alive.

Pug turned and said, 'I think—' Then his legs went weak. His son let go of the books in his arm and grabbed his father. As Pug was gently lowered to the grass, he muttered, 'Damn. I so wanted to bring that gate back here.' Then he closed his eyes and fell into darkness.

Pug awoke with a massive headache. He found his son sitting at his bedside and said, 'How long?'

'All night and half the morning.'

Pug sat up and felt light-headed.

Magnus said, 'It was a prodigious feat punching a rift through from the tower to the meadow in so short a time. No wonder you passed out.'

'We didn't have a lot of choice.'

Magnus said, 'It got me thinking. Even if we know a world has a rift we've visited before, it might be a good idea to send a vision orb through first, just to be safe.'

Pug nodded. 'I think you're right. Had we stepped through as that shock wave washed over the plateau rather than a half-hour before, we'd all be dead now.'

'Caution,' said Magnus with a nod. 'What next?'

'Look through what we've found, see if there's anything there that has any bearing on what we face, then you and I and the demon experts take a journey down to Kesh.'

'I'll have food sent up.'

Getting out of bed, Pug said, 'Don't bother. I'm in need of a lot of water as well as food. I'll get some down in the kitchen. Have you been studying your grandfather's books?'

'Of course,' answered Magnus. 'There are a couple I've put aside for you, but I think he made copies from our library and took them there after he left this island, before you found him wandering around mindlessly.'

Pug paused. 'That would explain part of his absence. But what was he doing on that world, and who was he serving? And does it have anything to do with the approaching demon host? I find it difficult to believe that Macros visited a world infested with demons by coincidence, and left behind his library so that we just happened to find it when we were facing a demon army.'

'With grandfather anything was possible.' Magnus had never met his grandfather, but he had encountered a Dasati called The Gardener who had possessed the memories of Macros the Black; it had been a ploy by Kalkin, the Trickster God, but had provided Pug and his son with information that saved Midkemia from a dreadful invasion, but at great cost: the utter obliteration of the world of Kelewan. Even if the Dasati's memories had not been his own, his belief had given Magnus the opportunity to get to know his grandfather slightly.

Magnus went down to the kitchen with his father, and they found Amirantha and Brandos waiting at a table, just finishing a meal. 'Where are the others?' asked Pug.

Brandos said, 'Gulamendis is studying that demon book you found on Queg, and Sandreena is busy being somewhere else.' The last was said with a glance at Amirantha, who almost winced but managed to keep his reaction to the comment minimal.

Pug said, 'Anything interesting in the books we brought back?'

'Not really,' said Magnus. 'There are a couple of things that are probably worth a little study, but I think this was Grandfather's work from a long time ago. I remember you told me about the time you came here after the Riftwar ended and found a letter from him, giving you his library. What he took to Telesan were copies. Exact copies, so I think they were magical duplicates, not made by scribes.' Magnus sat, 'Perhaps if we had saved everything, knew all of their titles, we might get some idea of why he went there after leaving Midkemia and what he was hoping to accomplish.'

'You have a better memory than most, Magnus,' said Pug, 'and I can remember a dozen titles I tossed aside. Let's draw up a quick list and compare them with those we brought back with us, perhaps we'll get some understanding of this new jaunt of your grandfather's.'

Magnus exhaled slowly and said, 'Another reason to miss Mother.'

Pug reached out and took his son's hand; he squeezed it slightly and then released it. 'I know.' Both father and son mourned Miranda and her insight into what her father might have been doing on that other world. 'There is one thing,' said Pug. 'Macros lived on Telesan for a time, and in some station of importance; this clearly indicates a connection between our world and that one. It seems a little too coincidental that the brothers would flee from their Hub world and end up at the former residence of Macros the Black.'

'Kalkin?'

'Who knows what the gods are doing?' replied Pug. 'I have long accepted that I will never fully understand this struggle, our part in it, or just how much good we are accomplishing.'

Amirantha said, 'I'd say you're accomplishing quite a bit, even if not intentionally.'

Pug asked, 'How do you judge that?'

'Your friend, Kaspar, is doing remarkable things in Muboya. The region has never been this peaceful in my lifetime, and that's over a hundred years.

'You've got people from various nations around the world putting the safety of this planet ahead of their personal interests and national interests. I am hardly anyone's idea of an honourable man, Pug, yet here I am doing my bit for the greater good.' He smiled slightly and said, 'That's no mean achievement.'

'Perhaps,' Pug said. 'I wish I felt it was worth the price.'

No one at the table said anything. Amirantha and Brandos had both witnessed Miranda's death at the hands of a demon who had been playing dead.

Finally Brandos said, 'So, if I might presume to ask, what's next?'

Pug said, 'We head down to Kesh and inspect that thing being built in the Valley of Lost Men. From Sandreena's description, I don't have any idea what they are doing.'

Amirantha said, 'Neither do I. Gulamendis and I have talked into the night about demon lore and what we are now discovering.' He shook his head in wonder. 'I am not ashamed to admit that I have been humbled to discover how little I truly understood.'

Brandos grinned and clapped his old friend on the shoulder. 'That's a good start.' He stood and said, 'Well, if we're off again, I think I should go spend a little time with my wife. She's starting to feel neglected and that's never a good thing.'

Pug nodded, a slightly sad expression on his face.

A young magician came into the kitchen and said, 'Pug, we've just had word that Lord Kaspar will be here in an hour.'

Pug stood up and said, 'Good. That means we can leave after sundown. I wanted his military expertise.'

Amirantha said, 'Well, I think I'll leave Brandos and Samantha alone and find Gulamendis to see if he's come up with any new insights from his reading. And a little rest before we go would be nice.'

Magnus and his father were left alone at the table. Those in the kitchen tried to ignore them as much as possible. Finally, Magnus said, 'I wonder how Laromendis is doing up in Elvandar?'

Pug absently nodded. 'I wonder, too.'

*   *   *

Laromendis stood before Tomas. Despite understanding what he'd been told about the human transformed by ancient magic into the shape of a Valheru, or Dragon Lord, he still had to fight his urge to kneel, or to run in terror. He wondered if he would ever get over that feeling, no matter how many times they met.

'Laromendis,' said Tomas, motioning for the taredhel conjurer to take a seat at the small table in the Queen's chamber. 'You wished to speak to me in private?'

'Yes, My Lord—' Tomas held up his hand. 'Err, yes Tomas.' Laromendis laughed slightly. 'I will never get used to that.'

Tomas smiled, showing a youthful humour behind the warrior's powerful visage. 'It took a while for a lot of people around here to get used to it, Laro. You don't mind if I call you that? I over-heard your brother use it.'

Laromendis was startled, but the smile directed at him was infectious, even charming, and he said, 'Why, no. I'd be flattered. He's the only one who ever did, but please, feel free.'

'So, why did you wish to see me alone?'

'Not alone, for I am certain you'll need to consult the Queen. I'm here at Pug's behest.'

At the mention of his childhood friend, Tomas's expression became concerned. 'How is he?'

'Well, I suppose. He took Miranda's death very hard.' The elf said, 'I don't know how such things are with humans, but I felt his sense of profound sorrow. Lately however, as the matters that bring me here have arisen, I think he's beginning to come out of his darkness.'

'That's good to hear,' said Tomas, adjusting the white tunic he wore when not armoured. Even without his helm and gold armour, he was an impressive sight. Laromendis was one of the few beings Tomas had met who was taller than him, yet the Star Elf was still in awe of the imposing Warleader of Elvandar.

'To the point, then,' said Laromendis. 'Pug asks if you might be disposed to convey the following to the Regent Lord at E'bar: The Demon Legion may be arriving in Midkemia soon. Would he be willing to discuss a mutual defence?'

Tomas was silent for a moment, then laughed. 'Why is he asking you to ask me, why not go yourself?'

'Because I am not in a position to influence the Regent Lord and, frankly, you are the only other being he holds in . . .'

'Fear?' said Tomas with a slight smile.

'I was going to say respect, my lord.'

Tomas inclined his head slightly, as if considering his next question. 'Your Regent Lord is a complicated person. He exhibits a certain deference to my Lady and myself, yet I sense he also views us with suspicion.'

'He is proud, full of ambition for our people and personally.' Laromendis said, 'My brother and I have spent more time here than any other taredhel, so we have begun to understand, at least a little, how profoundly the eledhel are tied to this world, this Home.' He fell silent for a moment, then said, 'But even we have no doubt that our branch of this far flung family is . . .'

'Superior?' supplied Tomas with a slight narrowing of his eyes.

'I was going to say more advanced.' He glanced around the room, fashioned from the living bole of a majestic Star, as Laromendis's people called these magnificent trees. 'I feel a fundamental rightness here, Lord Tomas. Those who remained kept the line of service intact and in harmony with the most important aspects of our world.

'We who fled the Chaos Wars took only what we could carry, nothing more, and from that humble beginning, a ragged band of refugees conquered the stars.' He looked Tomas directly in the eyes for perhaps the first time and said, 'If we tend to be arrogant, we have earned the right.'

'I have lived the life of a human, Laromendis, and recall the mantle of a Valheru; I have lived here with My Lady's people for more than a century and I can only tell you this: power in and of itself is neither worthy of respect nor fear; it simply is. It is how power is employed, and towards what ends, that ennobles or denigrates the wielder of power. When I don my armour, there are few beings on this world who can rival my abilities, Pug being perhaps the only one able to best me.' He smiled, revealing a boyish quality that was very unexpected, and added, 'It's certainly a good thing he is my closest friend and ally.' His smile faded. 'But during the early days of coming to my station I did things under the sway of my own power, things that I know now to have been cruel, base, and completely unworthy.

'I tell you this to make it clear that while the eledhel may appear rustic, even primitive, to your people, they are far from it. The Spellweavers's magic is subtle, but no less powerful than those of your people who can raise mighty cities by making the rocks flow and move as they wish. Your cousins, the Eldar, who reside with us, have much the same lore as your own 'mancers, yet they did not try to reshape Elvandar, rather they have adapted to it.'

He closed one eye and smiled. 'Now, to the real reason you wish me to speak to the Regent Lord, rather than carrying Pug's message yourself.'

Laromendis was forced to laugh. 'As I said, the Regent Lord

respects you. And, somewhat less importantly, he holds my brother and I in great disregard; our crafts are not highly valued by our people . . . Lastly, he most certainly thinks Gulamendis and I are dead, lost in the battle of the Hub.'

'You've neglected to inform your people that you survived?' Tomas said.

'We're not entirely sure our abandonment was an accident of war. In fact, it may have been designed.'

Tomas said nothing.

'If I might be so bold, should you decide to undertake Pug's charge, it would be most useful if you could discreetly deliver a message to Tandarae, Lorekeeper of the Regent's Meet. He will let you know if we can return as honoured survivors of a hopeless battle, or if we would be executed for desertion in the face of the enemy.'

'That information would certainly prove useful before showing your faces in E'bar,' Tomas agreed. 'Until then, what are your plans?'

'I would like to return to my brother on Sorcerer's Isle. He's quite enthused about the opportunity to learn from other cultures. I must confess I am more dubious than he, but his enthusiasm about the things he has learned from a human warlock named Amirantha is intriguing. And while my arts don't plumb the depths of dark mysteries as his do, I am always looking to improve my craft.'

'A wise choice,' said Tomas. 'Though you are certainly welcome to stay in Elvandar, should you wish it.'

Just then the curtain moved aside and Aglaranna, Queen of Elvandar, entered. 'Greetings Laromendis.' Coming from the court she wore a simple, but regal gown of sky blue cloth, trimmed with white at the collar and cuffs. Her only jewellery was the simple gold circlet embedded with a ruby gem, which held back her mane of auburn hair.

Laromendis stood without thinking, then bent a knee before the Queen, bowing his head. 'It is a joy to see you again, My Lady.'

'Please, rise,' she bid him.

He did, but would not sit in her presence. He was as over-whelmed by the Queen as he had been the first time he had come to this court. She was as powerful a presence as her husband, but in a completely different fashion. Tomas evoked ancient fear and a need for obedience, impulses that could be battled and overcome. Aglaranna overcame the senses with her beauty and majesty. There was nothing challenging in her nature and that made her irresistible. Softly, the Conjurer said, 'If possible, My Lady, Lord Tomas, it might prove useful if the Regent Lord could be persuaded to visit Elvandar.'

'We have already extended such an invitation,' said Tomas.

'Perhaps you should be a little more insistent, Lord Tomas.' He studied the queen, her flawlessness, her wonderful reddish brown hair and finely sculpted features. She possessed a type of beauty he did not find attractive in the women of his own race; he preferred a more robust looking female, and by taredhel stan-dards the Queen was small, almost petite. Yet her beauty was something that transcended the merely physical, defied the logic of attraction; it was the same beauty he found while walking in the sacred grove; if Home had a soul, it was Elvandar, and if Elvandar could be embodied in a single being, it would be the Queen.

'If you will excuse me, My Queen, Lord Tomas, I will use this clever creation to return to Sorcerer's Isle.'

The Queen gave her consent, and the Conjurer removed the device from his belt pouch, thumbed a switch and with a faint humming, was suddenly gone.

Aglaranna looked at her husband and said, 'What word does he bring from Pug?'

'Dire warning, and a request for us to reach out to the taredhel.'

She moved out of her chair to kneel before her husband, girlishness lingering in her fluid grace. She rested her head on his knee, as a child might to a parent, and said, 'What are we to do with our newly returned cousins?'

'That is the problem, my love', said Tomas, stroking her hair. 'They have not returned, and I don't think they ever will. Like those of the ocedhel who remain across the waters, they feel no need to come here.

'We shall endeavour to respect their independence, and we will try to be friends.'

'An alliance? You don't sound hopeful.'

Tomas said nothing. He knew in his heart that the Star Elves posed the gravest threat to Elvandar since the coming of the Tsurani invaders; a threat greater than the army of the Emerald Queen, even more than the Dasati invaders.

• CHAPTER FIFTEEN •

Strategy

*P*UG SIGNALLED FOR SILENCE.

Kaspar, one time Duke of Olasko and now General of the Army and First Advisor to the Maharaja of Muboya said, 'Pug has asked me to take over conducting this next bit of business.

'As I understand it from what Sandreena saw,' he nodded to the newly minted Mother-Bishop of the Order of the Shield of the Weak, 'and what Kendra said about his captivity, we have two tasks.

'The first is to gain intelligence, which has to take precedence over any other consideration. The second will be to effect a rescue. Sandreena, explain how, if you please.'

'If any guard or worker wears a talisman around his neck marked with something like a red wolf's skull on a black background, they are under some mystic control. They are compelled to attack anyone not wearing the same device.' She looked around the room. 'When I struggled with Kendra, he regained his own volition as soon as I tore it off him. My suggestion is we find sentries, overpower them and then free them. They are not being fed or rested well it seems, so it should not be too difficult.'

Kaspar continued. 'They can help us, if they're up to it, if not, we shall direct them up the trail to the abandoned Keshian fortress and from there arrange safe transportation back to their homes.' He looked at two young magicians, Jason and Akeem and said, 'You stay at that fortress and coordinate getting the wretches safely away.'

'This is not a military adventure, and while it may sound like a raid, it is not. If we are there longer than an hour, we are dead,' said Kaspar. 'The switchback trail prevents a fast assault, so we will approach stealthily, and if we have to leave in a hurry—' He nodded to Pug.

'Each of us will carry a transportation sphere, set to bring you back here.'

From the corner of the room a voice said, 'I count eight of us going down there, Kaspar. That's either too many or two few.'

Kaspar smiled, 'Jim, I wondered where you were lurking.'

Out of the shadows stepped the head of the Kingdom's intelligence service; he wore a black cloak over dark grey tunic and trousers. 'Too many, or too few.'

'That's why we will split into two groups.' Kaspar pointed to Pug. 'Pug, along with Gulamendis, Amirantha and Brandos, will investigate the device, and try to discern it's magical purpose, assuming there is one and it's not just a monument to demonic vanity.

'I will take Sandreena to scout out the military aspects of the place, with Magnus to provide any magical aid we might need. Feel free to join either group.'

'I think I'll tag along with you, Kaspar.' He grinned. 'Keeps the groups even.'

'Wise,' said the former Duke of Olasko. 'Given that there is little time difference between here and the valley, we leave at sundown. Get something to eat, some rest, and meet out in the courtyard just before the sun sets.'

Laromendis entered the room as the group disbanded, and came to stand before Pug. 'Tomas says he will travel to E'bar and speak with the Regent Lord,' he said.

Pug studied the elf's face and said, 'And . . .?'

Surprised that the human could detect the subtleties of elven expression, Laromendis said, 'I hold little hope you'll get any cooperation from the Regent's Meet. They're handpicked to agree with him. If the demons come, he will not help; he'll just order us to dig in and look for another escape route while the rest of you fight them.'

Pug nodded. 'Will you go back?'

Laromendis paused, thinking, then said, 'They think my brother and I are dead; it might serve all our causes if they continued to think that for a while longer. I will stay here with Gulamendis if you will accept me.'

Pug nodded. 'Talk to your brother about tonight's expedition; I wouldn't mind you along to look for things the rest of us might not see.'

Laromendis said, 'Of course,' and went to where his brother still sat.

Magnus came to stand next to his father and whispered, 'What are we expecting to see down there?'

'Nothing I can imagine, and I can imagine a lot, my son. Let's get something to eat then rest a little. I have a feeling it may be a very long night.' The two magicians left the meeting room.

Amirantha sat alone on the steps leading into the keep. It was late afternoon and he had just eaten. Sunset was an hour or more away, but he didn't feel the need for rest. He instead tried to keep his mind calm as he contemplated what they were to investigate in a few hours.

After the wet cold weather and series of storms, the sunshine had been a welcome respite, a balmy hint of the spring and summer to come. Amirantha felt a deep mix of anticipation, the idea of discovery, the risks. It had been easy to throw in his lot with this bunch, the mad magicians and happy warriors who served an abstracted greater good.

Then he had watched Miranda die.

He had seen death before, had lost those for whom he cared, but his coping mechanism had always hinged on the fact that they had always been fated to die before him. He realized with bitter self-loathing that this had been a facile attitude, no reason why he shouldn't care. In Miranda he had come to know a woman of stunning abilities, magic knowledge that rivalled Pug's and dwarfed his own. Moreover, she had been long-lived, older than he by a century, despite looking no older than middle-aged. She could have expected another century or more, yet she died suddenly in a brutal and bloody fashion before those around her could help.

Nothing else in his life had made Amirantha more aware of the fragility of life than that instant. None of them, not Pug, Magnus, himself or the other magic users of considerable ability, could have reacted quickly enough to keep her alive. It was like watching someone drown as you stood helpless on the shore.

The memory left a sick feeling in the warlock's stomach that had lingered. It had been a year since the event, and he still felt as if he should have been able to do something, for he was the warlock, he was the master of demons.

A stirring caused him to turn, and he saw Sandreena standing behind him. He started to rise, and she pushed his shoulder, forcing him back down. Trying to regain his poise, he said, 'If you're going to hit me again, please don't. I'm really very tired of picking myself up off the floor.'

She smiled a sad smile and softly said, 'Sorry. You bring out the worst in me.'

He tilted his head slightly, and said, 'It's a gift.'

She surprised him by sitting down next to him. 'I've given some thought to this situation.'

He was about to ask which situation she meant, the need to scout the demon site once more, her elevation to high office, or them finding themselves together, but in a rare attack of wisdom, he said nothing. 'Really?' he said, in as neutral a tone as he could imagine.

'You find that surprising?' she asked, her tone accusing.

He tried to remain even-toned. 'I don't find it surprising that you think about things, but rather that you'd speak of them to me.'

'Really?' she echoed, her tone very confrontational.

He knew he was rapidly losing any hope of having a civil conversation. In the time they had spent together he had found her a perplexing combination of keen intellect and impulsive behaviour that bordered on reckless. Her order taught that quick evaluation was sometimes necessary in determining which side of a conflict to join, but the lesson seemed to have denuded her ability to take a moment and consider. He just nodded.

'I have been known to give consideration to weighty matters,' she said, her eyes narrowing and her tone rising. 'I only came to speak with you because despite the fact you are a horrible excuse for a man, you still know more of demon lore than anyone else I've met. Besides, Magnus told me of your discovery in Queg and I need to know what you uncovered about the creatures we face.'

Amirantha studied her face for a moment, unsure what exactly she expected of him; he decided his best course was to take her statement at face value. 'Do you want to know what we've un-covered about demons in general or what we think about the bunch we're going to go face down in Kesh?'

'I've seen the ones we're facing in Kesh personally, remember,' she retorted with her eyes narrowing in anger. 'Brandos says you and the elf have come up with all manner of new ideas about demons and that you're so giddy from it, you're barely able to contain yourself.'

Amirantha looked pained at the thought of being portrayed as 'giddy.' 'Brandos tends to colourful characterization at times. In any event, what we've found is, if accurate, a completely different perspective on what is known as the "Fifth Circle" of Hell.

'Demon summoners like Gulamendis and myself are self-taught, although occasionally we meet others with whom we can share our knowledge. In Queg I found a . . . book, for lack of a better word, but it's more than that. It's a comprehensive examination of the Fifth Circle. The author was often viewed as a madman, and the work a fabrication to thrill a rich patron or terrify the gullible, but both Gulamendis and myself find the work credible.'

'Why?' asked Sandreena, setting aside her personal ire towards Amirantha for the moment in favour of genuine interest in what he had to say.

'The first thing I noticed was the demon stench; the book reeks of them. Whoever scribed this work did so in the presence of demons.' He got a faraway look and said, 'It's almost as if the demon recited the facts and the scribe simply wrote them down. The other thing is, what he said about familiar demon lore was both accurate and . . .' He looked at her. 'You are aware that I have, in my time, engineered a number of ploys to separate the gullible from their gold. A weakness of a bad confidence is to overstate things; while his work is sensational in scope and depth of subject, it is not overly grandiose. If anything, it's a little dull and academic.'

'Or exceptionally clever in execution,' said Sandreena.

'But toward what end? It's one thing to convince some minor baron that a demon is running around his woodlands, and that for a small price you'll spare the villagers from having their children devoured. It's quite another to spend years writing this tome, and then what? Sell it? No, the author was earnest.'

'What does it contain that will help us?' asked Sandreena, now genuinely interested.

'Our experience with demons appears to have only touched a portion of their population. There are many details I will skip, but here's one: Demons when summoned must be confined, else they run amok, or flee into dark places and hide, waiting for their opportunity to venture forth, then run. That's the difference between the powerful demons and the clever ones.

Occasionally, we find a clever one with some talent for magic; they are especially difficult.

'Gulamendis and I have skills which can confine a demon's choices when summoned. They are called into a circle of power that limits their ability to move without our permission. When I summon one, it must become subject to my will or I return it to the demon realm. If it becomes my servant, then I can give it permission to leave the confines of the circle.'

'To terrorize villagers so you can part the gullible baron from his gold?' Amirantha nodded. 'Or perhaps put on a fetching visage and climb into your bed?'

Amirantha closed his eyes for a second, then said, 'I will not tell you I am sorry one more time, Sandreena. I did what I did and you have continued to punish me for it every time we meet. Enough!' His tone was sharp, but not loud. 'Dalthea is . . . You bury three lovers over a century and see if you find the idea of comfort from an immortal become appealing.'

'Three?' said Sandreena. 'You never said—'

'And you never asked.' He looked her in the eyes. 'I thought of us as strangers who chanced to meet in a village with the improbable name of Yellow Mule, and we both sought a moment's comfort for the body and the heart. I was a travelling mountebank and you were the serious young knight trying to do some great good in the world. I thought it but a passing thing, not what it turned out to be; I never meant to hurt you.'

'You lied to me!'

'I lie!' he retorted. 'That's what charlatans do. We lie. We cheat. We act on our own best interest.'

'Then what brings you here?' she said, her eyes bright with emotion.

He let out a long sigh, leaning one arm on the step above him and his shoulders sagged. 'Honestly, I don't know. I look at the grey in Brandos's hair and realize that if he doesn't get killed in a brawl first, I will bury another person I love in ten, or twenty years. And then there's Samantha ... I'm over a hundred years your senior, Sandreena. I was an old man when your grandmother was a baby. For all I know, I might have bedded her. I need to be something more than a confidence trickster, a liar and cheat. I need to do something bigger than myself.' He let his voice fall. 'I thought I might stay with others like me for a while. Pug is older than I, as was Miranda.

'When I saw her killed, I realized that no matter how long or short our lives are to be, we must do something with them.' He shrugged and gave her a sad smile. 'That's when I decided to stay and help.'

She studied his face and remained silent then finally said, 'Tell me about these demons.'

He realized that in some way she had just forgiven him, or at least agreed to forget how he wronged her. What that meant was unclear, but at least he could turn his attention to the matter at hand.

'The demons that we conjure are from the outer precinct of hell, a region of sheer chaos and confusion, where life is a non-stop struggle for dominance.

'Think of the Fifth Circle as a disc, and the rim the outer precincts, the closer you get to the centre the more organized it gets.' He paused. 'It's hard to describe, because if I make it sound as if demon kind resembles us in any way, I'd be giving you a false comparison.

'They have a high king, whose name is not known, but who

reigns over other kings. The king we knew as Maarg has almost certainly gone, but his legend maintains a semblance of order to that outer precinct.

'He may have been replaced by Dahun, the demon my brother and his mad followers seem to worship, or perhaps Dahun's the ruler of a different region of hell.

'There are a thousand more questions than answers, but two have come to the fore: why are the demons fighting among themselves, and how can some of them exist in this realm without magical protection?'

Sandreena said, 'I thought the act of summoning gave them the protection they required?'

'Yes, the circle of confinement is also a circle of protection and when they bow to our will, we protect them from succumbing to this environment. But what of those demons we didn't summon?'

'Pug told me of the demon he faced, who replaced the Emerald Queen—'

Sandreena interrupted. 'The Temple has long had dealings with demon possessions, Amirantha.'

'Yes, discorporate demon spirits, but they are simply another lesser type of demon, a minor creature of the mind that can take over a weak individual. But even that tenure is brief.

'But the demon Jakan didn't possess the Emerald Queen; he killed her and took her place, with a conjured likeness that even those closest to her couldn't penetrate.'

'Impressive.'

'Laromendis is considered a great conjurer among the Star Elves and he says he could not do this. Who was this Jakan? A weak spirit demon that preyed on weak souls until it had the strength to do what it did? Or was it something else?'

'You love questions, don't you?' She spoke softly and there was a resignation in her voice.

He smiled. 'And you always seek answers.'

There was a faint smile, then suddenly her eyes narrowed and the moment was gone. 'Demons,' she insisted.

Amirantha stood up and said, 'It's easier if I show you.'

She followed him to the keep and they passed the kitchen workers preparing a meal for those who hadn't eaten already. Brandos and his wife sat in the corner holding hands and saying nothing, her head resting on his shoulder. Samantha had seen him off to enough battles to know that there was nothing to say, so they enjoyed their last moments together in silence.

Amirantha led Sandreena up the stairs of the tower, to the room that had been set aside for his use. There they found Gulamendis reading the volume avidly. He looked up and smiled, the first openly friendly and genuinely excited expression either of them had seen from the elf.

'This is amazing!' he said. 'Every time I read it, I find new things to wonder over.'

Amirantha said, 'If you don't mind, why don't you explain to Sandreena why this book is important?'

'First, it is genuine,' said the elf. He slowly reached out and said, 'Give me your hand.' He gently placed it on the book and she instantly snatched it back.

'Demon,' she said. 'I can feel it.'

Like a delighted child, Gulamendis asked, 'Where to begin?'

Amirantha asked, 'Did you make any sense of that battle you and your brother witnessed on Telesan?'

'I think so,' said Gulamendis. 'It would probably be better if I showed you.'

He opened the back cover, laying it flat on the desk. He carefully unfolded the last page, until the map was revealed, four times the size of a normal page. The map had been drawn in a vivid style, illustrations of demons of all stripe were painted in garish coloured inks along the edges, with small narratives below each drawing telling something about that creature.

But Sandreena was instantly taken with the map itself, for it showed a massive disc, divided into two circles, outer and inner, with the centre circle being divided into further segments. 'This outer circle is where we have plied our craft,' he said to Sandreena, while he pointed at Amirantha. 'The beings we summon from here are similar to those you have faced in your travels. The author of this work calls them the "lesser infernals".'

'Lesser?' Sandreena shook her head in disbelief. 'I've confronted some very big and nasty demons in my time.'

Gulamendis nodded slightly and said, 'As have we all. No, lesser doesn't mean strength or magic power, I am certain. It's about organization, or rather a lack of organization. It's a demon eat demon realm.'

Sandreena put her hand near the map, just outside the border and said, 'What's here, beyond the edge.'

Gulamendis looked annoyed at the interruption, but it was Amirantha who spoke. 'The Fifth Circle is no more a disc than it is a circle. It's a region, and I'm sure it has boundaries, but what's beyond those boundaries . . .? The void perhaps, or some other realm we do not know of, or maybe it is the boundary of the Fourth circle or the Sixth. In any event, it is this realm with which we are concerned, o' seeker of answers.' The last was said in a friendly manner, but

Sandreena's dark look told the warlock she wasn't in the mood for banter.

'May I continue?' asked the elf.

'Please,' said Amirantha before Sandreena could ask another question.

'It's within this inner realm that all our answers lie.' His finger moved around on the vellum and he said, 'It appears that chaos is part of the demonic nature, but at least in the inner circle – the circle of the greater infernals – some form of order has emerged over ages. These areas, what the author calls "cantons", are each ruled by a demon lord, a self-anointed king, arch duke, or some other like title.'

'Like Maarg?' asked Sandreena, having heard from Pug about the demon king's corpse found on the Saaur world of Shila.

'He ruled in the outer ring, as best I can tell,' said Gulamendis. 'It is an every-demon-for-himself sort of place, and he literally clawed and bullied his way to the top. Amirantha and I feel that what we had discerned about demons before all of this began was mainly true; demons hold a loose organization of alliances and services. They either destroy their rivals, absorbing their power, or take service. The weaker ones find a stronger demon to serve in exchange for protection, and the stronger demon then has a retinue ready to aid him in conflicts with his rivals. Much of rising and falling among the demons of the outer circle was the result of betrayal, ambush, and treachery. And it always raised the question in my mind how could anything remotely like a society arise from this chaos? How could they evolve beyond animal states, to have a language and magic?

'But here,' he said, indicating the inner circle, 'is the answer. Each canton has its own society, apparently an army, and a ruler.

Demons who somehow evolve enough to escape the outer circle but who don't contest for domination, they find their way to one of these cantons and . . .' He shrugged. 'I'm not certain. Service? Slavery? Freedom?'

'We struggle to apply mortal concepts to a race more alien to us than any other we've encountered, even trolls and goblins.'

'Certainly true,' said Amirantha. 'The author of this work labelled these cantons with a variety of colourful names, "Pandamonia", "Discordia", "Despair", "The Miasma" and "The Fallen". We have no way of knowing much about them, what the demons called them, or even if the number is correct.

'He writes a great deal about experiences here on Midkemia, and the rest is inference.' Gulamendis sat back and crossed his arms over his chest. 'Putting aside the colourful embellishment, at the heart of this work stands this truth: another realm threatens our own, at the heart of which stands a society, or societies, we know almost nothing about, one that we were completely ignorant of until recently.' With no vanity, he pointed to Amirantha and said, 'And it is most likely that we are more expert on the subject than any other being in this world.'

'Speaking of the heart,' said Sandreena pointing to a dark spot in the middle of the map. 'What is that?'

Gulamendis shrugged. 'Another, tiny realm perhaps? It is only marked with a single word, "Void," and there is nothing written about it anywhere in the book.'

Laromendis arrived at the door and said, 'Ah, there you are. Time to gather below. We are leaving.'

Sandreena, Amirantha, and Gulamendis all looked through the window and saw the sun hanging low in the western sky. They hurried down to the marshalling yard without further discussion.

• CHAPTER SIXTEEN •

Reconnaissance

KASPAR SIGNALLED.

They had ventured down the first trail to the rim of the valley, where they would begin the tedious descent down the switchback trails unless Pug decided he and Magnus needed to get everyone down in a hurry. All the magic users had been cautioned to not use their art in any form, active or passive, unless they were attacked, as the defenders might have placed wards to detect it. Looking at the long downward trail, and out beyond the distant rim, Amirantha turned to Gulamendis and said, 'We should have a quicker exit, at least. I'd hate to have to run back up those trails.'

The elf nodded. 'Some of my people are able to trek like this for days; sadly I am not one of them.'

They had discussed the plan in detail, but the sight when they arrived at the valley's edge, caused them all to stop. 'My gods,' said Kaspar. 'What is it?'

The construction looked finished. The four large arching towers now stretched towards a central point above the vast open area at the heart of the structure.

Pug said, 'It looks something like the portal used by the Dasati when they invaded Kelewan, though they didn't have all this fortification around it. They used a magic shield that was very difficult to breech, and it expanded as they sent more and more of their Death Knights through.'

Sandreena said, 'Where are all the labourers?' She pointed and said, 'There were hundreds of them working ... And the demon overseers patrolling the walls?'

Pug said, 'We need to get closer. I can see some movement in the distance, but it's too far away to make out who it is.'

Kaspar said, 'Sandreena lead us to that gully, please.'

His band had worked their way down the switchback trails cautiously, until they reached the gully Sandreena had used to circumvent the guard post at the bottom of the slope. In single file they followed her to the rim of the dry river basin, and after motioning for the others to wait, Kaspar and Sandreena crawled on their bellies up to the rim and looked over.

'It's quiet,' whispered Kaspar.

'On the wall,' said Sandreena.

Sentries could be seen walking the battlements, but between the basin and the wall was only empty ground. 'It's going to be difficult to get close,' said Kaspar.

'We should approach from the back,' said Sandreena. 'There's a dry river bed that runs near to the wall.' She pointed off to their left.

Kaspar motioned for Pug to join them and when he did, Kaspar said, 'Are you going to be safe using magic?'

Pug said, 'Magnus and I have been testing as gently as possible, and we don't sense anything unexpected.' He looked at the massive construction ahead of them and said, 'Something in there is very powerful, but it's dormant for the moment. There are a few wards to detect scrying, but they're basic, nothing we can't avoid.' He looked at the five crouching figures around him and said, 'I think we stick to the original plan.'

Kaspar nodded. 'Wait until we have worked our way around to the back of this fortress and then do what you think is best. If we hear any sounds of alarm from your group, we will have Magnus take us back to the plateau.

'If you hear any trouble on our part, do what you think best.'

Pug and Magnus and Amirantha provided a formidable magic force, and one that might make the difference between the others getting back alive or not. After a long argument, Kaspar had relented as Pug insisted that he should be the one to decide if he should come to Kaspar's aid or not. Kaspar was secretly relieved.

Sandreena, like Kaspar, Laromendis, Magnus and Jim dashed up the dry river bed, while Pug rejoined Brandos, Amirantha and Gulamendis. They slowly counted for ten minutes, then Pug said, 'Laromendis, be ready to make us look like a pile of rubble.'

The elf smiled slightly and said, 'That should be no problem, assuming that no one is looking very hard at our pile of rubble and we don't have to be rubble for too long.'

Brandos chuckled, then turned to listen. 'Someone's coming,' he whispered. The group quickly moved near the edge of the basin, and looked upward.

A demon sentry walked above their position, and it glanced

downward, blinking for a moment. It had a bovine head with massive red eyes, and a prodigious pair of horns that swept up and out. Grunting once, it blinked, then moved on.

When it was away, Pug turned and asked the elf, 'Rubble?'

'Rubble,' answered Laromendis. 'Next time, try to give me a little more warning.'

'Those cattle heads tend to be fairly stupid,' said Amirantha.

'It also helps that they're nearsighted,' said Brandos. 'That fact alone has saved my head more than once.'

Pug shook his head. 'A nearsighted sentry?'

Brandos whispered. 'It makes them nervous. They jump at any motion they detect. If we stay in the dark and don't move, they'll probably miss us even without the illusion our brother elf just cast.'

Pug said, 'Let's go that way,' indicating the direction from which the sentry had walked. They crouched and moved up out of the basin, keeping low along the edge of the depression.

They reached the road that led to the switchbacks up the hill and found that the sentry post Sandreena had described was gone. Pug assumed they had removed everything from the perimeter once the gates and wall were finished, clearing the area around the walls free of any possible concealment.

They crept into the darkness on the opposite side of the road, finding another depression to crouch behind. Slowly they moved away from Kaspar's group.

Sandreena held up a balled fist, indicating that they should stop. Kaspar gently put his hand on her shoulder to let her know he was behind her. She signalled there were sentries ahead, indicating two of them. He slowly rose to peer over the edge of the dried river bank and saw two demons walking a patrol before a small gate.

The small group had traversed half of the structure's perimeter and had yet to see a safe approach. The fortification looked as if it were built to withstand a short, not a long siege. There was no structure beyond the walls, so any storage and quarters lay in small buildings nestling just inside the walls, or were nonexistent.

Kaspar indicated they should move away and when they were at a safe distance from the gate, he whispered, 'I don't know what this place is; it's like nothing I've ever encountered. But it's easily defensible with a hundred soldiers, and near impregnable with twice that number, but I'll be damned if I can see much sense to it beyond that.'

'My best guess,' said Sandreena, 'is they built it as a temporary defence, in case someone stumbled onto what they were doing and tried to stop it. I see no water source, no decent supply route, and no barracks for a garrison. It's as if they are planning to abandon this place once they've accomplished whatever it is they are doing here.'

'My thoughts as well,' said Kaspar. He turned and motioned for Magnus to come close. Still whispering, he said, 'Do you have any sense of what this place is for?'

Magnus's expression was grave. 'There is some very dark magic occurring within those walls. It's . . . muted, waiting for something to be unleashed, but it's there.'

Suddenly, a fine silver net appeared out the darkness and landed upon the white-haired magician. Magnus stiffened, then his eyes rolled up into his head, as if he had been struck from behind. Kaspar and Sandreena crouched low and drew weapons as figures rose out the soil of the plateau before them. Sandreena turned towards Laromendis and Jim Dasher, but couldn't see them, so she raised her mace as Kaspar drew his sword, and a pair of finely woven nets descended upon them.

Sandreena felt a shock course through her body and her mind become a tumbling cascade of thoughts and images. Part of her knew she was under attack, but years of training, both martial and magic, wilted under the effect of that silver net. Her defensive spells refused to coalesce in her thoughts; moves as basic as raising her shield or hefting her mace, ingrained in her body's memory as much as her mind, became jerking attempts to control herself.

Kaspar was likewise overcome; he spasmed and twisted as he sought to command his body to meet the coming attack. But like Sandreena and Magnus, he quickly fell to the ground.

Looking up, they could see three figures covered from head to toe in suits of fine cloth, with only the smallest slits for eyes. The cloth was the same colour as the earth that had hidden them, and they must have been lying in ambush for quite some time, perhaps hours, waiting for the intruders to get close enough to render them powerless.

Another figure appeared a moment later, a grinning bearded man who looked down at the three prone bodies and said, 'Bring them!'

As he turned away, Sandreena managed to whisper, 'Belasco!' She didn't know if Magnus or Kaspar could hear her.

Pain coursed through her body when she tried to move, but if she remained motionless, the pain faded. Her thoughts were still chaotic but she witnessed enough and remembered enough to have a sense of time passing as they were lifted and carried towards a small rear gate in the wall.

Then her thoughts fled and darkness arrived.

Jim crouched motionless behind the smallest of rocks, his cloak pulled over him. He expected to be discovered any moment, but he had an instinct for when to flee and when to remain still. Right now his 'bump of trouble' was telling him to get as close to the ground as humanly possible. He could hear muffled voices and sensed some movement ten yards ahead.

He had felt rather than seen the ambush, and his first re-action had been to leap backwards, away from the fight. It was not cowardice but caution that motivated him; he wanted to be sure no one was coming at them from behind. Those three steps backwards, as their attackers had jumped down the side of the dry riverbank, saved him from detection. Something had happened to Laromendis, but he couldn't be certain. One moment the elven magic user had been there, the next he wasn't.

Jim had his dagger ready, but kept still. He waited until he could hear no sound, then risked a peak from under his cloak.

The river bed was empty.

He had heard the brief struggle and knew they were over-matched the instant Magnus went down without a sound. Whoever waited for them had expected a powerful magician; he assumed the same magic trap prevented Sandreena from using her abilities, and the nets had quickly rendered both her and Kaspar unconscious.

Pug and Kaspar had been clear in their instructions to him; he was the last link to the outside world if all else failed. Given the level of power and talent in this reconnaissance team, he considered himself a desperate choice.

He crouched low, not willing to risk moving just yet. Where was that elf?

Then suddenly the elf was standing before him. He turned, looked down at Jim and whispered, 'They're gone.'

Jim stood up and Laromendis reached out to touch his cloak. 'That is impressive.'

'I'm good,' whispered the noble-turned-thief, 'but I'm not that good. This didn't come cheaply. The artificer who wove it for me called it his "cloak of blending", and I suspect it uses magic similar to your own.' He looked around for any sign of lingering danger. 'What just happened?'

'Your guess is as good as mine,' whispered the elf. 'They waited for us; they knew we had magic users with us, and they were ready.'

'They knew we were coming.'

'Apparently. What troubles me is how the ambush was executed.'

Jim's brow furrowed. 'Explain.'

'We were not moving quickly, in fact we were very cautious. For our three ambushers to have secreted themselves in that location, in anticipation of our arrival, they had to be lying in those shallow depressions for quite some time, perhaps an hour or more.'

'How did they breathe?'

Laromendis nodded emphatically. 'I don't think they did breathe.'

Jim's face became a mask of concern. 'Necromancy?'

'Pug mentioned that one of his concerns was trying to understand how death magic and demon magic were linked.' The elf paused, then looked at Jim. 'There may be a more prosaic explanation, but if those were . . . reanimated dead?'

Jim was, for the first time in years, uncertain what to do next. 'We need to send word to Pug, and we need to follow those captors.'

Laromendis said, 'I'll find Pug. I can hide better than you can, but I cannot track or skulk, and that cloak gives you more flexibility than my magic does.' He asked, 'What should I tell Pug?'

'Tell him what you saw, nothing more. Don't speculate unless he asks, and tell him that if I don't find you within one hour he's to assume I've been taken as well.' Jim glanced over the verge and said, 'Good luck,' then he wrapped his cloak around him and almost vanished.

'Good luck,' returned Laromendis, fascinated by Jim's subtle bit of magic. He could see him moving along the verge of the dried river, but only if he looked closely and concentrated. He knew that if he took his eyes off the human, he'd vanish from sight. The cloak did not render him invisible, but rather let him blend in with the surrounding terrain.

Laromendis decided he'd ask more about that cloak if they ever got out of here. He glanced around to ensure he wasn't being watched, then started back the way he had come, hoping to overtake Pug before they ran into trouble.

Pug motioned for the others to halt. They'd been making very slow progress, frustrated by the need to loop far to the north-west and then return towards the wall in tangents. There was simply no cover until they reached a point further to the west, and from there they could hardly see anything. Kneeling behind an overhang that sheltered them from all but the keenest observation, he whispered, 'This is getting us nowhere.'

Gulamendis also spoke quietly, 'Amirantha and I sense demons, but there are not that many, and they are scattered.'

'Where?' asked Pug.

'All over,' answered Amirantha. 'There's a heavy concentration of them near that big gate where we first crossed over the road, but after that . . .' He shrugged.

'How about here?' asked Brandos.

'Few,' answered the elf.

Looking at Pug, he said, 'Perhaps the direct approach?'

'What do you propose?' asked the magician.

Glancing around at the night sky and shrouded landscape, he said, 'Unless they have night vision like our elf friend here, I can get closer and take a look. It won't be the first time I've crawled on my stomach to get a look at an enemy position.'

Pug thought for a moment and said, 'I'm loath to use magic that might be detected until I know what we face. Get as close as you can, then get back here, but secrecy is paramount.'

'Understood.'

Brandos crawled over the edge and on to the beam at a surprisingly efficient rate. Amirantha said, 'Enemy position?' He chuckled softly. 'He means spying upon the local sheriff or city watch waiting for us.'

'As long as it works,' whispered Pug.

Time dragged slowly until they heard Brandos returning. He snaked down on his stomach to where they crouched, rolled over and sat up. 'There's a small gate about a hundred yards southwest. It looks like it's the one part of the wall that's not quite finished. They have to move a wooden barrier to bring wagons in or out, and there's only one guard. A demon,' he said to Amirantha with a grin.

'What manner of demon?' asked the Warlock.

'Big battle demon, ram's head, all decked out in black armour and carrying a huge double bladed axe.'

'A Ram's head?' said Amirantha, looking at Gulamendis.

The elf said, 'They tend to be tractable if you can subdue them.'

'If you can subdue them,' echoed Amirantha.

'What are you thinking?' asked Pug.

'If we can control that demon, even for a few minutes,' said Amirantha, 'that could provide us an ingress. If you have the means to get in unseen and look about—'

'I can do that,' said Pug. 'I can render myself unseen for a short period of time.'

'That's good,' said Gulamendis with a slight smile, 'as we should only be able to subdue that demon for a short period.'

'What do we do with it when it's no longer subdued and starts shouting alarm?' asked Brandos.

'I expect it will be dead by then,' said Amirantha, pointedly.

Brandos rolled his eyes. 'They tend to stop being cooperative as soon as you start killing them.'

'Then do it quickly,' he said to Brandos and Gulamendis.

'You hook him,' said Brandos, 'and we'll gut him and cook him.' Gulamendis nodded. 'I've got one banishment that's very quick, but tends to be messy.'

'I don't mind messy,' said Pug. 'If we need to leave in a hurry, we can.'

'What about Magnus and his group?' asked Brandos.

'If they hear trouble, they know what to do,' answered Pug.
'I hope so,' said Brandos. 'Because I certainly don't.'

Pug said to Amirantha, 'Take the lead.'

Amirantha nodded, but instead of crawling forward as Brandos
had, he stood, motioning for the others to follow, and started
walking straight to the gate.

The sentry was looking the other way when Amirantha loomed
upon it in the darkness, and when it turned its sheep-like head
in the Warlock's direction, it uttered a curious sound, 'Uh?'

Before it could make another, Amirantha used a single word
spell that stunned the creature, causing the huge axe it held to
drop from limp fingers. Amirantha said to Pug, 'You have perhaps
five to ten minutes; more likely five.'

Pug said, 'I'll be back in four.' He stole a quick glance at
Amirantha who stood with hands outstretched, his magic controlling the demon. Brandos stood ready to strike a killing blow if
needed, with Gulamendis ready to banish the creature.

Then he took a deep breath, and started walking towards the
now unguarded entryway. As he moved around the makeshift
wooden barrier, he unleashed a spell he had never used before.
It was a difficult cantrip, that caused him to be ignored. Not
truly invisible, but when someone glanced at him, he didn't
garner their notice, as if he wasn't important enough to
remember. It was a spell taught him by Laromendis the week
before, and while the elf had proclaimed Pug's mastery of it
sufficient, Pug still had doubts.

He walked through the opening and paused, glancing in all
directions.

The four towers rose overhead, arching towards the open

centre. This close, Pug could sense their power; it was faint, or perhaps dormant was a better word, but it was there. A tiny flicker of light danced across each tip from time to time, but otherwise they were quiet.

Pug could not enjoy the luxury of investigating any one aspect of this place, no matter how much he wished he could. He moved towards the massive excavation at the centre of the ring, glancing from side to side to see if he was being observed. A sentry on the wall looked directly at him for a moment, then turned away to look out over the dark narrow path outside the wall. Either the spell was working or the guard expected to see humans in dark robes trekking around the facility during the night.

Pug reached the edge of the pit and glanced in. His stomach knotted. The pit was less than thirty feet deep, but he could see the pile of bodies. The stench clearly indicated they had been dead for days. Elves, humans, dwarves, and even some demons sprawled in the mass.

Pug stepped back and felt a fresh breeze blow the foul smell away. Had the air been still he would have sensed the dead at the outer gate.

He hurried towards the only feature inside the ring that offered an invitation, a small building of some sort, with a single door and no windows. As he hurried to reach it, a voice from nearby hissed, 'Pug!'

It was only by the scantest margin that Pug didn't incinerate Jim Dasher where he stood. 'You have no idea how close that was,' Pug whispered. 'Where are the others?'

'In there,' Jim pointed to the door. 'There's a stairway leading down to an underground chamber.'

Pug said, 'I have one minute before I must start back to where

Amirantha and the others wait.' He pointed towards the unguarded entrance.

'Magnus, Sandreena, and Kaspar were taken.'

'What?'

Jim motioned for him to remain silent. 'A trap. I think they knew we were coming.' Before Pug could ask how, he continued. 'I used my cloak and Laromendis employed his conjuring skills to stay hidden. He's gone after you, and if he hasn't overtaken his brother and the others by now, he will be with them by the time you get back.'

'Me?' said Pug. 'My son is down there.'

'And I'm better able to slip in and out than you. You're spell is good, I had to look at you long and hard before I realized, but I did eventually recognize you. If you go down the stairs, you'll be in such a small space that those at the bottom won't be able to ignore you, so let me go. I'll meet you by the gates in five more minutes.'

'If you're not back by then, I'll come after you,' said Pug.

'What about the plan?' hissed Jim.

'Everyone is in place, and I'll send Brandos with instructions if I must. I've lost too much to not go after Magnus if you don't return.'

'Understood,' said Jim. 'Now, let me go down there and then I'll find you.'

Pug hesitated, hating to leave this in another's hands, but one complaint he had always had about his wife Miranda was her seeming inability to delegate important tasks to others. Feeling a rush of bitterness thinking of her, he nodded and turned away.

*　*　*

Jim Dasher knew it had been difficult for Pug to let him go. The recent loss of his wife and younger son made him much more protective of Magnus. Still, Jim knew from experience that this was exactly the type of situation where emotion could get you killed.

They had established a plan, and it was the third option that only he, Pug, Kaspar, and Magnus knew of. Three companies of soldiers were assembled and ready to attack at a moment's notice.

Each was under the command of men whom Pug trusted implicitly, his adopted grandsons, Tad, Zane, and Jommy. Jommy waited in a nice quiet estate on the island of Roldem, with three hundred Royal Marines under his command.

Zane was down in Kesh with half a legion of Kesh's finest border guards, the dog soldiers; and had control of nearly a thousand men.

And Tad was in Krondor with five hundred more of the Prince's own, and Kaspar had another five hundred hand-picked shock troops from the army of the Maharaja of Muboya assembled half a planet away with the young magician Jason ready to bring them here.

Any or all of them could be here in minutes. The only critical thing was the one person who must use a Tsurani orb to get back to Sorcerer's Isle, where a simple order would trigger a full-scale assault on this fortification.

As long as one person could get away.

Jim made his way slowly into the building, and down the circular stairway, which began as a hole in the floor. He kept one hand on the wall on his left, while the other held the cloak around him firmly. The nature of his marvellous garment adjusted in proportion to his movement, but the staircase was barely wide enough to allow someone to pass, so he felt the need to reach the bottom as quickly as possible.

He made five full circles and knew he was approximately thirty feet below the surface, with the bottom still not in sight. Ten more and he saw light, and when he reached the bottom, he estimated that he was easily a hundred and fifty feet below the ground. It would be a wonderful climb back up, he thought, especially if he were being chased.

At the bottom, Jim discovered a large room with ancient stone walls. Another of those damned ancient Keshian fortifications, he thought. His adventure had started at a similar site on the plateau called the Tomb of the Hopeless, and now he found himself in one even more remote and dangerous than that.

Looking around for some idea of what to do, he noticed that only one of the four tunnels held a distant light, so that was the direction he chose.

The tunnel was also made of ancient stone, dry and dusty, but the floor showed the tread of many feet. He still had no concept of what this place was and why the mad magician Belasco and his demon minions had chosen to occupy it, but he suspected he was going to regret the discovery.

Reaching the end of the tunnel he hesitated, clutching his cloak around himself and looking into the room with surprise.

A massive altar, ancient and stained black from sacrifices centuries past, was now stained with fresh blood. Before it knelt three figures, bound in chains and forced to kneel: Kaspar, Sandreena, and Magnus.

Well, at least they're still alive, thought Jim.

On top of the altar lay the still form of Belasco, his eyes closed. Dead, unconscious, or sleeping, it was difficult to judge.

And standing on the other side of the altar was a slender man, whipcord strong and stripped to the waist. His torso was covered in clan tattoos, and his teeth had all been filed to points. Jim had never seen one before, but still recognized what he was: Shaskahan cannibals were practitioners of particularly dark magic.

Only this time the magic didn't seem to be intended to destroy the body on the altar, but rather he appeared to be trying to revive it. When the chanting stopped, the Shaskahan reached over and gave Belasco a gentle shake. 'Master?' he whispered, loud enough for Jim to make out the word.

From out of the air came a voice. 'Yes, my servant?'

'Are you with us again?' asked the man. He appeared genuinely frightened by what was taking place.

'Not yet,' came the answer.

'What must I do? We trapped those who came, as you told us to. We have them here, bound in chains that stop their magic.' He looked at Sandreena and Magnus, then at Kaspar. 'We can spill blood if it will help?'

Dryly, the voice in the air said, 'Nothing can help.'

Then another voice sounded, and it was as if the winds of hell had been given the power of speech. 'Let me out of here!' it commanded, and the body on the altar shook; the Shaskahan pulled back, obviously terrified.

Jim hung back in the shadows, totally uncertain what to do next.

CHAPTER SEVENTEEN

Summoning

*T*HE PIT EXPLODED.

Pug and the others were thrown to the ground as a tower of green energy ripped through the air from the pit. The brilliant energy lashed out like angry lightning, sizzling through the air with a hiss loud enough to make Pug's group want to cover their ears.

'Gods!' said Brandos. 'What was that?'

Pug felt the hair on his arms and neck stand up as an all too familiar and evil power began to coalesce. 'Oh, gods, indeed,' said Pug as a deep thrumming sound and a powerful vibration emanated from the ground beneath them and set their teeth on edge. 'It's a summoning!'

'What?' asked Gulamendis. 'I have never experienced anything like this.'

Laromendis said, 'I have never seen its like either.' The taredhel had found his brother, Amirantha, and Brandos while Pug had encountered Jim. Pug had just finished explaining what he was going to do when the energy erupted.

Pug turned to Brandos and said, 'Here, take this.' He handed him a Tsurani orb and said, 'Push that button and you will find yourself in the keep on Sorcerer's Isle. A magician named Pascal will be there waiting for you. Tell him to bring everything. He'll know what to do.'

'I'm not leaving,' he said, looking at Amirantha. 'He'll get himself killed if I'm not here to watch his back.'

Amirantha took the sphere from Pug and pressed it into Brandos's hands. 'I have been staying alive since before you were born, boy.' If anyone found it strange that the younger looking warlock called the grey-haired fighter 'boy', no one felt the need to remark on it. 'Do as you're told and then get back here if you can; otherwise wait at the keep with your wife. Understand?'

Looking from face to face, Brandos realized that he was the most expendable person there, so he grabbed the sphere and suddenly he was gone. 'What now?' asked Gulamendis.

'Something beyond our ability to imagine may be coming through that portal soon.' Pug saw that the guards in the area were hurrying back inside the wall, with looks of panic on their inhuman faces. 'If you see anything heading for the small building against the far wall, kill it,' he shouted, taking off at a run.

Amirantha and the two elves didn't hesitate and were only half a step behind Pug, who sprinted past the wooden barrier and through the empty gate. Several demons of varying size were screaming at one another, looking for anything to vent their rage and terror against. Amirantha shouted, 'Pug, to your right!'

Both the Warlock and Gulamendis began banishment rituals, but before they could get halfway through, Pug put out his palm and unleashed a withering beam of silver energy that tore the demon closing on him in two. The pieces fell to the ground smoking, and then erupted into flames, while the two demon masters and the conjurer looked on in awe. 'Remind me never to make him angry,' said Laromendis.

Gulamendis nodded, then shouted, 'That got their attention.'

A dozen demons had seen the display and Pug had provided them with a convenient target for their fear and rage. They bellowed and shrieked as they charged him and the others. Pug made a sweeping gesture with his hand and a curtain of flames erupted on the ground in front of the demons. They were engulfed as they screamed and roared in outrage and pain.

Gulamendis came to stand next to the nearly frantic magician. 'Those are demons. Fire will only annoy them.'

'It has slowed them down for a couple of minutes,' said Amirantha.

They reached inside the building and Pug made a quick decision. 'Amirantha, go down the stairs and find Jim Dasher. Be careful.' To Laromendis and Gulamendis he said, 'We have to keep those creatures back.'

The Warlock hurried down the circular stairs while Pug's right hand shot outward, palm forward, through the door. A rippling in the air, tainted green by the light from the summoning device, showed a wall of force striking a dozen demons and knocking them backwards. Several lay stunned and motionless, but the others seemed only to get madder.

Gulamendis took a talisman from his belt pouch and pointed it at one particularly nasty looking demon, a thing of scales and crocodile teeth, bat wings, and blood red armour. He spoke a quick phrase and suddenly the demon's yellow eyes blinked as it reached over and ripped out the throat of the demon next to it. Laromendis closed his eyes and muttered, 'Something big.' A moment later the ground shook from the enraged bellow of a massive golden dragon as it sprang into being above the thirty or so demons ringing the hut.

Gulamendis said, 'This will only buy us a few minutes, Pug. The bigger and angrier the illusion, the faster Laro fatigues.'

The dragon was a thing of beauty, looking exactly like the one the brothers had ridden upon with Tomas. It opened its maw and a scorching blast of searing fire rolled over the demons, scattering them. Pug felt the heat wash over him until he noticed that while the demons ran screaming, batting at the flames as their flesh blistered, there was no fire, no smoke or char on the ground. The moment he realized this, the heat stopped. He could still see the dragon, but it was now insubstantial and clearly an illusion.

Knowing the demons would soon come to the same understanding he sent out another blast of flame, which exploded in a tower of orange and yellow that inflicted real burns on the demons. 'That will keep them confused a little longer,' said Pug.

'Confusion will only work for a while,' said Gulamendis. 'Their reserves from outside the walls are now joining in.'

Pug said, 'They were probably given orders to return when the summoning started. I wonder what chance let these ones live while their companions lie at the bottom of that pit?'

'That battle we saw on Telesan was not an illusion, Pug,' said Gulamendis. 'There's a demon war taking place, and its our good fortune that the demons are now warring against one another.

I've lived through losing two worlds to them. A third would be one too many. Look out!'

Pug saw the flyers attacking the dragon illusion and Pug responded with a lance of purple light, which caused one demon to burst into flames above the dragon. As the corpse fell, it passed completely through the dragon and several of the other demons realized something was amiss.

'They're stupid,' said Gulamendis, 'but not that stupid. They'll turn on us in a minute.'

Pug shot out another great bolt of energy and said, 'If we can hold out for another ten, fifteen minutes, the marines from Roldem should be the first here.'

As more demons swarmed into view, Gulamendis said, 'I think they're going to be overmatched unless we can help them.'

'We'll help,' said Pug.

Gulamendis used his ward and reached out to take control of the largest demon he could see, then set it against its neighbour. It didn't take much provocation for that conflict to escalate as several other demons were drawn in. 'Something in their conditioning is breaking down, Pug. The battle demons are reverting to their old habits and starting to fight for domination.'

'Why?'

'I have no idea, but that whatever was controlling the creatures is losing command of them.'

As they watched the demons began to turn on one another, but enough continued to rush the small building that Pug was forced to use all his skills to knock them back with another pulse of energy. 'I can't keep doing this all day,' he said, obviously fatigued. 'There are so many of them.'

'If they all turn on each other, we will only need to bar this door.' The demon master selected another demon in the fray and turned it on its neighbour. Then the illusion of the dragon vanished.

'That tears it,' said Laromendis, coming out of his trance. 'I've got little left to offer.' He pulled out the wand he had harboured since they fled the battle of Hub and pointed it at a particularly nasty beast charging the door. It went down in convulsions as energy consumed it.

Pug said, 'I wish I knew what was going on below.' He pushed aside thoughts of his son and the others and returned his attention to the battle before him.

Amirantha waited in the shadows, uncertain of what was occurring before him. He saw Jim Dasher hugging the wall by the door; the only hint of the noble-turned-spy was an odd refraction of the light, which moved only slightly. If Amirantha stared at the spot, he could just make out the vague shape of a man between the door and the room beyond.

He watched the scene in the room for a moment, and his eyes widened. His brother, Belasco, lay motionless across a sacrificial altar, and Sandreena, Kaspar, and Magnus knelt before him. Amirantha assumed their bindings prevented the two magic casters from using their abilities, or this situation would have been resolved before either Jim and he had arrived.

A strange looking man, thin with ragged hair, and an impressive looking set of pointed teeth, appeared to be weeping piteously over Belasco, imploring his still form for instructions. Even more perplexing was the dialogue he could hear between two invisible entities. Amirantha stopped to ensure he wasn't losing his mind, because even though his brother lay motionless on the altar, he could hear his voice, and then another, both demanding some sort of behaviour from the witless man.

Amirantha came up behind Jim and as the cloaked figure tensed, he said, 'It's me; what is happening?'

Jim gripped the Warlock by the arm, pulled him back into the tunnel and said, 'I have no idea. That lunatic cannibal has been talking to your unconscious brother for five minutes. I have no idea who the other voice belongs to.'

Amirantha said, 'I need to explain the subtleties of demonic possession to you, but now is not the time. Can you kill that man without giving him time to harm anyone else?'

'Easily, but why?'

'Because if he makes the wrong move, we're all going to die.'

'That's a good enough reason,' said Jim, and Amirantha saw him produce his dagger out of thin air.

'Wait,' said the Warlock.

'Why?' asked Jim. 'Either we want him dead, or not. Which is it? Our friends are stupefied and our enemy is overcome. As I see it, our problems could be resolved with two quick kills.'

Amirantha whispered, 'Ah, if only it were that simple.' He pointed to the confused cannibal. 'Why is he so perplexed?'

'Because his master lies prostrate and he has no idea what to do,' said Jim. 'I don't know a lot about magic, but I know that sometimes the real price is unanticipated. If that evil bastard on the altar has made a mistake, why not take advantage and end this?'

'We can't end it like this,' said Amirantha. 'Not yet. His minion is confused because there are *two beings* within his body!'

'Two beings?' whispered Jim. 'What does that mean?'

'It means my idiot brother has summoned a demon who tried to take over his body. Now they're struggling for control.'

'Is that why he's lying there motionless?'

'Apparently. Neither one has enough control to command the body and fight off the other.'

'What should I do?'

'Regarding Belasco, nothing, for the moment,' said Amirantha. 'As for that sharp toothed fellow, can you kill him without bringing harm to our friends?'

'At any time.'

'Do so now, if you don't mind, then cut the others loose. I will probably need Magnus and Sandreena's help with whatever happens to Belasco.'

Jim faded into the shadow and for a moment Amirantha felt as if he were alone in the tunnel. Then there was a blur of motion on the left wall and the wailing Shaskahan went rigid and slumped to the floor. Jim pulled back the hood of his cloak and stood over Belasco, and then motioned for Amirantha to enter. The kingdom spy then moved to unfetter his companions.

Magnus and Sandreena were both tied with the silver netting, while Kaspar was bound and gagged in a more conventional fashion. Kaspar gasped for breath when Jim pulled the gag from his mouth. 'Gods! I thought I was going to suffocate they pushed that so far back.' He cleared his throat and said, 'Help me up. My knees are not what they once were and I have been too long in one position.' Jim gave him a hand and said, 'What did they do to Magnus and Sandreena?'

Both magic users remained mute, wide eyed, and staring into space. Kaspar said, 'They became like that when the nets were cast on us. They removed mine, but kept those two under them the entire time.'

Jim nodded. 'Slavers nets. They use them in Durbin when they're trying to snag a magic user. The really fine ones are costly, and not only dampen magic, but render the magician tractable.'

'Help me get them out,' said Jim.

Kaspar was stiff legged for a minute and then applied himself to removing Sandreena's bindings, while Jim cut through the netting holding Magnus. When they were free, both went limp; Kaspar caught Sandreena and lowered her to the floor gently, while Jim did the same for Magnus. Jim said, 'Now we wait for them to recover.'

'How long will it take?' asked Kaspar.

Amirantha stood over the prone figure of his brother, whose eyes were trained on him. He said, 'The effects should wear off shortly.'

The body on the altar didn't move his lips, but a voice sounded in the air. 'Is that you, little brother?'

Amirantha said, 'It is, big brother.'

'You don't find me at my best,' came the hollow reply.

'I never have.' Pulling out a dagger, he said, 'Is there any compelling reason I shouldn't end this now?'

'Besides my reluctance to die any time soon, you mean?'

'You've shown so little inclination to grant me that consideration, I hardly feel moved to give it to you.'

'Fairly stated,' said the disembodied voice of Belasco.

Suddenly another voice, loud, raspy and harsh, commanded, 'Kill him, and I will make you powerful beyond your wildest dreams, Warlock!'

'There's another reason,' said Belasco. 'If you kill me, Dahun will be free. I'm the only thing keeping him from entering this world.'

Amirantha glanced at Magnus and Sandreena who were blinking as if slowly coming out of a trance. Knowing that he needed to buy a little more time, Amirantha said, 'If Dahun is in you, what is that contraption on the surface about?'

'Ah, that would be telling,' said Belasco with an evil chuckle.

'What madness have you undertaken now, brother of mine?' said Amirantha, prodding Belasco's shoulder with the point of his dagger.

'That hurt!' said Belasco petulantly.

'Injure me at your peril!' shouted Dahun's voice. 'I will accept a clean kill to set me free, but torment will earn you repayment a thousand times over.'

Kaspar said, 'Not very reassuring, is he?'

'Neither of them are worth saving,' said Amirantha. His eyes flickered between Kaspar and the others, and with a twitch of his head, he indicated he needed the General to play along. 'Still, they know some things that might prove interesting.

'Belasco, I can only assume you're controlling this monster inside of you for two reasons, your usual spite and self-serving interest, and because you believe you have some way out of this impasse?'

'You know me well, brother. But until revealing these things works to my advantage, I think I shall keep my reasoning to myself.'

'Well, you always were unwilling to share.'

'Blame Sidi. He was always beating me and taking my things.'

'True, and both of you treated me the same until I started summoning help.'

'That was an unfortunate day,' said Belasco's voice.

'Warlock!' came the demon's voice. 'Release me and I shall make you a prince of men, my first servant on this world.'

Amirantha sighed, and shrugged at Kaspar. 'Sorry, Dahun, but experience tells me your promises are small currency.'

Belasco said, 'Actually, he might keep that one. He doesn't plan to eat everything in sight. He wants to settle in and run things. That was our original arrangement, and he has been as good as his word.'

Amirantha closed his eyes as if he couldn't believe what he was hearing. He sighed slowly and then said, 'Until you betrayed him,' he said flatly.

'Of course.'

Amirantha was silent for a moment, then said, 'So, if I kill you, the demon prince inside you is freed, but if I let you live . . . well, sooner or later you'll die anyway as you can't eat or drink, unless you tell me of your plan.'

'Not yet.'

Amirantha saw Magnus and Sandreena begin to rouse and said, 'Speaking of Sidi . . .'

'Yes,' said Belasco.

'He's dead.'

'Pity,' said Belasco.

'Why? You hated him.'

'Because I wanted to be the one to kill him; Mother may have been an evil witch, but she was our mother.'

Amirantha glanced at Kaspar who said, 'Now that I've met all three of you, I can just imagine what she must have been like.'

'Who speaks?' asked Belasco. 'I glimpsed him before, but he keeps moving.'

'Kaspar, formerly Duke of Olasko, and now General of the Army in Muboya.'

'I'd bid you welcome, General, but I suspect you're not here to wish me well.'

'Exactly,' said Kaspar. 'We came here to kill you.'

'Ah, always murder in everyone's heart.' That was followed by an evil chuckle.

'Now what?' Kaspar asked Amirantha.

But it was Belasco who spoke. 'We wait until I decide what course of action is in my best interests.'

CHAPTER EIGHTEEN

Attack

*P*UG UNLEASHED ANOTHER SPELL.
Demons of all shapes and sizes were flung back, and Pug shouted, 'Something is very wrong.'

Gulamendis shouted over the shrieks and bellowing, 'What?'

'I'm not sure, but I sense something strange.'

Laromendis was so exhausted he was nearly unable to stand; he had conjured every conceivable illusion he had learned over the years. His myriad of threats, taredhel sentinels, animals and monsters of every stripe, had distracted and delayed the onslaught of demons long enough to give Pug time to unleash his considerable power.

A voice from behind said, 'Do you need some help?'

Pug turned and his face became alive with relief, as he beheld Magnus standing there. 'Are you up to it?'

Nodding, he said, 'They used a spell binding net on Sandreena and myself, but the effects have worn off.' Then his eyes narrowed and he said, 'And I'm quite angry.'

He moved to stand between Gulamendis and Pug, and with outstretched hands released a blast of crimson energy that moved like a thundering breaker on the beach. The demons, irrespective of size and shape, were hurled back again. Those at the rear of the pack were cast down into the vast pit from which the green energy rose.

A shout from behind caused the remaining demons to turn and see what new threat approached them. Into the emerald glow cast by the tower of energy ran armoured humans, each dressed in the garb of Roldem's Royal Marines. Adept at battle on ship and land, they were the island kingdom's toughest combat soldiers. Leading the charge was a familiar face, though his usual boyish grin was missing. Jommy Killaroo, now Knight of the King's Court of Roldem and Captain of Special Services to the King, shouted orders as he raised his sword and lashed out at a man-sized demon standing before him.

Pug let out a long breath. 'Three hundred marines from Roldem will keep them busy until the rest get here, which should only be minutes now.'

As if to punctuate his words, another shout from outside was followed by the arrival of Tad, another of Pug's adopted grandsons, leading a contingency of the Prince's Own, from Krondor. Their orders were simple; kill every demon in sight.

Pug said to Magnus, 'Save your strength. We may need it soon.'

Magnus nodded, 'My tantrum was satisfying, but fatiguing.'

'How's Sandreena and Kaspar?'

'Alive,' said Magnus. 'Belasco is incapacitated and struggles with some sort of demon presence,' he held up his hand before his father could ask a question. 'I'm sure Amirantha can explain it later, but for the moment all you need to know is that if Belasco loses this struggle, then an entity named Dahun will appear in this realm.'

Gulamendis said, 'Dahun! He's one of the regional kings, and if he does get through, it'll take all of us to contain him.' He shook his head in doubt. 'I don't know if Amirantha and I could banish him back to the Fifth Circle.'

'We should have another half a dozen magicians here within a few more minutes,' said Pug.

'That should do it,' said an exhausted Laromendis.

'Yes,' agreed his brother. 'If you damage him enough, wear him down, then Amirantha and I should be able to send him back to where he came from.'

'It's not like we're going to have any choice,' said Pug. Looking at Magnus he said, 'We could use Amirantha and Sandreena up here.'

'They're trying to puzzle out what Belasco is doing.'

'I thought you said he was incapacitated.'

'It's difficult to explain, Father, I'm not sure I even understand, but it appears that Belasco is a host for the demon, and killing him will only release Dahun into this realm. Belasco has kept him in check, but at the price of his own freedom.'

Hearing this Gulamendis said, 'By the Ancestors, I need to get down there.' He left the struggle as more human soldiers arrived to fight the demons.

'This should be over soon,' said Pug, as the company of Keshian dog soldiers and another of Royal soldiers from Muboya hove into view.

Then a loud noise echoed from the pit and a company of flyers erupted out of it, followed by another host of monstrous creatures who scrambled their way up over the edge of the pit and launched themselves into the fray.

'Perhaps not,' said Magnus as he sent a massive fireball into the midst of the flyers circling over the attacking human armies.

Gulamendis found Amirantha and Kaspar hovering over the prone form of Belasco, while a disembodied voice bellowed, 'My minions will be here shortly, humans! This cursed magician who confines me will perish, then I shall be free and your deaths agonizing and eternal! Release me now and I will reward you, but my patience is nearing its end!'

Jim Dasher stood ready to end Belasco's life with his dagger, if there was any need. He threw a questioning look at Amirantha.

Amirantha shook his head, and then looked at the elven Demon Master and asked, 'Have you heard anything like that before?'

'I've never heard a demon use the word "patience", nor have I heard of one being confined when in possession of a mortal host.'

Sandreena, now fully recovered, said, 'I've been threatened before, but usually by a demon trying to rip out my throat, not by one trying to strike a bargain.'

'This is unique in my experience, as well,' said the Warlock. 'And my brother, holding true to everything I know about him, refuses to cooperate.'

'You've given me no reason to cooperate, dear brother.' Belasco's voice hung in the air.

'Give me a reason that will persuade you, Belasco.'

'The conundrum is that for me to emerge victorious, I must

first rid myself of my demon possessor, and the only means to accomplish this is to first perish.

'Should I perish, however, Dahun will revert to his body, one that will soon be in this realm.'

'Soon?' asked Gulamendis.

'Perhaps it's here now,' laughed Belasco. 'Had you killed me an hour ago, perhaps even minutes ago, he would have been cast back into the Fifth Circle of Hell, but now . . .? It may already be too late.'

'I could kill you and find out,' said Amirantha.

'But if you do that, and he appears, what then, dear brother?'

'We may have enough strength to send him back?'

'Ah, *may*. What if you don't?'

'What is the truth?' demanded Amirantha.

Gulamendis said, 'I may not be able to get the truth from your brother, but I can try to compel the demon within him to speak the truth, at least for a while.'

'You have a compelling enchantment that powerful?'

'I think so,' said Gulamendis. He looked exhausted, but closed his eyes. 'I will try.'

Long minutes dragged by. The distant sounds of battle punctuated the silence from time to time, until Kaspar asked, 'Is it safe to leave you here?'

Amirantha indicated the dagger in his hand, held mere inches from his brother's throat. 'I don't think you being here makes much difference.'

'Good,' said Kaspar as he turned to leave. 'From the sound of things, they could use a general up there, or at least one more sword.'

Jim looked at Kaspar, who said, 'You stay here. Amirantha

might hesitate, but I have no doubt you'll cut Belasco's throat if needed.' Jim nodded.

Amirantha was forced to smile. During the months since he had met Kaspar, he had developed a genuine affection for him. Given the former Duke's reputation, he found it surprising that a former enemy of the Conclave and friend to his mad, dead brother Sidi would prove such affable company; but then he knew what Sidi had been capable of, and judged much of Kaspar's villainy had been Sidi's doing. Jim was also someone the Warlock found likeable, despite having a hard, cold side to him.

Gulamendis said, 'It is done.' To Dahun he said, 'To truth are you bound. What reason have you for this possession?'

It was a question shared by all three of the demon experts in the room; possession was rarely used by more powerful demons. It was against their nature; why trade a more powerful body for a weaker, more vulnerable one? Disguise was the only possible reason, but disguise was hardly necessary given the huge conflict above.

Silence was their answer.

After a long minute, Belasco chuckled. 'Your spell must have worked, elf.'

'Why do you say that?' asked Jim.

'Gulamendis compelled the demon to tell the truth, but did not compel him to answer. His silence tells you he cannot lie to you, so he elects to say nothing.'

Gulamendis looked from Amirantha to Jim to Sandreena, with a beseeching expression on his face. They both shook their heads.

'What do we do now?' asked Sandreena.

'Come up with a bargain for my brother,' said Amirantha.

'What do you propose?' asked Belasco.

'Jim could cut your throat and we could deal with the demon when he gets here,' said Sandreena, her tone leaving little doubt she considered it the most viable option.

Amirantha held up his hand and said, 'A last resort.' To his brother he said, 'We could banish the demon back to the Fifth Circle, now?'

'An exorcism?' said Belasco incredulously. 'You must be joking.'

'Sandreena is the Mother-Bishop of the Order of the Shield of the Weak,' said the Warlock.

'I think I liked her better when she just wished to bash my head in with her mace,' said Belasco. 'That would be quick and easy; death by exorcism is far too slow and painful.'

Sandreena and the two demon masters exchanged knowing looks, and they conceded wordlessly that Belasco was right, the more powerful the demon driven from the host, the more damage endured by the mortal. And no one in the history of any temple had successfully banished a demon king or prince.

Amirantha said, 'Your choice, brother. A quick death and we deal with your demon, or we can try to save you, and then most likely be forced to kill you.'

'You know me well, brother.' There was a long silence, and Belasco said, 'Give me your word that should I emerge from this intact you'll grant me one day's grace to find a safe haven.'

'After all you've done?' said Sandreena.

'That's the bargain,' said Belasco.

'I vote for a quick death,' said Sandreena.

'I think we should try the exorcism,' said Gulamendis.

Jim shrugged. 'I really don't know what's best.'

'That leaves it to you, brother,' said Belasco.

Amirantha said, 'Give me one reason to grant you any mercy. You've been trying to kill me for a century.'

'Well, that's a regret, really. I count it a bad habit, really. I just got so annoyed with you and Sidi . . . I didn't really think things through.'

Amirantha closed his eyes a moment, then opened them and said, 'You may not be as mad as our brother was, but there's nothing sane about you.

'Let me be clear, I'm leaning heavily towards ending this rapidly, which involves cutting your throat, unless you provide me with a good enough reason why we should risk letting you live, and still have to deal with a powerful demon anyway.'

There was a long silence, then Belasco said, 'I will tell you the truth.'

Amirantha laughed. 'That would be unusual.'

'By the blood of the old woman of the moons, the nightmares of the child in the village, and the bones in the wicked man's hidden grave,' said Belasco.

Amirantha fell silent. He looked at Sandreena and Gulamendis and softly said, 'When we were children we made a pact; we imitated a curse our mother used . . .' He shook his head. 'It was as close as any of us came to anything sacred. Even Sidi never broke a promise or lied after making that oath.'

'It's the best I can do, brother.'

Amirantha was silent again. After a long moment, he said, Very well. Begin.'

Pug saw the demons before the doorway turn from his group to answer the attack from Jommy's marines. Kaspar arrived and said, 'What's the situation?'

'Chaos,' shouted Magnus. 'Our forces arrived, then a horde of demons appeared out of that pit!'

'It's a massive summoning pit; even Amirantha and Gulamendis didn't recognize it for what it was: a demon gate.'

'We have to shut it down!' said Kaspar.

'The problem,' replied Pug, 'is that it might take a while.'

Kaspar looked out at the battle raging beyond the door while Magnus sent another blast of searing energy at a demon charging in their direction. 'Keep discouraging them,' said Kaspar, 'while I get a better look.' He tapped Laromendis on the shoulder and said, 'You up to giving me a boost up to the roof?'

'Certainly,' said the elf. They stepped out the door and Laromendis made a stirrup with his hands. Kaspar stepped up and the tall elf thrust him high enough to allow the General to clamber onto the tiles of the roof.

Magnus stepped outside just in time to destroy a flyer that had spotted Kaspar as an easy target, and the General shouted, 'Thanks!'

Kaspar saw that the activity from the pit had ceased and shouted down, 'I think that's all of them!'

He looked over the battle and cursed himself for not having had a better notion of how this struggle might unfold. He had made one poor assumption, that a quick strike by overwhelming forces would obliterate a disorganized band of cultists and a few demons.

He hadn't expected that the demons would be armed, organized, and sending reinforcements. Still, his forces were slowly gaining the upper hand through sheer numbers. Which was a good thing, he considered, as it seemed to take three or four human soldiers to best one of the larger demons.

The stench from demon blood was making his eyes water and another flyer almost took his head as it came hurtling out of the night sky. He felt the heat from its flaming body as Magnus dispatched it.

Kaspar sat on the eaves and then dropped to the ground, with an audible grunt. 'I'm too old and tired to be doing this,' he said to no one in particular.

Pug and the others came out of the small building as the ebb and flow of the struggle had drawn most of the combatants to the other side of the large fortress. Kaspar said, 'We've got the upper hand if something doesn't change unexpectedly.' He nodded. 'I've got to find my commanders and see if we can coordinate this a little better.'

He hurried off and Pug turned to Laromendis. 'Why don't you see what your brother and Amirantha are up to down there? Magnus and I will protect this position.'

Laromendis said, 'Of course,' and ran back into the building.

'There's a new war underway,' said Belasco. 'It's been underway for centuries, now. The five demon kings have battled for supremacy since time began, but this new war is something different.'

Amirantha said, 'How is it different?'

The sound of laughter filled the room, both Belasco's and the demon's. The monster's was filled with hate and bitterness, while Belasco's held genuine amusement. 'I don't really know,' said the motionless magic user. 'Lies are as much a part of a demon's nature as they are of mine, dead brother.

'When I first began to dabble with summoning it was for the usual reason: I wanted to best you. I tried to kill Sidi once by creating a lich, did you know that?'

'No,' said Amirantha.

'It wasn't well conceived, really, too much emphasis on irony and not enough on learning my craft. Sidi disposed of the monster quickly and I spent the better part of a year living in a very cold cave up in the Northlands, surrounded by ice bears, snow leopards and dark elves.' He sighed, more as an emotional footnote than a real exhalation of breath. 'You'd think I'd have learned, but I really didn't.

'I decided not to conjure a random demon and turn it loose on you; I knew you'd easily defeat it, so instead thought I might subvert one of your spells so that you summoned a creature you weren't expecting. I thought that was very clever.'

'It almost worked,' said Amirantha.

'Almost?'

'I had help. I would have perished had I been alone.'

'Well, that's some sort of consolation.' He paused, then said, 'To learn how to do it I began studying demon lore, much of it familiar to you, I assume. But I did find a few unusual odds and ends; a scroll here and a book there revealed that there was far more to the demon realm than you'd ever suspected. I wasn't doing this for scholarship, really. I was looking for a clever way to kill my brothers.'

Gulamendis looked at Belasco and then at Amirantha and just shook his head. Sandreena kept her eyes fixed on Amirantha's face.

Amirantha said, 'The demon war?'

'Something is driving the demons. Something came into their realm and struggles with them for supremacy in their own realm,' said Belasco. 'Millions of demons have been destroyed in the fight and three of the kings have united to oppose the invaders.'

'Who?' asked Amirantha.

'I don't know,' replied Belasco. 'I only hear vague references to "them", or "the invaders". One time I heard that they were "from the darkness" . . . Other than that, all I know is that this force has destroyed the order, such as it was, of the Fifth Circle.

'Of the two kings who did not ally, one took a wait-and-see position: my friend here, Dahun.'

That brought forth the sound of snarling, but no coherent speech.

'The other was Maarg. Some fool on a world in this realm opened a Demon gate into Maarg's realm, and he unleashed the outer horde into this world. There were great battles, but in the end, the demons found themselves stranded on another world with no way back.'

'Shila,' said Sandreena. 'Pug has spoken of that world and the demon battles with the Saaur.'

'But it was Dahun who saw the potential in *this* realm. The demons have their own magic users and before Maarg devastated Shila, Dahun sent spies and agents into that world, to pillage the libraries. They returned with everything they could carry and for the better part of half a century they simply studied.

'Dahun first recognized the need to solidify his own position so he annexed Maarg's realm, trapping Maarg on the mortal realm knowing the demon king would eventually starve to death after he devoured everything.

'He then allied with the three remaining demon kings and sent forces to battle the invaders; but the forces he sent were those he inherited from Maarg's realm, he kept his own loyal army close.

'He then began preparing to leave the Fifth Circle.'

'And come here?' asked Gulamendis, as his brother walked into the room.

'The battle goes well,' said Laromendis, as his brother nodded, but held up his hand to indicate silence.

'Yes,' said Belasco. 'This realm is weak compared to the Fifth Circle, but Dahun is by far the most intelligent of the demon lords. He realized that changes would be needed before his entrance into the realm.

'You know as much about demons as any man can learn on his own, brother. You know that without control, a demon will continue to feed until he devours everything he can find. Dahun created that control. He created a hierarchy that went further than the one that already existed in the demon realm, one that relied not only on power and alliances, but loyalty, as well. He orchestrated betrayal, infiltrating spies into the domains of the other rulers, and began a series of conflicts between his neighbours.

'Dahun created the illusion that Maarg had returned, feigned his own defeat at the hands of the demon king, and allowed the other rulers to believe what he wanted them to believe. Then he escalated the demon war to a new level, setting allies against one another and against the mortal races he encountered in this realm, against anyone who might pose a threat.

'In short, he readied himself to enter this level of reality and assume supremacy.'

'But we somehow managed to frustrate that plan,' said Amirantha.

'More than you realize,' said Belasco. 'At first I thought this merely another opportunity for some grim fun, a little nasty play that might net me some personal gain, but when I discovered what Dahun's plans were, in truth, it was too late.'

'You were in his trap,' said Gulamendis.

'Ahh, another new voice,' said Belasco. 'Yes, demons are creatures that cannot be reasoned with, negotiated with, or pleaded with; they can only be forced to reach an accommodation, and the only thing you can be certain of is that they will betray you eventually, given an opportunity.

'Amirantha, you would not believe what your so-called minions think of you. Before you take offence, understand they feel that way about all humans. We are cattle to them. We are food. We provide things they desire, nothing more. To get what they desire, they will serve if they must, but it is always about what they want.'

'And Dahun desires to live on this world?'

'He desires to rule it. He sent every demon he could herd through his gates to vanquish the elves on a dozen worlds. He came here because—'

'No!' came Dahun's voice. 'You may not speak of that!'

There was silence.

Amirantha said, 'Belasco?'

More silence.

Gulamendis looked at Sandreena and then Amirantha and said, 'What do we do now?'

'I have no idea,' said the Warlock.

CHAPTER NINETEEN

Demon Unleashed

*P*UG CAST A SPELL.

A wave of pulsating energy rose above the heads of those struggling on the ground and swept the sky clear of the few remaining winged demons. Somewhere in the midst of the fray Kaspar was bringing order and the diverse Midkemian units were beginning to coordinate their efforts. Demons still crawled out of the pit but the rate had slowed to a trickle and Pug sensed they were on the verge of defeating this invading host.

A dozen magicians had accompanied the soldiers and they used their arts to contain the more fractious creatures, or to neutralize the magic-using demons. Pug turned to Magnus and said, 'I think it's almost over.'

Before Magnus could reply, a loud thrumming filled the air

and a huge pulse of blinding green light shot up each of the four towers to explode at the top of the columns.

The effects were almost instantaneous, the ground heaved beneath everyone's feet and knocked most of the combatants to the ground. Pug quickly regained his footing and pointed to the towers, which now pulsed as ripples of green energy ran up to their tops to feed a growing, bright white ball of energy.

'Oh, gods, I know what that is.'

Magnus said, 'It's a summoning device of some sort, as you said.'

'But it's also what ties the necromancy and demon lore together!' said Pug. 'It's why those death rituals that Jim reported occurred, and why there were bodies in the pit, and it's why Dahun doesn't care how many demons we kill.' He pointed to the energy running up the towers, increasing in frequency and tempo. 'When the gate is fully open, he'll come through.'

'But he's here, already,' said Magnus. 'He's possessed the body of Belasco!'

Pug said, 'It's a ruse! He's buying time.' He gripped Magnus by the arm and said, 'Get back down there. Tell Amirantha and Gulamendis what is occurring.' He looked at the massive battle and said, 'I've got to come up with a way to stop the killing!'

The human forces were coalescing around Kaspar who was orchestrating a containment attack, pressing in on all sides around the remaining demons. The tactic forced demons to confine other demons, so only those on the outside could engage the human soldiers.

Then another wave of demons exploded out of the pit. 'Oh, damn!' said Pug.

*   *   *

Magnus hurried into the chamber. 'They're using death magic to activate the Demon gate!' Amirantha looked at Gulamendis and said, 'Now, I wonder who thought up that idea?'

Dahun's contempt cut through the air. 'Your brother thought to use me, human! He was bending power to his own ends! He envisioned a demon army here, serving him on this world, as he conquered it! The fool!'

Amirantha's brow furrowed. 'I've never known him to be that ambitious.'

Gulamendis said, 'People change.'

Laromendis said, 'Whatever the motivation, am I correct in assuming this melding of death magic and demon summoning has created an unexpected problem?'

Magnus said, 'Each life taken up there fuels the device, and it appears as if it has begun to open a Demon gate. Lesser demons are coming through in waves.'

'Can you shut that creature up?' asked Sandreena.

Gulamendis closed his eyes and said, 'No. But I think I have a trick.' He chanted something and abruptly the sound of Dahun's voice in their minds retreated to a distance.

'What was that?' asked Magnus.

Amirantha smiled. 'A nice little trick that I'm going to get him to teach me if we live through the rest of this day.' Looking at the still face of his brother, Amirantha shouted, 'Belasco! Can you hear me?'

A distant whisper answered, 'Yes.'

They had to strain to hear him over the ranting demon. Amirantha said, 'Was it you who created the death magic portal?'

'Yes,' said Belasco. 'I almost killed Sidi once in Kesh, forcing him to abandon his lair. I found several interesting tomes and books.'

'You always wanted to better our skills,' said Amirantha.

'Because I am better!'

'Well, you're about to get everyone here and probably half the world murdered to prove you're not as clever as you thought,' snapped Sandreena. She was obviously tired and did not feel this was going well.

Jim narrowed his gaze and gave her a silent warning to keep still.

The still magician's ethereal voice took on some urgency. 'I can feel the tug! The gate is opening! Our bargain? If I tell you how to defeat this monster, do I get my day's head start?'

Jim started to say no, but Amirantha's eyes warned him this was coming to a head. Finally, Jim nodded.

'One day,' said Amirantha. 'You get nothing else, no food, water, horse or weapon.'

The sound of laughter drowned out the railing demon. 'Done! Here is what you must do. You must render me unconscious within the next ten minutes.'

Sandreena hefted her mace to where the prone figure's eyes could see, and held in a menacing fashion. 'That's no problem.'

Belasco laughed at the threat. 'I like her!' In faint tones that seemed to be growing more distant, he said, 'No; brother, you know what to do.'

Amirantha nodded and looked at Gulamendis. 'His body isn't the issue; it's his mind. You need to keep aware of what Dahun is doing while I stun Belasco's consciousness.'

'Excellent,' said the recumbent magic user. 'As soon as you

do, I will lose my hold on him between the realms and he will come through the gate.'

'This is your plan?' said Sandreena. 'I thought we were trying to keep him out of this realm!'

'You must destroy the gate while he is still within. You will have less than a minute once he begins to manifest, but he will be completely vulnerable during this translation. That is when you must strike.'

'Then revive me and I will be on my way, dear brother.'

Amirantha said to Magnus, 'You need to alert your father. It's going to get very nasty up there in a couple of minutes.'

Magnus closed his eyes. 'I'm not the best at this, but I'll try to save the time needed for me to run up there.'

Father, Pug heard in his mind.

'Magnus?' he whispered.

Yes. Listen closely as I don't know how long I can maintain this link. In less than ten minutes Dahun will manifest within the Demon gate. He will be vulnerable for a minute, perhaps two. If you destroy the gate at once, you destroy him before his full power is manifested.

Pug let out a long breath. 'I have it.'

Pug saw Kaspar a short distance away, but he was blocked by half a dozen demons. A particularly brutish one, that looked almost like a rhinoceros with two large curving horns coming out of its shoulders, lowered his head, hefted a massive sword and charged. Pug shouted, 'Get back!' to the soldiers nearby and sent a pulse of energy at the creature.

Pug was trying his best to stun or disable the demons without killing them, but it was not going well. Several of the monsters were so determined that nothing short of a killing blow seemed to slow them down, let alone stop them.

Pug reached Kaspar and said, 'We need to withdraw.'

'Why?' said the General, his sword smoking from the black demon blood on it. He had a nasty gash on his right cheek, but ignored it. 'We've taken command of the field, have them surrounded and are forcing them into a knot. We can cut them down from the edges and should see them all dead within a half hour!'

'Because in about ten minutes, each death here will cause that thing,' he pointed to the green column, 'to bring a Demon King here and he will have to be put down using enough magic to level this entire structure. Nothing within a quarter mile of this place is likely to survive.'

'Withdraw!' shouted Kaspar, not waiting to hear any more. He had known Pug long enough never to doubt him in matters pertaining to magic. Zane, one of his key captains and a foster grandson of Pug hurried over and looked as if he was about to question the order. Like Kaspar, he knew the human forces had the upper hand in the field.

'Get them south of here! We don't want to be trapped on those bloody switchbacks! I want everyone at least a quarter of a mile away in the next six minutes!'

Zane knew better than to question an order like that, and began relaying the command. The order was quickly passed and the soldiers confronting the demons launched a fierce assault for thirty seconds while those behind turned and began a hasty retreat.

Kaspar said, 'This is where I'd normally use archers, but as I didn't bring any . . .'

Pug said, 'I understand.' He raised his hand and launched a red ball of light. It was a signal every magician in the field had been prepared to see, though not if they saw the battle going well. Still, it was an order to cover an orderly retreat.

Those magicians who could fly or hover took to the air, laying down withering blankets of flame and shocking energy like lightning. Others climbed to the walls and used wands and staves raining all types of destruction on the demons. Pug cursed the need to retreat. They had almost repulsed the demon legion and if he had time to investigate the gate, he was sure he could render it inoperative without destroying the entire structure.

Still, what one wishes for and what one gets are often two very different things, the magician thought. He thought of Magnus, *Are you safe down there?*

I'm coming up. This chamber is deep enough to keep the others safe, but you may need help with Dahun.

Pug knew better than to argue. His son was most likely right. For a brief moment he pushed aside a rising fear, for he knew he was fated to see Magnus dead alongside his mother and brother, and he wondered if this would be the moment. He prayed it wasn't as he rose into the air and began blasting demons back into the pit.

Kaspar's soldiers were as well-trained and disciplined a group as Pug had ever seen, despite most of them not having trained together. They withdrew in rapid order, leaving it to the magicians to hold the demons at bay. The advantage to the human forces was enough that even during the soldiers withdrawal, the demons could not pursue them due to the punishing magic raining down on them from all sides.

Magnus appeared in the air next to his father and said, 'You've become adept at rising into the air, father!'

It had been something Miranda had been able to do with ease, but Pug always had trouble managing it. It was a point of pride that he laboured to master those skills at which he was not gifted and he smiled as he said, 'I can't let you get better than me at everything, now, can I?'

Magnus tried to chuckle at the quip, but knew his father was nearly frantic with worry. 'It will be fine, father,' he said trying to reassure him.

Both magicians unleashed as much destructive energy as possible, creating a curtain of death between the demons and the retreating humans. 'Now it gets dangerous,' said Pug, as the last of the human soldiers turned and ran.

Only the magic wall of flame and crackling energy confined the demons, and Pug said to Magnus, 'Tell Amirantha to do whatever it is he's going to do.'

Magnus sent word to the Warlock.

Amirantha's eyes widened as he heard Magnus's voice in his mind. *Father says the area will be clear in two minutes.*

Amirantha said to the others, 'Two minutes.'

Belasco's voice said, 'Good. I am getting very tired holding this beast in check.' There was a dark chuckle, a humour rooted in pain and anger. 'I guess we can both say I overreached myself this time, brother.'

Amirantha looked around the room and saw Jim ready to cut Belasco's throat, Sandreena ready to bash his head in with her mace, and the two elves ready to do whatever they needed to subdue him should the need arise. 'Given that there are five people here longing to see you dead, and you're stuck in a mental struggle with a demon king, putting thousands of lives at risk . . . Yes I can agree you overreached.'

'Well, I'd tell you I was sorry, but we both know that it would be a lie,' he said with what seemed to be an echo of evil glee. 'You may be right, you know.'

'About what?' asked the Warlock.

'About me being insane; I'm not sure, because I've always felt this way. I know Sidi was mad, but that was easy to see. But I realize now that a lot of what I've done . . . Don't get me wrong on this, dear brother, I still don't care, but I do realize that one must be a little crazy to try what I've tried.

'I saw myself as just too clever—' There came a hollow laugh. Then suddenly Belasco's tone changed, 'It's starting! You must do it now!'

Amirantha nodded, and Gulamendis said, 'I will delay the demon within for a few minutes.'

Sandreena said, 'I can pacify your brother, Amirantha.'

'Begin,' said Amirantha.

'Fare well, brother,' came Belasco's voice. Amirantha's eyes widened slightly, for in his lifetime, his brother had never offered him the slightest good fortune. As if understanding this, Belasco added, 'For if you do not fare well, I most certainly perish.'

They began their spells.

Demons withered under the blistering attack of the magicians surrounding them. Pug could sense more than see that some of the magicians on the walls were failing, exhausted from using so much of their magic in so short a time. Only Magnus seemed unaffected by the demands placed on him.

A massive wave of energy swept up the four towers and suddenly a slightly translucent figure began to appear suspended in the air.

Twenty feet tall, Dahun's massive torso was heavily muscled, and descended into huge legs and a scaled lizard's tail below his spine. His black legs and tail blended to red at his stomach and turned crimson at his chest. His face was contorted in pain, as if the transition from the demon realm caused him great agony. He bellowed: a distant, hollow sound. His eyes were solid black orbs, opened wide and seeking; and as his head moved from side to side, his hair, braided with human skulls, swung around his shoulders. The demon king's brow was adorned with a massive golden circlet set with a dark stone, which pulsed with purple light. The fingers of his left hand ended in black talons and flexed slowly, as if in anticipation of tearing apart his enemies. In his right hand, he held a flaming sword. His hips were girded with a metal-studded kilt, and two large leather bands crossed his chest with a massive golden emblem at their centre.

Pug said, 'Now!' to Magnus, and they unleashed every destructive magic they possessed.

Two waves of sizzling light shot from their hands to strike the figure full in the chest. Dahun trembled and started to fall backwards, his hands outstretched, as if in supplication. A single word escaped his lips. 'No!'

As he fell from the confines of the four towers, purple lightning erupted from his body, striking the pillars above him. The demon king screamed in outrage and pain, his arms flailing as he tried to reach for the nearest pillar to keep from falling out of the pit boundaries.

'Destroy the towers!' Pug said to Magnus.

Pug focused on the demon while his son sought to topple the towers. His bolts of searing energy raised smoking welts on the demon's body until Dahun struck the ground between two of the arching structures. A piteous cry escaped from the demon king as he touched the soil.

Magnus noticed that while most of the other magicians nearby were fleeing, a few of the stronger ones remained on the wall, directing their magic at the demon in aid of Pug. He reached out with his mind to find a keystone in the foundation of the tower closest to where his father and he floated. Using his power, he then ground the stone to dust in moments, and sent a massive wave of energy at the sudden void in the masonry. The entire tower shuddered and began to collapse, stones falling as the construction moved side to side. As it crumbled, massive discharges of green magic swirled upward, like mad dust-devils spinning away into the night sky.

Dahun shrieked in agony as the unbalanced forces in the pit began to discharge massive explosions like lightning and balls of fire. Pug could feel waves of heat rising and instinctively raised a protective shield around himself and Magnus.

With the shield in place, they could only watch.

Dahun lay writhing on the soil, gasping like a landed fish. His body contorted in spasms, while flames roared all around him. His legs and tail still hung over the pit and they now began to smoke and blister; he screamed in pain, but was unable to move.

Magnus sent to his father, *It's over*.

Pug replied, 'Not quite yet.'

A second tower began to tremble and Pug used his magic to send a warning to the remaining magicians. 'Get out!'

Two of them flew away and the other leaped from the low wall to the outside of the fortress and ran as fast as he could.

The third and fourth towers also began to come apart and

tumble inward. As they did, another tower of flame erupted from the pit. All of Dahun's lower body was now consumed, and his vacant eyes had rolled up in his head.

Then suddenly a loud sucking sound could be heard, followed by a trembling through the earth. Dahun's remains were ripped from the earth and vanished back into the pit in an instant. All the masonry and dead bodies nearby were also sucked into the pit as if a massive vacuum had inhaled everything. Anything without foundation within the confines of the walls disappeared, including discarded weapons.

Then it was still.

'Is it over now?' asked Magnus.

'I think—'

The explosion was massive.

A visible shockwave rolled out of the pit, pushing earth, parts of dead bodies, and debris before it. It blasted outwards with enough force that the small building and the outer walls of the fortress were swept away like a child's hands knocking away toy blocks.

Only Pug's shield kept his son and himself safe, but the ferocity of the blast caught him off guard.

The speed and power of the shockwave cleared the area in seconds, and when they looked down, there was no sign of the pit, or any construction. The blast area was also devoid of any plant life and as smooth as polished marble.

'What happened?' asked Magnus.

'The rift closed,' said Pug. 'We unbalanced the magic and it rebalanced itself.'

'It looks as if there's nothing left down there.'

'Well, our friends are still down there, if they survived.'

Lowering himself and his son down, Pug said, 'We'd better start digging them out.'

'I hope Kaspar got his men far enough away to survive that blast,' said Magnus.

'I suspect he did,' said Pug. 'I'm not so certain about poor Timothy. He was running when last I saw him.'

Magnus said, 'He's fast.'

'Let's hope he's fast enough. They reached the ground and Pug said, 'Now, where was that building?'

'Somewhere over here,' said Magnus, as he closed his eyes and started probing with his magic to locate the entrance.

Amirantha was the first to regain consciousness. It was pitch black in the room. The massive explosion above had momentarily sucked all of the air out of the chamber, extinguishing the lights and rendering everyone within it unconscious.

His lungs burned and he felt his head pounding as he reached around blindly and felt the base of the altar. He used it to steady himself and got to his feet. The air had quickly returned to the room, but the sudden decompression really had caused some damage.

He reached into his belt pouch, took out a crystal, and incanted a single word. The crystal began to glow, casting enough light on the room that he could see the others. Sandreena was stirring with a groan, and he knelt next to her shaking her shoulder gently he said, 'You're alive.'

She shook her head and focused her eyes on him and said, 'What?'

'In case you were wondering; you're alive.'

She grunted, then said, 'I was wondering.'

He helped her to her feet as Jim and the two elves began to review the damage. Looking at the prone figure of Belasco, Amirantha said, 'Did he survive?'

As if prodded by the question, Belasco groaned and moved slightly.

A thump from above and a sudden cloud of dust from the corridor was followed by Magnus's voice in their minds, *Is everyone all right?*

Amirantha shouted, 'We're alive, if barely.'

A moment later, the two magicians entered the chamber and Pug said, 'It's over.'

'The demon's gone?' asked Jim, blinking, trying to clear his vision.

'Everything's gone,' said Magnus. 'The pit is filled, the ground is flattened, and the stones are scattered for miles. It's as if this place never existed.'

'Good,' said Jim. 'That means no explanations to the Keshian government.'

Belasco groaned again as he sat up. In a gravelly voice he asked, 'It's over?'

'Yes,' said Amirantha. 'And your day's grace to find a safe haven begins this moment.'

Moving gingerly from the altar stone, the magician stood on uncertain legs for a moment, then he said, 'I'll go.'

He began walking in a halting fashion, stopped, took a deep breath, then repeated, 'I'll go.'

He was almost to the door when Amirantha said, 'Wait.'

Turning, Belasco said, 'What?'

'Give me your word one more time.'

'You already have it,' he said with a contemptuous snarl.

'Again, say it again.'

'What?'

'The oath.'

Belasco was silent for a long minute, then said, 'Very well. By the old woman's blood—'

Amirantha shouted, 'Kill him!'

Pug, Magnus, the elves, and even Sandreena hesitated, looking at the Warlock as Pug said, 'What?'

Jim Dasher, however, didn't hesitate. The dagger that had not left his hand since coming into this chamber now flew straight across the room, and took Belasco in the throat. The magician's eyes grew round, and he reached up as if he could staunch the blood flow with his fingers.

Crimson gushed from his mouth and nose as he tried to speak, then his strength gave way and he fell to his knees. With blood pouring down his face, neck, and chest, he fell over on his right side.

'Why?' Pug asked.

'Because that wasn't my brother,' said Amirantha.

'What?' asked Sandreena.

'Belasco would never recite the oath incorrectly. It begins, "By the blood of the old woman of the moons", not "By the old woman's blood".' Pointing a finger at the corpse on the floor he said, 'That was no longer my brother. That was Dahun.'

'It was the demon king?' said Gulamendis.

'Yes,' said Amirantha. 'When we were being so clever, he was outwitting us. He manipulated everything we did. We believed there was a struggle between him and his host, because he wanted us to. Belasco remembered the oath correctly, but when the time came, Dahun cast him out into the demon body emerging from the Fifth Circle. It was a foregone conclusion that you two,' he pointed to Pug and Magnus, 'would destroy Dahun's body; Belasco had no ability to use the demon's magic. He was an easy target.'

Magnus said, 'It required a lot of magic to destroy that construction, but before that, there was no real fight.'

Pug said, 'But why? Why go to all this trouble to come here, just to possess your brother?'

'I can only speculate,' said the Warlock.

Jim said, 'Well, we're going to be back on Sorcerer's Isle soon, so let's leave it to discuss then.'

Pug said, 'Agreed. Now, let us leave this gods forsaken place and go home.'

No one in the room objected.

Aftermath

*P*UG MOTIONED FOR EVERYONE TO SIT.
The mood in the room was subdued. Despite their victory over the demons, they had lost lives.

Pug said, 'With Belasco dead, I hope our days of conflict with your family are over, Amirantha.'

The Warlock smiled. 'Assuredly. My brothers' service to the dark agency who caused so much harm is beyond my ability to amend, but I will do what I can to help, Pug.'

'It's welcome. It's clear we have very little understanding of the demon realm.'

The two elven brothers were speaking softly, and Gulamendis said, 'My brother is going to return to E'bar, Pug, to see if we are able to help our people,' dryly he added, 'and find out if we're at all welcome.

'I'd like to remain here for a while, and study with Amirantha.'

'Of course,' said Pug. 'You are both welcome here at any time.' He looked at Laromendis and added, 'Your task may prove difficult, if I understand what your Regent Lord and his Meet plan. But if we must, we shall endeavour to extend our hand and offer friendship.'

Laromendis smiled. 'Remember, we are a long-lived people, Pug. Give Tomas a few more years to come to terms with the Regent Lord, then we'll introduce you.'

Dressed once more as the ragged leader of a Krondor street gang, Jim Dasher laughed, and drank his wine. He had announced earlier that although the Kingdom could do without his services for a few more days, he doubted the Mockers, the thieves of Krondor, could. Wiping his mouth with a dirty sleeve, he said, 'I must be off in a few minutes, but I have a question, and this seems the perfect time to voice it, while you're all here.'

Pug nodded, looking around the room. Only Kaspar was missing, having returned with his soldiers to his responsibilities in Muboya. Brandos was sitting next to Sandreena, and for most of the day had complained about missing the fight, much to Amirantha's amusement.

They had all returned a few hours before sunrise, and had bathed and rested before enjoying this late breakfast, or very late supper, depending on one's perspective.

Jim asked, 'What was really going on down there, Pug? I know what I saw, both of the times I visited, but what did I *really* see?'

Pug looked around the room and said, 'One way or another you're all members of the Conclave, even if you don't consider yourselves as such; you've all shown a steadfastness in defending this world beyond the duty you owe to any crown or faith,' he looked at Sandreena as he said the last. 'You deserve to know what I know.

'For over a century, I have been confronted by a dark agency. I have had suspicions as who the manipulator is, but twice now I've had to rethink my assumptions.' To Amirantha he said, 'That your brothers were servants of the same agency is, I think, a coincidence.'

Amirantha nodded. Putting down his wine he said, 'It must be. They would never knowingly work together; they were as anxious to kill each other as they were to kill me. Sidi was driven, and quite mad, and Belasco was . . . less so, but certainly not sane.'

'Which tells me that this evil agency you speak of, Father,' said Magnus, 'draws to it those inclined towards madness.'

'Because you can't cheat an honest man,' said Jim Dasher.

'What?' asked Gulamendis.

'It's an old saying among confidence tricksters. To inspire confidence in a mark you need two things: they must be greedy and must think they have an edge over you.' He sipped his wine, then continued. 'Your two brothers were conned, Amirantha. Whoever they worked for lulled them into thinking they were getting something more than they were giving up in service, that somehow they had the advantage.'

Amirantha nodded. 'Anything that appealed to Sidi's need to hoard power, or to Belasco's vanity, yes, that would work.'

Pug said, 'However this agency recruits its servants, it has many, and they come at us when they think they are strong enough to win.'

'So you think they'll come again?' asked Sandreena.

'Almost certainly,' said Pug. Then he smiled. 'But we will be ready. We have strong resources, as you have seen; our members and allies hold high office.'

'Creegan?' asked Sandreena.

'He is in the Conclave. I recruited him when he was a young Knight-Adamant. Now he's Grand Master of the Order. We have closer ties with your temple than any other, though we have a good relationship with some others.'

Sandreena said, 'I assumed as much.' She took a drink from a mug of tea, then said, 'I'm not sure about this Mother-Bishop role, though.'

'Oh, that,' said Pug, smiling. 'It was only temporary. I think Creegan failed to mention that to you.'

Sandreena was caught between outrage and relief. 'Yes, he did. Who will he choose in my stead, and why?'

'Who is Brother Willoby, a loyal member of the Conclave and an adept administrator. You are too good at what you do to be trapped in an office all day. As to why, Creegan had no idea how much assistance you might require from the temple before we were done. A Knight-Sergeant would command some authority, but the title of Mother-Bishop would get you anything you asked for.'

Sandreena considered this for a moment, then laughed. 'Sneaky bastards, all of you.'

'We need to be,' said Pug. Returning to Jim's question, he said, 'I don't know exactly what we witnessed. He looked from Gulamendis to Amirantha and said, 'Have you given it any consideration?'

Gulamendis said, 'We have. This was so unlike what we know about demon behaviour, we must stop using old assumptions and build a theory based only on what we saw.'

Amirantha said, 'We know there's civil war in the Fifth Circle that has raged for centuries, and as far as we can tell, it has spilled over into our world for the first time. But that doesn't mean it won't happen again.'

Gulamendis said, 'I doubt that's the last we've seen of the demons, but perhaps we won't have to confront them as we did on the taredhel worlds.

'While it probably didn't seem like it at the time, what we saw down in Kesh was nothing compared to the onslaughts my people endured.'

'So then, why was Dahun trying to sneak into this world with a smaller force?' asked Jim. 'Or rather, why commit magic, murder, and mayhem on that scale? Why not just take over Belasco when no one is looking, or arrive like a normal demon and rip things apart.'

'That's the heart of the mystery,' said Gulamendis.

'I have a theory,' said Amirantha.

'Let's hear it,' said Jim, sitting back in his chair. His beard was starting to grow and Sandreena had no doubt that by the time he walked the streets of Krondor the next day, he would be his disreputable looking self again. One day, she might forgive him, for the part he played in the most painful period of her life, but she'd never forget his hand in it.

Amirantha said, 'Dahun was fleeing. He came here to hide.'

Pug and Magnus exchanged glances, and Gulamendis said, 'That would explain a great deal.'

'Hide from what?' asked Brandos. 'I've faced enough demons in my day to know they're hardly timid.'

'That I don't know,' admitted Amirantha.

'Perhaps those other demon kings?' suggested Laromendis.

'Perhaps,' said Pug, 'but I doubt it.

'There's something else behind all of this, a deeper cause of all the troubles that have visited this world since before any of us were born.' He let out a long sigh. 'It will eventually make itself known, but until it does, we can only pride ourselves on this victory and wonder how long we have to enjoy the newly won peace before we must prepare for the next attack.'

'You're certain there will be one?' asked Sandreena.

'As certain as I am of anything,' said Pug.

The conversation ceased leaving them in silence.